Leeford

CW00524304

Tales of ordinary and no
folk

written by

Michael Braccia

and

Jon Markes

Based on the first year of the fortnightly serial originally
published by the Express and Star newspaper

expressandstar.com

michaelbraccia.co.uk
jonmarkes.com

First published in this format 2023

© Michael Braccia
© Jon Markes

FOREWORD by Billy Spakemon
(Black Country Radio)

From a very early age, stories were part of my life. When I begin to outline my journey, when talking to various groups, I explain how I have realised just how 'shaping' the first five years of my life were. Sitting on the red quarry floor at my Nana Murray's in Oldbury, I listened to the stories and songs that were always filling the rooms every day. All my family worked in the local factories and would come back at dinner time to have their 'fittle', exchanging stories from the factory floor, many of their own childhood memories, characters and tales that had been passed down. The notion of community and community life was embedded in me without knowing in those early years. Words transport us into different worlds. It can be a completely fictional world or one which resonates close to home, sparking a dialogue that brings our own stories back onto the screen of our imagination. To me, the seed is all important. Within the lines is a place that begins to grow until the narrative is like a root searching for a bloom. That bloom is your own engagement flower, which is totally subjective. You immerse yourself as much as the bloom opens, as much as you become within whatever you are reading, or listening to. It is one of the most wonderful experiences.

I discovered while completing my doctorate that I was dyslexic. Once a diagnosis had been made and I re-examined my life it was obvious I had been carrying this weight all my life. 'Creative, but jumbled' were common remarks written in the margins. 'Seems to take a long time to read passages'. That negative has in many ways been a positive because I have to read and re-read text several times in order to grasp what is going on. This process enables me (although it takes time) to really get under the skin of narratives, discourses, the construction of characters. Although at times it can be frustrating, particularly from an academic perspective, as with most things I take it as a positive in how I form a relationship with stories.

I came across the Leeford Village stories a few years ago when Mike asked if we could serialise some on the radio show I do for Black Country Radio. I think we probably did half a dozen over the period of a few months. I listened to them as they came in, enjoying the characters and storylines. Mike had told me it was loosely based on Kingswinford, very much conveying that community spirit and localism so common of the region. I'm not sure if there would have been the same reaction had I read these first pieces rather than heard them, but as I listened there was a rhythm that I find common in local writers. Poets, writers, songwriters have an underlying Black Country rhythm in how they write. I feel it is inherent in how we have absorbed our past and legacy without knowing. There is a certain subtle pace to how sentences are written, words are formed. It's maybe me almost searching for this 'identity' through the text. What it does do is bring this warm familiarity. A sense of place which lifts itself off the page. There is a sense of belonging, in knowing, becoming acquainted with each character, each shift of narrative. I felt almost an ownership of the village, a friendship with its daily passage. It mirrors 'life' as it is.

Leeford Village is a drawer of tranclements. A broth bubbling away, stirred with each of the individual's own personality. How these individuals interweave across the canvass of daily life. There are sparks that are ignited that send the reader back to their own childhood. My own the world of Eel Street , Little Eels Street, Portway Road and bits of Churchbridge in Oldbury. This tiny bit of the world was full of Leeford Village characters , each with their own unique slant on the world . As in this book they fill the world with colour, joy. Michael and Jon have carefully crafted a series of landscapes that roll into one another. We journey through the tracks they take us down discovering something new as we turn each corner. Read this book out loud. Laugh out loud, shout out loud and become part of Leeford Village life. It is a book that can be read and re-read, finding new marks made by the different characters and how they knit the stories together. I'll be studying every person I see when I'm next in Kingswinford thinking: are you George, Clara, Suptra? Ha! Bostin!!!

Billy Spakemon 2022

PREFACE

In Leeford Village, we get to know (and maybe even love!) many different characters who are simply living their day-to-day lives in a small village. They don't always get it right but, generally, their intentions are honourable, and they find a way of entertaining us along the way!

This collection is based on the first year of the serial originally published by the Midlands regional newspaper, Express and Star.

In 2019, two friends, both writers trying to complete and publish novels, decided to collaborate in a very different project. Midlands-based writer, Michael Braccia, originally conceived the world of Leeford Village and was joined by York-based writer, Jon Markes.

Leeford Village is located on the western outskirts of Banfield, (the fictional town Michael uses in his stories, including his short story collection: *Banfield Tales*), near the beautiful Staffordshire countryside.

Variously described as a 'soap opera', 'light drama', even a 'gentle sitcom', the serialisation of Leeford Village began in September 2019, following an interview by the Express and Star with Michael and Jon about the unusual way they co-write. Michael writes an episode, Jon edits it for grammar, spelling, and continuity. He then writes the next one and emails that to Michael. At the outset of the project, they made a firm rule: only spelling, grammar and continuity errors can be corrected. Neither author can influence his writing partner in terms of plot. Each writer can decide to take the other's plot in a different direction if they choose – and they often do!

The serialisation of Leeford Village is inspired by the books of Alexander McCall Smith. Michael loves the Edinburgh-based *Scotland Street* series (originally serialised in the Scotsman newspaper). Once he introduced the concept to Jon, they discussed how they could develop stories about fictional characters living in a small village.

They have now created over 60 characters with an array of personalities. There is Vera Cleeve, gnome-fanatic; Stephen and Gary, the local cops, never knowingly efficient; Ted the publican, who speaks Swedish but is not understood by his wife; Cody and Agnes, who own the local fish and chip shop and are way past the seven-year itch; George Dennis, Clara's husband, with his particular way of communicating, constantly irritating overly officious parish council leader and businessman, Frank Watson, who seems to irritate everyone else. There is Ethel, who hears the gossip in her coffee shop, including the reasons why Suptra Singh cannot return to his native India, and what Clara has done with a precious ring. We also meet a local hero after a night of flood and fire. Many more characters will greet you, including sisters Linda and Sherry, apparently vying for the amour of market trader and launderette manager, Allen Gomez. And then there is the band, trying to put a set together for the inaugural Leeford Village fête, without falling apart.

At the time of writing, the serial continues on both the Express and Star and Shropshire Star websites.

Welcome to Leeford Village - a story with all the drama, humour, quirkiness, romance and tragedy of village life!

Chapter 1: No Place Like Gnome

A small village on the western edge of Banfield, a Midlands town known many years ago for heavy industry and mining. A quiet place, bordering the countryside sweeping west, land that climbs over the Welsh mountains until it reaches the Irish Sea. Leeford may be quiet, but its characters and their activities keep the village alive and vibrant. None more so than Vera Cleeve, who is in danger of falling into a life of crime, the sort of crime many people wouldn't even notice. Or care about.

Gnomes. She loves them, does Vera. Any sort of gnome, not just the bearded guy sitting on a stool fishing all day. No, Vera will 'collect' any gnome from anywhere. Living opposite the vicarage in Market Street has given her lots of opportunities to add to her collection. The Reverend John Peterson and his family have a huge garden (ideal for fêtes) and his wife, Hilda, also has a liking for gnomes. She's has been known to scour Amazon or eBay for the gnome she wants. The last order she placed was for a 'Posh and Becks' pair. No accounting for taste. Gnomes have been going missing all over the village for years. The 'Great Leeford Gnome Mystery' is not really a mystery at all. Everyone knows it's Vera, but two years ago, Hilda Peterson had an embarrassing run-in with Sergeant Miller when someone had an entire West Bromwich Albion team of gnomes stolen from their front garden.

'But Hilda, the evidence is there for everyone to see. In your garden.'

'Stephen, you're not going to be stupid, are you?'

'Sergeant Miller when I'm on duty if you don't mind.'

'Alright, Sergeant Miller. You can call me Mrs Peterson. Anyway, what makes you think I did the great Albion Gnome Heist?'

'Well...' Sergeant Miller splutters over the cappuccino he had collected before confronting the suspect. 'Hil... Mrs Peterson. The Albion team disappeared from a garden in Green Crescent, not a hundred and fifty yards away, and, well, they're here. In YOUR garden.'

'I have a receipt from Amazon. Bought them two weeks ago.'

It takes Hilda five minutes to produce said receipt. The colour drains from the sergeant's face.

'Sergeant Miller, I'm not the only person who likes gnomes. Might I suggest you cross the road and check in the Cleeve back garden?'

Life can be strange in Leeford. For the past six weeks, Swedish phrases have been found written in various places in the village. On beer mats in The Cross, the local pub, on the advertising board at Spendfield supermarket. They've also been found on scraps of paper left in books in the library. The phrases are usually accompanied by drawings of the Swedish flag and an illustration of a moose (maybe an elk, no one seems to have sufficient knowledge to decide). The phrases themselves are nondescript, even mundane. It's as if the artist (or linguist) is making basic statements or asking questions. This is only known because, by chance, Ted Coleman (publican) has been doing a basic online Swedish course.

'Well, Ted, what the hell does this mean then?'

'Har du en tidning?'

'Good tidings? Christmas thing, is it?'

'No, it means "do you have a newspaper?"'

Doug Taylor, a young man obviously impressed by the knowledge of his elders, places another beer mat on the bar. 'What about this one, Ted?'

'Strange one this, Doug. "Vargen tar en ren." The wolf takes a reindeer.'

'They have reindeer in Sweden, don't they?'

'Yes, but why tell people in Leeford Village about wolves chasing reindeer?'

George Dennis, a retired headmaster, is popular in the village. No one takes him seriously, particularly his wife, Clara. He does have a rather strange way of speaking. 'Yes, me old drainpipe, the poor old girl is simply lonely. Craves male company.'

'She's got you, George,' says Doug, forever helpful.

'You don't understand old potato, she needs canine company.'

'Well, she is a poodle. Depressed, you say?'

'Old fruit, you've hit the nail on the head. Any concrete suggestions?'

Frank Watson can't take any more. He likes George but making a fuss about a dog (and a poodle at that) is not in his makeup. Nine years younger than the ex-teacher, and still running a business in East Banfield, he convinces himself that he, F. Watson, has his feet on the ground. This doesn't include pampering to poodles. 'For pity's sake, George, nip down the RSPCA and ask for a boyfriend for Tiddles.'

'Chloe, if you don't mind, young ginger biscuit.'

'Chloe? You've got to be kidding.'

'After my second wife. She ran off, like the first.'

'You've had no more luck than Tid - er - Chloe,' observes Doug, trying to sympathise.

Ted Coleman steps in, urging his regulars to contribute to his meagre income for that day. He encourages banter but has a distinct preference for the type of banter that could be pursued whilst holding a container for a drink in one hand or the other.

'Come on lads. Let's get some refills in, eh?'

'Hey, Ted,' enquires Frank, 'have you seen that strange bloke hanging around?'

'What strange bloke?'

'You know, duffle coat, scruffy hair, complete stranger. He scuttled away to the library when I tried to say "hello".'

'Probably one of those refugees the council has brought in.'

'That must be it.'

Banfield Council had agreed to take fifty Syrian refugees. Most of them were allocated places in the high-rise flats of East Banfield. However, a family of four was offered a flat above the shops in Leeford. This had been unoccupied for over a year. Everyone you speak to in the village sympathises with the refugees, but it seems that more than a whiff of nimbyism can be detected if one searches for it.

The empty flat, above the fish and chip shop, needed extensive renovation. Cody and Agnes Thornton, who run the shop, found the whole process particularly disruptive. Sadly, the Thorntons placed the burden of responsibility on the family earmarked for the flat.

'Why here, Agnes?'

'Cody, you're asking the wrong person. I'm on your side. Phone the council.'

'Waste of time. It always seems to be you and me that cop for it.'

'Not always love. We've done okay.'

'Until now. Anyway, I'm off to The Cross.'

All shades of opinion on any matter are heard in The Cross, and everyone is asked for their thoughts - Cody being no exception as he enters the pub.

'What's your take on it, Cody?'

'What about?'

'That refugee.'

'Now, Doug, we don't know he's a refugee,' contributes Ted.

'What does he look like?' asks Cody.

He had seen the family when they first arrived to view the flat. The father is a rather portly chap and sporting a neat beard, contrasting with a distinct lack of growth in the cranium area. 'No, that's not him, and I don't know if any other refugees are heading for the village. At least not yet. You know Agnes, she's on the ball when it comes to local politics and stuff.'

'Mystery man, then,' offers George.

Following the Hilda incident two years ago, Sergeant Miller never did check the Cleeve garden. There is a simple reason for this - he knew that Vera Cleeve stole gnomes. Everyone knew. He was going through the motions, knowing full well that the gnomes were being 'borrowed', maybe a sort of gnome holiday, with Vera as the landlady. Recently, however, there has been a spate of gnome robberies from shops and market stalls, not just temporary transfers from garden to garden. Everyone had got used to Vera. They knew the gnomes would eventually return to their rightful owner. Unfortunately for Vera, the sergeant also has a piece of evidence - the only market stall not losing gnomes is Vera's stall from which she sells books, bric-a-brac and ornaments, including gnomes.

'Are you going to arrest me, Sergeant?'

'If this carries on, I might have to.'

'I've been framed.'

'Vera, this isn't New York. This is Leeford market. Why should you be framed?'

'You'll soon find out if you look hard enough.'

A quiet day at The Cross. No one in the bar except Ted. The man doesn't open the door fully, but peers round it at the publican. Ted stares at the man, recognising him from the description Frank has provided.

'Good morning. Coming in for a drink?'

'Money... not much.'

Ted thinks he recognises the accent. 'How much do you have?'

The man approaches, holding an old leather purse and empties the contents onto the bar. 'You see.' Ted counts £1.78. 'Not enough for a pint - have a half. I'll throw in a bag of crisps.'

'Tack.'

At this, Ted's interest surges. 'My God, you're Swedish, aren't you?'

'No remember.'

Ted realises the man has a problem. He calls Sally, his wife, then opens the side-door leading to their private rooms, beckoning the man through. 'What is your name?' Ted asks, in both English and Swedish. The man doesn't know who he is or how he arrived in the village, but he admits to creating the drawings and phrases. The stranger's English is limited, but Ted starts to piece together the man's story, such as it is. Now he understands.

'Sally, call Doctor Roberts. Get him to come over as soon as.'

'Why, Ted?'

'This poor man has lost his memory.'

'What'll it be Suptra? The usual?' Ethel Lucas knows it will be the usual. It has been the usual for the past twenty-odd years, even when her poor Billy ran the cafe. In fact, she is so confident it will be the usual, she has prepared it beforehand, at 9.42 precisely, in time for when Suptra makes his entrance at 9.45 precisely. He enters the cafe without saying a word and sits down glumly. Ethel notices he is not wearing a tie and there is a tuft of hair sticking out from the side of his head. She places two slices of toast smothered in Marmite and a cup of very milky tea on the table - the usual table, at the far end of the cafe, where Suptra will sit for the next hour, before slowly making his way to the over-60s bridge club, at the Community Centre. Suptra Singh gazes at his plate.

'Something wrong, love?' asks Ethel, knowing there probably is.

'No, no, no,' says Suptra, emphatically but not convincingly.

'No, what, love? No toast? No Marmite?' Ethel looks at the tea, or rather the tea-flavoured milk. 'Tea too strong for you, Suptra?'

'No, no, no,' repeats Suptra, 'the toast is fine. The Marmite is fine. The tea...,' (Suptra pours out a saucer of tea and slurps it noisily, smacking his lips), '...the tea is a little strong to be honest, Ethel.'

'It's the tea, then,' says Ethel, impatiently placing the cup back onto the saucer. A splash of milky liquid spills over the side and onto the table.

'No! It's not the bloody tea.' Ethel is sure the beginning of a large tear is forming in Suptra's eye.

'Well, if it's not the...'

'It's Nita.' Suptra almost shouts out the name.

'Nita? Your niece? The teacher?'

'Yes, she wants to go to India. She says she wants to explore her heritage.'

Ethel breaks into a smile of relief. 'Oh, how lovely! You must be so pleased.'

Suptra shakes his head. 'Pleased? Why should I be pleased?' he shouts. 'She wants me to go to India with her!'

A customer, whom Ethel has never seen before, comes through the door and sits at the first table. 'And what's wrong with going to India? It'll be lovely for you both', she says.

Suptra puts his head in his hands and lets out a strange wailing noise that causes the new customer to turn around quickly. Ethel mouths 'sorry' to him.

'No, no, no. I can never go back to India,' says Suptra once he has recovered. 'Never. Do you understand?'

Ethel frowns. 'Can't say as I do, love, to be honest.'

'I can never go back to India. They will kill me!'

Monday is always the busiest day for Clara Dennis – and the most frustrating. Twenty years ago, when she first became an Oxfam shop volunteer, people would donate interesting items, items of value inherited from their grandmothers, or crusty aunts who had spent a lifetime hoarding *bric-a-brac*. These days, all the valuable items are being sold on eBay and the left-over worthless junk is deposited on the shop's doorstep over the weekend, after people have cleared out their cupboards and attics, or failed to sell items at the car boot. Today was no exception and Clara had arrived at the shop to find three black bin liners full of clothing, unwanted by anyone, particularly Clara. She had arrived early, knowing there would be the usual rubbish to sort through, to repack in bags ready for the recycling van to take away.

George, her husband, is away for a long weekend at an Old Boys' function at the school where he had been headmaster for thirty-two years and she had spent her Sunday in the garden, taking the opportunity to relocate plants without George's interference. She had pruned, tidied the shed and thrown George's failed horticultural experiments out of the greenhouse. George will be so full of the conversations with his old colleagues and students when he returns that it will be at least a week before he notices what she had done. She will deny it and convince him that they had done it together before he left for his weekend away. Sometimes, George's increasing forgetfulness serves her well.

Two bags of clothes, smelling of mothballs and goodness knows what else have been emptied and there has been nothing worth putting onto the racks. The third bag is more interesting. There is a nice pair of shoes that appears to have never been worn and an imitation fake-fur stole that is quite trendy these days. She puts both items to one side for pricing later. A few more clothes and then, right at the bottom of the bin liner, a handbag. A very nice handbag. *Real crocodile skin*, she thinks, and wonders who in Leeford would possess such an expensive bag that they were prepared to donate. 'That should fetch a few quid,' she says out loud.

She unzips the pockets at the side to check for any loose change or tissues that might have been left inside. Nothing. Then she sees a small, zipped pocket on the inside of the flap. She unzips this, but there is only enough room to put her finger in. At first, she feels nothing. Then, as she wriggles her finger to one side of the pocket, she feels something solid. She prises the pocket open a little wider and there it is, a ring nestling in the corner. She scoops the ring out with her little finger and hears it drop onto the laminate floor. She hears it, but does not see it and, for the next ten minutes she is on her hands and knees crawling along the floor, as if taking part in a fingertip search for a murder weapon. When she can stand the pain in her knees no longer, she slowly pulls herself up using the leg of the large table spanning the centre of the room. As she takes a step backwards, she hears the sound of metal sliding across the floor. 'There you are!' she says, bending down to pick up the ring which had lodged itself beside the table leg; a gold ring, encrusted with a row of five diamonds. 'Oh, my life!' she exclaims, holding the ring up to the light. 'This is worth a fortune!'

Clara tries the ring on her fingers, but they are too swollen with arthritis, and it does not pass beyond the first joint. The ring is so beautiful it brings a lump to her throat. She holds it up to the light again and watches as each facet of the diamonds reflects colour as she turns it, this way and that. She is mesmerised and fails to hear the first knock on the door. The second, much harder knock rouses her from her reverie with a start. It will be her volunteer assistant for the day, arriving just before opening time. Clara goes over to the locked glass cabinet where the more expensive items are kept. She pulls the key out of her pocket and unlocks the cabinet. There is a further knock on the door. Clara unlocks the cabinet, pauses and takes a deep breath. She closes and locks the cabinet and puts the keys into her pocket. And the ring.

Linda Cross loads the first service wash of the day. The machine gurgles for a couple of minutes then begins to fill with water. 'So, you're saying that Jesus was Italian?' says her sister, Sherry, sitting on a bench by the window eating her lunch, as she always does at 8.30 in the morning.

'Of course, he was,' says Linda, with an air of authority. 'Think about it. The Pope's Italian, and he's a direct descendant of Jesus. Therefore, Jesus was Italian.' Linda's strange logic never fails to amuse Sherry, though it always fails to convince. She lets out a laugh, which annoys her sister, who is convinced of her own assertion and pleased that she had worked out this connection for herself.

'Also, if you think about it, the Bible was written in Latin, right?'

'Er, right.'

'And Latin used to be Italian, right?'

'Well, wrong way round, but I see where you're coming from.'

'So, the Bible is Italian, and Jesus wrote the Bible.'

Sherry very nearly chokes on a mouthful of sandwich.

'Well, I never. I learn something new every day, Linda.'

Linda fills the next machine and slams the lid shut.

Chapter 3: Ring of Fire

Six months ago, Banfield Council devolved some powers to local parish councils in the borough. Leeford Village, used as the guinea pig for the devolution roll-out, embraced the scheme with enthusiasm. Determined that only local people could be elected to the parish council, they insisted that to qualify for a seat the representative must not only live in Leeford Village, they must also own their own home. Causing even more of a stir, it was decided that only the head of each household could apply. A maximum of eighteen delegates could take seats, but only fifteen applied - no election required. Nick Allthorpe, the Community Centre manager, brings out his best golden drawing pins (reserved for special occasions and official council business) to attach the list of representatives to the notice board. The irony has not been lost on him that as he rents a flat in the village with his partner, Jessica Townley, he does not qualify. Frank Watson, never short of an opinion, feels compelled to comment.

'Bit of a shame, you being Community Centre manager.'

'Quiet day in East Banfield, Frank?'

'Don't take it to heart. Let's see the list anyway.'

'No real surprises, Frank. You're there, obviously,' says Nick adding, in a subdued tone, 'as the current parish council leader.' Frank, owning a house in Green Crescent, has to rub it in, and reads out the other names:

'Steve Adams, Banfield Avenue; Nigel Cleeve, Market Street; Ted Coleman, East Banfield Road; George Dennis, Market Street; Ethel Lucas, Green Crescent; Stephen Miller, Mossy Grove; Rev John Peterson, Market Street; Dr Jeremy Roberts, Market Street; Suptra Singh, Green Crescent; Ken Taylor, Kidderminster Road (A449); Cody Thornton, Market Street; Daniel Windrush, Market Street; Adam Stringer, Green Crescent; David Ward, Market Street. No one in Spring Hill has applied to join the committee. Three places going begging. Shame you can't apply, Nick. First council meeting Thursday night, isn't it?'

'Feel better now, Frank?'

A predicament for Clara. The ring is safely tucked away in her 'special' jewellery box, positioned next to her late mother's carriage clock on her dressing table. She hasn't mentioned it to George for a number of reasons. First, he's still away at the Old Boys' function, the current headmaster asking him to stop on for a few more days. Second, he would forget what Clara said within minutes, with some comment about carrots or assorted fruit if questioned. Third, she doesn't want to tell anyone. Instinctively, she knows it was wrong to take the ring, but George has never bought her anything nice or expensive (or nice AND expensive) and this piece of jewellery, she thinks, is exquisite. What to do? Clara often talks to her cuddly Snoopy, also positioned by her late mother's carriage clock.

'What do you think, Snoops? I would like to keep it, and I deserve it. I don't get paid for the work I do. Don't tell me, volunteering is volunteering, the clue is in the word. I don't have to do it.'

No answer.

'I don't know. Why should I feel guilty?'

Still no answer.

'Tell you what, if it makes you happy, I'll put flyers up around the village about the bag. It's a nice bag – worth getting back if it was a mistake - and if the owner comes in and mentions the ring, they can have it. I'll say that we kept quiet about the ring in case we had a flood of people who wouldn't mind a free piece of jewellery.' At this, Snoopy falls off the dressing table. Clara doesn't even notice.

Sheri Lyons is on the afternoon shift as Clara continues the debate with the prostrate cuddly dog. She had noticed something in Clara's manner the day before, as they carried out their usual handover. *Shifty*, she thought, *but why?* They had chatted about the bag, and the flyers, and of course no mention of the ring. There was something, though, definitely something. The last time Sheri had this feeling was the occasion of the Scrabble dispute. Someone had mistakenly donated a valuable first edition Scrabble game made in 1949. They had returned the next day to understandably swap it for a rather battered 1970s edition. Clara was having none of it, telling the generous donor to 'sue me if you must', locking the valuable artefact in the cabinet. The donor had sufficient self-control to prevent himself issuing physical threats to Clara but did indeed insist that legal proceedings may well follow. On Sheri's return to the shop, Clara said nothing, but Sheri has a knack of spotting an atmosphere as she enters a room. It took her two days to discover the truth about the game, and that was only because the donor had stormed into the shop shouting the odds. On this occasion, Sheri checks the cabinet – no Scrabble games.

I'll get to the bottom of it, whatever it is, Sheri thinks. The flyer has been posted on the Community Centre notice board for less than an hour when Vera Cleeve enters the shop.

'What can I do for you?' asks Sheri.

'The bag is mine.'

'The bag?'

'You know, the nice bag you've found.'

'Oh, Clara's flyer?'

'It's brown with cream flecks.'

'From what I've seen of Clara's flyer, anyone could say that. The photo she took on her phone is very clear. Can you describe it in more detail?'

'What do you mean?'

'You know, the colour of the material inside the bag, possible contents...'

'Forget it, Sheri. Thanks very much.'

Sheri shakes her head with an expression that says 'typical' as Vera blunders out of the shop. She doesn't seem capable of entering or exiting a room or building in a, shall we say, normal way. Vera likes to make an entrance, and her style of exiting depends very much on the result of the current negotiations. She is always having negotiations, often with Sergeant Miller. She tries it on for personal gain, usually gnome-related gain, but a nice bag will do.

'I'd like to call this meeting to order.'

'This isn't the Commons, Frank.'

'Mr Chairman, if you don't mind.'

'Point of order, Mr Chairman,' shouts Ken from the back of the room. 'You said there are no elections because only fifteen people applied for seats.'

'Yes, that's right Ken. What's your point?'

'My point is – does that mean you don't have to be voted back in as chair?'

'That's up to you. Show of hands those who would like the committee to vote on the positions of chair and vice-chair?'

Unanimous. Frank asks if anyone would like to put their name forward for either position. No takers. So, he asks if someone could propose his name for chair and Stephen Miller for vice-chair. No one else wants to run the committee, so the coronation proceeds. Frank is in his element.

'We have no specific agenda items for tonight's meeting. Any other business?'

'Clara sent in apologies on behalf of George. He's still at that Old Boys' thing.'

'What about missing gnomes?' asks Ted Coleman.

'Stephen, would you like to take that one?'

'As you know, I have been investigating the mysterious disappearance of a number of gnomes.'

Giggles splutter from a small section of the committee.

'Any leads, Stephen?'

'No one will be named unless and until they are charged, but we do have some significant leads.'

From the same spluttering section could be heard, 'wonder if Inspector Morse will turn up in his Jag for this one?' Stephen Miller, police sergeant for Leeford Village and vice-chair, Leeford Village Parish Council, ignores the splutter. Nigel Cleeve coughs as necks are stretched to catch the expected defensive glare on behalf of his beleaguered mother but makes no comment.

'I will be interviewing Mr Gomez, who as you know runs a stall on the market, in addition to managing the launderette. He has lost two gnomes from his stall in the last week, and he has made a formal complaint. I will report back at the next council meeting.'

'Mrs Dennis?'

'Yes, who is this?' asks Clara, eyeing the phone with suspicion.

'John Tonks. I took over from your husband as headmaster.'

'Is there anything wrong?'

'Well, yes. You know that George stayed over for a couple of days. My wife was very happy to accommodate him, until, well...'

'What's happened? Has he been drinking?'

'Not sure, but his behaviour is very odd, and he seems quite confused. He told my wife he is still headmaster and keeps calling me "young carrot". That's what he called me over thirty years ago.'

'Oh, I see. I'm so sorry. I'll arrange for George to be collected. Will tomorrow morning be alright?'

'Yes of course. Goodnight, Mrs Dennis.'

Jeremy Roberts examines the stranger. He has, indeed, lost his memory. He doesn't know his own name, where he's come from, or why he's in Leeford. The doctor and Ted Coleman begin the process of speaking to everyone who has seen the man around the village. They need to piece together his movements and track down his family - if he has any family.

'I'll talk to Stephen Miller. He'll know what to do.'

'Thanks, Jeremy – he had a good night's sleep. He's welcome to keep the room for a few days until something is sorted out. Poor guy's been sleeping rough.'

'What about these drawings, Ted?'

'At least we know there's a Swedish connection.'

'I'm a GP, not a psychologist, but it seems to me that he's trying to remember and he's getting flashes of things, like the flag, the moose and something about, what was it, a newspaper?'

'One thing's for sure. At least this will distract Stephen from the stupid gnome mystery.'

Chapter 4: Vera

Vera was born two years after the end of World War II. Rationing is in place, the implementation of the new National Health Service is just round the corner, and her mother is driven into the ground by the time of Queen Elizabeth's coronation through sheer toil, after losing her beloved Arthur to a sniper in Northern France. Ellen Carter would not see her little girl's sixth birthday. It was left to her older sister, Rosemary, and her brother-in-law, Harry, to try to give young Vera a loving home.

Vera's Uncle Harry was what you might call a 'Jack-the-Lad', running a post-war service carrying anything – literally anything – on his handcart. By the age of ten, Vera was helping him to load the cart with a wide assortment of goods. One day, he was doing a house clearance in Central Banfield, a long haul from the edge of Leeford Village, but worth it.

'What's that, Uncle Harry?'

'That? Well, it's called a garden gnome. Do you like it?'

'It's beautiful, can I have it?'

So began Vera's love affair with gnomes. She started to collect them, repair them, paint them, revere them. The day she left home Vera had an agonizing choice. There were twenty gnomes in the Carter back garden, some of them standing guard in Harry's vegetable patch.

'Look after me carrots, they do. Look Vera, you won't have room where you're living. Take four of your precious gnomes. I'll take care of the rest.'

'Watch out for the dog next door, Uncle, you know what he's like.'

'Young lady, your gnome friends are fierce enough to look after themselves.'

Vera married and left the family home on the day of the Kennedy shooting. The man she married, Bert Cleeve, was a market trader in Leeford Village, but they had met in Central Banfield when he was covering a stall for a friend. Initially, he didn't share her passion for gnomes, but over time allowed her to place one or two at the side of his DIY stall, from which he sold everything from nuts and bolts to screwdrivers and garden trowels. Vera runs the stall to this day, but the products have changed. She also loves books, and these days competes with Steve and Mel Adams who sell books via the Internet from a business they run from home. Ornaments, including painted gnomes, also adorn her long-running stall, which she no longer needs for an income, but which she has vowed to continue to run till she drops. The Seventies delivered a contrast of emotions for Vera Cleeve. The birth of her son, Nigel, was book-ended by the passing of Aunt Rosemary and Uncle Harry. She had lost the two people who loved her most, and whom she considered to be her parents, although the smell of Pears soap still induces a brief flashback for Vera as she recalls Ellen, her mom, tending to her grazed knee with a dab of antiseptic cream and a hug. Rosemary taught her to cook. Harry demonstrated gardening tricks and the trade secrets of how to run a market stall. He could hold an audience and sell something – anything – to a considerable proportion of that audience.

Nigel excelled at school and Vera had ambitions for him. Not for her son the cold, damp, November mornings on Leeford market.

'No, he won't be going into any ordinary trade,' she would say.

She wanted him to go to university and become a doctor or lawyer. Something 'respectable'. Eight good GCSE grades at Banfield Grammar, but, no, he would not stay on.

'Butchers' trade for me, Mom. My mate, John, has got me an interview for an apprenticeship at Banfield Chops in the town. They'll teach me how to make pork pies and everything.'

Vera knew it was useless arguing. She had made her case and Nigel followed his mom in the stubbornness stakes. Once Nigel had made up his mind, that was it.

She has always worried about Nigel. He met Mandy when she was still married to Greg Withall, but Mandy had been trapped in an abusive relationship with her husband and finally decided to make a break and divorce him when he went to prison for six months for assaulting a police officer. Greg made several threats against both Mandy and Nigel, and by the time they married, Greg was once again in trouble, going down this time for ten years. Her son and daughter-in-law never knew, but during the period of the Withall threats, Vera employed a private detective to follow him. At first, Vera didn't realise, but Sid Spade had taken a fancy to her, as the saying goes.

Sid, a sixty-year-old retired policeman, met Vera twice a week in a cafe in Banfield. She did not want Ethel putting two and two together, so she kept clear of the village. Vera, an attractive woman in her fifties, had no problem attracting suitors after Bert died the year before at the age of just fifty-six.

Sid didn't allow his feelings for Vera to have an adverse effect on his clandestine operations. If anything, it heightened the level of customer loyalty of which he was extremely proud. 'Look after your customers,' his dad would say, 'and they'll look after you.'

Vera did, eventually, succumb to his romantic advances. Only if Vera publishes her memoirs (or leaves them in a box under the bed) will Nigel and Mandy (or anyone else for that matter) discover the truth. A few long weekends in Weston-Super-Mare conspired to seal the passion that had flourished between them. A passion, unfortunately, that did not last more than a year. As Greg Withall became more involved in criminal undertakings and developed his own relationships with the police and the county judge, Sid's professional expertise was no longer required. He kept up the pretence of following Greg for a few months, but the inevitable happened. Sid gained a few more middle-aged, female, clients and fell for a lady in East Banfield who had seen off a string of husbands – some worryingly before their time – and Vera found herself in the odd position of hiring yet another PI to follow Sid. This time Vera used a female detective, Bridgit Peabody.

Vera, in a low moment, was concerned that the worst might happen, and the new detective might meet Sid and fall for him, but, as it turned out, she had nothing to worry about on that score. With Greg on his way to prison again, Vera cancelled Sid's contract and had no further need for the ultra-efficient Bridgit.

The Leeford Village enigma that is Vera Cleeve is not, to local folk who know her well, an enigma at all. She has on more than one occasion scuttled back to her study to peruse the dog-eared pages of her Oxford Concise to test the veracity or otherwise of inculpations offered to her as she makes her way down Market Street each day.

'Enigma, enigma, let me see…' Nigel and Mandy would hear.

'Ah, "mysterious or puzzling person, or thing". Nigel?'

'Yes, Mom?'

'Am I a mysterious or puzzling person, or thing?'

'Where on earth did that come from?' says Nigel, not the least bit puzzled, being quite used to his mother's quirky ways.

'Someone called me "an enigma" at the market today.'

'Mother, you can be the most infuriating, irritating, awkward person I know, but we love you and no, you're not an enigma. One of a kind, I'd say.'

Yet another occasion where Nigel has managed to pacify his beloved mother, whether or not the comment was meant as a compliment.

'Thank you, darling. Love you too!'

*

One thing the long-standing residents of Leeford Village do know is that Vera is a family woman. Not just within the Cleeve household, although she would do anything for her immediate family - particularly her precious granddaughter, Holly - she also considers the older denizens of the village to be her brothers and sisters, whether or not the sentiment is reciprocated. She is eccentric, demanding, impatient, but has a good heart. Her hobbies and passions cause passers-by to take a second glance at her stall or her garden (given the opportunity, which is not often as the garden is her private place for respite), but she is rarely accused of hurting anyone. Occasional spectators of the supposed feud between Vera and the lady of the vicarage, Hilda Peterson, would be surprised to know that they do have a friendship, of sorts, and they do share an interest – not just gnomes – that has seen them share a taxi once or twice a year to take them into the city - the ballet. Vera's granddaughter, Holly, has been taking lessons since the age of three, and she has an ambition to join the English National Ballet one day. Hilda has some useful contacts in the art of the glissade and the rond de jambe par á terre, and they have been known to talk for hours about the little girl who might one day grace the stage.

Vera Cleeve. Much misunderstood. Not the heartbeat of Leeford, but very much part of the arterial system that allows day-to-day village life to flow and thrive.

'Ah, there you are, Nick. And Jessica.'

Frank Watson leans on one of the tables laid out in preparation for the Friday morning mother and toddler group.

'Hello, Frank.'

Nick continues to lay out tables. Frank sucks in a large draft of air, expelling it a few seconds later, followed by a loud cough.

'Are you okay, Frank?' Jessica asks, more concerned than she ought to be, given hers and Nick's past run-ins with Frank.

'I am, yes. I am,' puffs Frank.

Nick glances towards him but continues laying out the tables.

'I'm here on council business, in my capacity as chair, having been re-elected unanimously at last night's parish council meeting.'

Frank straightens his tie, as a re-elected chair of the council should.

An uncomfortable silence is broken by Jessica.

'Was it a good meeting, Frank?'

'Oh, yes. An excellent meeting. In fact, that's what brings me here. Nick, could I have a word?'

Nick only meant to put out three tables, but in his effort to avoid talking to Frank there are now enough tables around the room to hold a large jumble sale. At first, he ignores Frank's request, but curiosity gets the better of him. Frank is sitting on a far-too-small plastic chair that Jessica has fetched him, out of fear he might collapse.

'What is it?'

Frank shakes his head.

'Oh, Nick. I sense a touch of bitterness there, my lad.'

Nick shrugs.

'So, the committee decided to hold our first ever village fête. It's been proposed for several years, but no one has ever grasped the nettle by the horns, as they say, and made it happen,' Frank tugs at his tie, 'until now.'

Jessica smirks.

'Of course, we want to use the Centre as the base, headquarters if you like, mission control, you might say, where the fête sub-committee could meet to put their collective heads together to formulate a strategy, so to speak.'

'You're saying you want to hire the Centre?'

'In a nutshell. Of course, it would only be council members attending, you understand. They would require the appropriate level of privacy, befitting their status and the task in hand, you might say.'

Jessica cannot hide her annoyance.

'Don't worry, Frank. We'll make sure we let them in and then beat a hasty retreat, as you, particularly you, would say.'

'Well, there's no need to be like that, Jessica. But good on you for understanding the importance of the endeavour.'

Nick decides the best way to get rid of Frank is compliance.

'So, which days and how many of you?'

'Well, the sub-committee is four. Reverend Peterson is the chair, not of the parish council, that's yours truly, but of the sub-committee, and three others.'

'There's a small room to the side of the kitchen they could use. What do you think, Jessica?'

Nick looks towards Jessica for confirmation, but Jessica is deep in thought.

'Jessica?'

'Sorry, I was just…Frank, what are the criteria for council eligibility, again?'

Frank sighs.

'We've been through this, before. You must live in the village and own your own home.'

'Thought so. So, if you don't own your own home, you can't be on the council?'

'That's the nub of it, yes.' Frank turns to Nick. 'So, can we talk dates, Nick?'

Before Nick can answer, Jessica speaks again.

'Reverend Peterson owns the vicarage, does he?'

Frank takes a few seconds to think about this.

'Of course not. But he is the vicar. He has to be on the parish council. He's, well, he's…well, anyway, you couldn't have a parish council that doesn't have the vicar on it.'

No response from Nick.

'Could you?' asks Frank. Nick shrugs. Frank's face reddens.

'I agree Frank,' says Jessica, clearly enjoying the moment. 'But the fact is, he does not own his own home. So, technically, the rule regarding home ownership is being broken.'

Frank begins to utter a word that comes out as a high-pitched squeal.

'So, it would be unfair to not consider others who may want to sit on the council, but do not own their own home, wouldn't it? Such as Nick and I, for example?'

*

26

'Could you make me up a cheese sandwich, Ethel?'

Nita Sangra is in a hurry.

'Of course, love.' Ethel takes a wedge of cheese from the fridge and slices it thickly.

'Off to school?'

'Well, yes and no. It's a training day, so there are no kids. I forgot to make my lunch and the buffet they provide is usually awful.'

Ethel arranges the cheese slices on a thick slice of well-buttered white bread. 'Anything on it?'

Nita wishes she had asked for granary, then doubts whether it would have been an option. 'A bit of pickle, perhaps?'

Ethel spoons pickle from a large jar and spreads it until hardly any cheese can be seen. Nita reassesses her opinion of the school's buffet provision. Ethel places another slice of thick white on top and presses it down with her hands. A few chunks of pickle escape the sandwich and fall onto the chopping board.

'How's your uncle, Nita?'

'He's fine, Ethel. Why do you ask?'

'Oh, he seemed a little agitated earlier, that's all.' Nita has no time to stop to talk to Ethel, but this worries her. She has noticed her uncle has not been himself over the past couple of weeks, but she has been too busy with lesson planning, two parents' evenings and various after school meetings to ask him about it. 'Thanks, Ethel,' she says, stuffing the doorstep sandwich into her bag and making a swift exit before Ethel can say another word.

Clara is cashing up and Sheri is straightening the bookshelves for the umpteenth time.

'Why would anyone in their right mind put back a Penny Vincenzi novel next to Monty Don's *The Complete Gardner*? It makes you wonder what their own homes are like.'

Sheri's words do not reach Clara, whose mind is on her husband, George. Having collected him from the reunion she had watched him spend the evening preparing a talk to give to the new school intake. Clara had tried to convince him he was no longer a headmaster and suggested he let someone else give the talk, just this once, to which he replied that if the first voice of authority the young whippersnappers heard was that of one of these long-haired good for nothing teachers, their education would be over before it had begun. No, he was determined to give the welcome speech himself.

'Penny for them.'

Sheri waves her hand in front of Clara who is staring at the till.

'It's George. I think he's finally lost it, Sheri.'

'The headmaster thing? Well, maybe it's just a passing phase and he'll come back to his senses.'

Clara sighs. 'I'm not sure he has his senses anymore. I'm really not.'

Sheri places a hand on Clara's shoulder. Just then the door crashes open.

'Oh, I'm so glad you're still open!'

Clara is about to say, 'we're not', when the tall, well-dressed woman utters the dreaded words: 'I've come about the handbag.'

Clara's blood drains down to her feet.

'It's my mother's. Well, it was my mother's. She's not around anymore. Well, she is, but in a home. We had to put her there when she…well, you know how it is with old people.'

Clara thinks of George at home, probably rehearsing a speech he will never give. Sheri, wary after Vera's attempt to claim the bag, asks the lady to provide more information.

'It's brown, with cream flecks.'

'And?' Clara is hopeful that the lady is merely describing the bag pictured on the flyer.

'It has a pink lining, two internal pockets and a gold buckle on the strap.'

Clara turns very pale.

'Well, that sounds like the bag,' says Sheri, 'I'll go and fetch it.'

The woman explains to Clara they had cleared her mother's house, putting clothing and accessories into bin liners which they donated to different charity shops. The lady's mother was pleased her possessions, for which she no longer had a use, would be sold for good causes. The only thing she wanted and which they were to not let go under any circumstances was a brown leather bag with cream flecks. The lady and the husband had spent a fruitless couple of days trying to retrace their steps to recover the bag, but to no avail.

'Then, my husband remembered he had dropped off the last bag at this shop.'

'Here it is,' says Sheri, handing the bag over to its owner.

'Oh, that's wonderful. It's not the bag she wants most. It's her engagement ring she has always kept in this pock…', the lady unzips the inside pocket and feels for the ring. She opens the other pocket, sweeps her hand around the bottom of the bag, tips it upside down, before finally, as much as she is able, turning it inside out. She emits a loud wail.

'It's gone!'

Sheri turns to Clara. Clara shakes her head.

'I'm sure you must have lost the ring elsewhere. It wasn't in the bag, love,' says Sheri.

'Was it a special ring?' Clara is staring at the woman. Her voice is barely audible.

'It was her mother's engagement ring, Clara!' says Sheri.

The woman's wails have turned to sobs.

'It's not just that. Mother had it valued last year. It's worth twelve thousand pounds!'

'Has Shakespeare been in yet?' Frank wheezes.

Ted's glance is almost sympathetic, but not quite.

'Sarcasm is the lowest form of wit, Frank.'

'You're beginning to sound like him. Anyway, here he is. Pint and a quote.'

'Evening lads. Pint Ted, please.'

'Alright, Jack?' queries Frank.

'Frank, what were you looking for on the market today?'

'Never mind what I was doing, what's up?'

'Nothing, I'm fine. Why are you asking?' asks Jack.

'You are currently quoteless. When you've finished on the stall, you come in The Cross and give us a quote. Anything wrong?'

'No, I just like to keep you guessing. Especially you mate. Anyway, here goes:'

'Wait for it, lads...'

'Over hill and over dale, we have hit the dusty trail, and those caissons go rolling along.'

'Who in the name of Mike said that?'

'Gruber,' Jack announces, puffing out his chest.

'Oh, 'im off "Allo Allo"?' chimes in Cody.

A glare from Jack suggests that he, for one, is not a fan of Messrs Perry and Croft, his facial expression suggesting that he may well have swallowed the fly that has persisted around the rim of his glass.

'He's the one that sometimes plays the piano when René's awful wife sings for the customers,' suggests Cody.

'Didn't he fancy René?' enquires Ted

'For your information, it's Edmund Gruber. Anyway, don't you start. As the owner of this salubrious establishment, I thought you were on the side of culture.'

'You mean on your side?'

'Exactly.'

'On that note, gentlemen, I bring this intellectual cogitation to a conclusion. Last orders please.'

'Do the elders still mention it?'

'What do you think?'

'Look, I need to know. Nita's into that family heritage thing and she wants an answer.'

'You could come over and take your chances.'

Suptra pauses. The pause and the length of pause he produces is the kind that sounds like the roar of a lion to his cousin in Kolkata.

'Suptra, what's wrong? Are you still there?'

'Yes, Filtra, I'm here.'

'What are you going to do?'

'Not talk to you much longer. This call is costing me a fortune and all you've suggested is "take your chances".'

'Just trying to help.'

'Ten thousand dollars is a lot of money. I can't pay it back - it would take years.'

'I must admit, Suptra, if you come over with Nita, they will hold you here. You might be put to work in one of their factories. Forced to pay your dues. You'll never get home.'

'That's what I'm afraid of. At least if they let me live.'

'I'll find out what I can and ring you next week.'

Lost, that's what I am, lost, she thinks as she shuffles towards the crossing. Transferring oneself from the Oxfam shop at the end of Market Street to the precinct area that curls around to Spring Hill is not, under normal circumstances, a dangerous affair. However, in her current state of mind, Clara imperils everyone. Not least the tall, well-dressed woman with a habit of crashing through shop doorways – she has a substantial vested interest in the matter – nor Sheri, who could (unfairly) be implicated as a close colleague. Nor husband George. He may not know it, but he needs Clara more than ever. What would Sergeant Miller make of it if brought to his attention? Has she already committed a crime?

She ponders over her thirty-odd years in Leeford, her depressed state convincing her that the end is nigh. Clara has no recollection of waiting for the green light to offer her safe passage to the market area opposite the charity shop. She ambles past one stall, then another.

Odd thoughts spring to mind, her inner consciousness attempting to distract her. *Gomez – he's on his stall again today. He's replaced his gnomes.* She turns to her left - the array of shops in a semi-circle encloses her, taunting her to enter. The flower shop, music emporium, butcher's shop, launderette, and Billy's Cafe. *No, I'm not being interrogated by Ethel. She'd have me in the Tower. Seventy years old. I should know better. Twelve thousand pounds. What we could do with twelve thousand pounds. George is going to need help - more than I can give him. But it's not mine, it's the property of the bag lady. She knew exactly what to look for, and it's hers – or her mother's. Not mine, not Sheri's. The ring is the legal property of the bag lady's mother.* 'Fix your mind on that girl,' she tells herself, out loud, as she passes customers leaving the hairdressers and card shop further up the street away from The Cross. *What are they thinking? Give it back, give it back, it's not yours!* Right now, it's in her jewellery box near her mother's carriage clock, jealously guarded by a cuddly Snoopy.

Her mind made up, Clara almost causes a pile-up outside the sandwich shop as she steps off the pavement with one thought in mind: it would be more courageous to hand it in than leave it at home but not admit to what she did. *Make some excuse - it fell into my shopping bag by mistake. I thought it was a cheap ring that no one would miss. I took it home to clean and mislaid it. I had one of my turns. I...* Clara has run out of excuses. She somehow manages to get to the other side of the road, ignores the hand gestures of the scaffolding truck driver and walks towards the library. It's not often Clara allows books to go overdue, but she's letting a few things slip.

A lady she knows vaguely, Louise Cooper, a retired teacher, brushes past her. Clara nods an acknowledgement. Mrs Cooper is known for her obsession with the weather.

'It's a bit black over Bill's mother's.'

'Really,' says Clara.

Sally occasionally despairs. She married her beloved Ted on the understanding that The Cross would be a profitable pub and provide the family with the quality of life they deserve. She is content to put up with the odd bit of banter, but of late she has noticed that most of her husband's time is taken up by schoolboy-ish in-jokes, name-calling and in particular the pointless exchange of useless information (the lads call it cultural reference). Ted's exchanges with the erudite Jack Simmons is the current fashion. For once, Ted is leaning on the bar taking it all in and not yet contributing.

'I am certainly not one of those who need to be prodded. In fact, if anything, I am a prod,' says Jack, introducing the first quote of the night.

'Give us another one, Jack,' pleads Cody, sounding in his excitement the young side of fifteen years of age, belying his mature fifty-six.

'Eating my words has never given me indigestion.'

'It's an extraordinary business, this way of bringing babies into the world. I don't know how God thought of it.' Jack completes a treble, stunning at least one of his captive audience.

'Pro – flaming – found,' slurps George Owens as he sinks into another pint.

'Okay, lads, here's your challenge for tonight. I've given you three quotes, all by the same person. Place a pound on the bar, have a guess and I'll double your money if you're right.'

'A pound?' A voice jumps in from the back of the snug.

'Why else would I call it the Pound Challenge? We've done this before.'

'I'll have first go. Here's my pound, Jack,' chimes in Meredith Park.

'You're not a Leeford resident,' jokes Cody.

'No, I'm North Banfield, but I work here, and it's not the flippin' parish council anyway,' she fires back, winking saucily at her challenger.

Cody turns a deep shade of vermillion when one of his friends suggests that Meredith is flirting with him.

'What will Agnes think?' asks Ken.

'Watch out Cody, she's got her eye on you, mate,' suggests a cheeky-faced George Owens.

'Stick to your scooters, George,' comes back Cody.

'Are we doing this or what?'

'Right, Meredith, what's your guess?'

'Kevin Keegan.'

Jack can barely cope with the wave of mirth rushing through his diaphragm.

'What's so funny?'

'Nothing Meredith. It's just wrong. Sorry sweetheart.'

A succession of 'goes' is attempted by the usual suspects. Cody offers Elton John, Ken goes for Marilyn Munroe, and Ted pipes up (pound in hand) with Harold Wilson.

There is a general consensus on giving up.

'Ted's the closest.'

'Who is it then?'

'Winston Churchill. Honest – you can check on the web if you don't believe me. Thanks for the money lads and, er, Meredith. Try again tomorrow perhaps?'

Young Zack Peterson slips out of the snug by the side door, smartphone still displaying the face of a man most school children would recognise. *The face of Britain in World War Two. I could have had him then,* he thinks. *Got that in fifteen seconds flat while all the old codgers were still thinking about it. Bide your time, Zack,* he tells himself. *Wait till the stakes are a little higher.*

Introduced to the fish and chip trade as an eight-year-old, Cody was destined to follow in his father's footsteps. Ron Thornton had run 'Thornton's Chippy' on the East Banfield Road since the mid-sixties, following redundancy. Cody's mother died not long after he moved up to Spring Hill Senior and she had never been actively involved in the business up to that time. The loss of his mom, Alice, created an emotional chasm in Cody's life that has never been satisfactorily filled.

Throughout the 1970s and into the 80s, Cody had a passion he hoped one day would become his profession. His calling: crime. No, he was not a budding cat burglar or con artist, but he loved detective fiction, and he dreamt one day of donning a Columbo-style raincoat and the Sam Spade trademark Fedora. But, but most of all, he was obsessed with Colin Dexter's Morse stories. Each one taught him something new – how to interpret a crime scene, understand the pathologist's jargon, and he was very excited when the stories were transferred to the box that was the focal point of the Thornton living room. Like the modern version of their family fish and chip shop in Market Street, 'Thornton's Chippy' also provided a family home above the shop.

After the loss of his mom, Cody never gave schoolwork the attention it deserved. Two main subjects dominated his life - learning the trade from his dad and his Morse obsession. He devoured every sentence of Dexter's books and all the lines of each episode of the detective series. Until he met Agnes.

Perched on the high stool nearest the new Space Invaders machine, he allowed himself to be distracted by four girls positioned at the table near the main window. *That's our spot,* he thought. It took him a minute to realise he was repeating the mantra of his father and grandfather before that. A bunch of lads meeting for a drink and a game of dominoes at the same table every Friday night as a prelude to the next stage – disco night. Geoff, Ted's predecessor at The Cross had, on occasions, found it necessary to gently persuade temporary squatters or gatecrashers to find another table. Geoff looked after his regulars – even the youngsters. For him, that was anyone under forty.

George Owens was one of the regulars. His older brother, Jason, used to tag along until something happened between them. George never divulged the details, but Cody was aware it was about a girl. As George stood next to him, searching for a coin to have yet another go at blasting the aliens into infinity and beyond, he followed Cody's gaze across the room.

'I'll have the blond, old son.'

'Eh?'

'The one with her back to the window.'

'You're on,' said Cody.

The blond girl's friend sitting opposite her turned to glance at Cody before George made his approach. Just once. That was enough.

'Agnes,' says Cody.

'Agnes? I think she's more like a Sharon or a Clodagh.'

'Clodagh?'

'You know, Clodagh Rodgers the singer.'

'Never mind that, what do you think, George?'

'What I think, old son, is that you picked one with a bit of a reputation. Anyway, when are you seeing her?'

'Saturday night disco. What's this reputation then?'

'You do know, don't you Cody, that she's been out with three blokes in the last month?'

'At the same time?'

'Yeah. We call her *Miss Concurrently*.'

'Funny, George. So funny. Whatever. I like her.'

'Out of your league, Cody. Out of your blummin' league.'

'We'll see.'

'Hello.'

'Hello, Cody. You look nice - new jacket?'

'Oh, this old thing? A man must look smart when he meets a new lady friend.'

Agnes suppresses a giggle. *He's old-fashioned, but nice,* she thinks.

'Shall we go in, Agnes?'

'You know what, Cody? No. Take me for a ride in the country.'

Cody tells Agnes what George said about her being 'out of his league'.

'You are silly, listening to your mates. What do they know? I like you. That's what matters.'

'Can I see you again, Agnes?'

'Give me a kiss and I'll tell you later.'

Six months later, they were engaged.

'Do you really want to run a fish and chip shop, Agnes?'

'Don't you want to marry me, Cody?'

'Of course, I do. It's a fantastic offer that your dad has given us.'

'What's the problem, then?'

'I wanted to make my own way.'

'You still can. Your dad's retiring. He's asked us to find £20,000 for the shop, the flat and the business. It's worth at least twice that. We'll still need a mortgage, but I've got a part-time job and I'll help as...'

'As much as you can.'

'Exactly.'

'You know, Agnes. You're the girl for me. I need direction. I need to be told what to do. I promise I'll never get tired of that.'

'I'll hold you to that, love. Now, about a date for the wedding.'

Inward-looking, pensive. Introspective –that's the word. It describes Cody. The way he is. Time moved on. Happy in his marriage, Cody nonetheless wanted more. No doubt he realised he was luckier than most, and in the early evenings when Agnes would team up with their sole part-time employee to provide fish and chips for the community, Cody sat and pondered. *Could he achieve more? What more did he want to achieve? Is this it?* he thinks. *She's just what I need. She said she would hold me to it, and she did. Boy, she did, and still does.*

'You've done enough today, Cody. Why don't you have an hour and do some writing while I finish up in the shop tonight? It's not Saturday - our only busy night, Saturday!'

'Okay, love. Only thing is, I, well...'

'What is it?'

'The muse doesn't hit me when I choose. Sometimes it happens in the middle of the day, and I have to jot it down on a pad under the counter!'

'The muse?' she asks. 'The muse?' Just use your imagination. You used to do that.'

I love her so much, but she doesn't get it. Creative people like me have to be patient. Colin Dexter didn't permanently have the 'muse' at his fingertips. Morse still came to life. Thank God I've got my Morse videos. Be lost without them. Now, I could watch one of those. What about the first one - 'The Dead of Jericho.' Dunno, seen that one six times. Still good, but 'Last Seen Wearing', about a school runaway, is one of my favourites. Can't do it, Agnes will be calling me in an hour to 'clean the fat from the fryers' or 'restock the pickled eggs, please.' Never stops. I should be more grateful. I married Agnes for love, and I still love her.

Another evening in The Cross with the lads. Two, maybe three pints then home. Nothing exciting happens. Unless you count the night that Frank Watson was speared by a misdirected arrow as Ken Taylor attempted to force one into double-top; nothing ever subtle about Ken. Frank's little toe would soon recover. Same stool, same table, wonder what the topic of conversation will be tonight. Hang on, she's looking nice.

'Eh up, Cody, I would blink if I were you,' says George.

If heaven has creatures, she is one of them. A vision in dark blue if ever I saw one. To be fair, she has made an effort.

'Anything the matter, mate?'

'Nothing George, nothing.'

She's more than nothing. She's everything. Dark, curly hair falling onto her shoulders. Obviously been to the hairdressers today. Blue, yes, her eyes are blue. She's smiling at me. At last, she's noticed me. She's coming over.

'Any idea who she is, George?'

'Young woman who recently opened the new card shop. Lives in North Banfield. Why, Cody?'

'Never mind, George, give me a bit of space...'

North Banfield. Only fifteen minutes away. What is she? Early twenties? Twenty-four maybe? She's going to speak to me. I didn't want someone new. Although she didn't know it, she entered my life in the same place that Agnes had first appeared. The Space Invaders machine may have been replaced by a more modern contraption, the decor upgraded, and the publican superseded by a younger model, but the lounge in The Cross will forever be an important location for me. I vowed that the family would stay together no matter what, and the arrival of the little bundle that was Adam should have solidified that vow, but now she's on the scene.

When did it change with Agnes? When Adam was born – almost twenty years before the night the girl in the card shop walked into The Cross. I love him – he's my boy – but, unfortunately, Agnes did start to lose interest in me as she focussed on Adam. Nothing wrong with that – she's a mother, and a damn good one – but the spark of romance was extinguished amongst an array of nappies, towels, doctors' appointments, sleepless nights, and thousands of portions of cod and chips.

38

'George.'

'Just a minute, dear. I've got one more to get! Seven down. "A letter for Socrates". Something, something, G, something, A. Hmm.' George sucks on the end of his pencil.

'Any idea?'

'No idea, love. George, there's something I need to talk to you about.'

'Okay, dear. Let me just finish this. Now, what word has a G in the middle? Funny it ends with an A. Not many English words do that. Could be Latin, I suppose.'

Clara sighs and picks up her crochet. Since rumours of a village fête began to circulate, she spends nearly every evening with her crochet needle and wool making baby clothes for the craft stall, assuming one of the younger women from the play group at the Centre will set one up. Perhaps she should suggest it herself.

'Magma. Could that be it, petal?'

It will never be known whether Clara was ever going to reply as George immediately answers his own question.

'Now, why would it be magma? What's that to do with Socrates?'

George sits at the opposite side of the room, underneath the standard lamp. *He's looking old*, Clara thinks, *and his behaviour is more erratic since he came back from the reunion. Still, he is my husband. I should tell him my predicament. A problem shared is a problem…*

'Sigma! That's it! By Jove! Socrates was Greek, so we're looking for a Greek letter. Sigma! Obvious. I wonder if Palmer got it. I'll ask him in the staff room, tomorrow. Now, Jove. He was Roman, wasn't he Clara?'

Clara shrugs.'George, can I speak to you now? I have a problem and I need…'

'Later, dear. Whatever it is, we can talk about it later. To celebrate my success, I'm going to The Cross for a swift half. Fancy coming along, old girl?'

'No, George, I'd rather stay here and…'

'Finish your knitting. Of course.' George folds his newspaper, shoves it into a magazine rack then stands and smooths the front of his trousers. He walks across to Clara and kisses the top of her head.

'Shan't be long, my dear. Make sure the boys stay in their dorms.'

Clara hears George in the vestibule, putting on his coat. He opens the front door, but, after peering out into the dark of the street, he turns

39

and goes back into the house. Clara is aware of his presence behind her in the doorway. A couple of minutes pass before George utters in an uncertain voice: 'when is the baby due, Clara?'

Clara strokes the nearly completed pink cardigan on her lap. She turns around and sees George looking like a lost child, wringing his hands as though he is about to be scolded for daring to ask a question. 'There is no baby, George,' she says, softly.

'Oh, my dear girl. I'm so sorry,' he says.

She hears George pad down the hallway. A single tear runs down her cheek. Then she jumps up and rushes to the still-open front door. She shouts down the street, 'George. You've still got your slippers on!'

It's nearly closing time. Linda and Sherry pull the last load out of one of the dryers, folding the warm clothing into a plastic basket.

'Want one?' Sherry thrusts a packet of Minstrels in front of her sister.

'Actually, Sherry, I don't, thank you.'

'Are you ill? You never refuse a Minstrel. Or anything else edible, for that matter.'

Linda places the basket on the top of the counter.

'For your information, I'm on a diet.'

'A diet?' Sherry tries and fails to stifle a small giggle.

'Yes. So, Minstrels are no longer for me.'

'Since when have you been on this diet, then? Can't say I've noticed.'

'A few days.'

'A few days?' Sherry almost spits out the Minstrel she has just put in her mouth, but manages to suck it back in. It hits the back of her throat, causing her to cough violently.

Linda looks at her sister, unconcerned that she might be about to choke to death.

Sherry regains her composure and pops another Minstrel into her mouth.

'What about last night? The two packets of Doritos you demolished before going to bed? Or the half bottle of Coke you drank when you got up this morning? How do they fit into your diet?'

Linda holds up a pair of slacks that have turned themselves inside out during the washing and drying process.

'Sherry, you can't waste the food you've already bought. Not when half the world is starving. But once that has gone, everything I eat will be low-fat.'

Sherry takes the last Minstrel from the packet. She waves it in front of Linda.

'No, thank you. Anyway, I've already started making a few changes.'

'Such as?'

'Such as, this morning, when I got my latte from Ethel's, I had it with semi-skilled milk.'

'Semi-skilled milk? From an apprentice cow, would that be?'

'I've no idea how they do it, Sherry. And if I get used to it, I'll go the whole way and drink my coffee de-caffeinated.'

Sherry laughs loudly. 'Because there are loads of calories in caffeine, obviously!'

Linda takes the basket of still-warm laundry into the back room, ready for ironing. She grabs their coats and switches off the light. She throws Sherry's coat at her and puts on her own. 'I've no idea how many calories are in caffeine, Sherry, but if they can take it out of the coffee, every little bit helps.'

Pippa Philpotts is about to turn the sign on the Post Office door to 'closed' when she sees Ethel walking up the path.

'Oh, glad I caught you,' says Ethel, a little breathless.

Pippa returns to the counter.

'What can I do for you, Ethel?'

'Just a book of stamps, please. How are you?'

Pippa hands the stamps to Ethel.

'Well, a funny thing happened today, Ethel. I received ten parcels for Vera Cleeve. They were all gnome-shaped!'

Ethel purses her lips.

'Yes, very strange, that. Very strange indeed.'

The regulars are gathered around the bar in The Cross, watching the Wolves match on the TV in the corner, communicating with a succession of 'oohs' and 'arrhs' and a collective nodding or shaking of heads. So immersed in the action are they that when Jack bursts through the door, no one notices. However, when he shouts: 'he's fallen in the water!' at exactly the same moment the referee blows the whistle for half-time, they turn towards the door.

Ted responds first. 'That's easy, Jack. Pickles, from the Goon Show.' He punches the air, as if celebrating a victory, then puts his hand to his throat and warbles 'he's fallen in the water' in a high falsetto. He expects an appropriate response from his customers, but none is forthcoming. Feeling slightly embarrassed, he turns towards Jack. There is no Jack.

'Oh, where's Jack gone?'

'Pickles?' Frank hands Ted his empty glass.

'That was his name, wasn't it?' Ted places the glass under the beer tap.

'No, not Pickles,' says Cody. 'You're thinking of Eric Pickles. He was in For Love of Ada, with Irene Handl.'

'That's right, Cody. That's who I'm thinking of. Now, what was his catchphrase? Jack'd know. Where is he?'

He puts a pint of mild down in front of Frank.

'Got it!'

Then, in the voice of a Victorian Liverpudlian washerwoman, he shouts, 'have you been, Walter? Have you been?'

He laughs at his own impersonation.

Frank picks up his pint and takes a long gulp.

'It wasn't Eric Pickles, Ted. It was Wilfred Pickles. Eric Pickles was the darts player, wasn't he?'

'At Conservative Party conferences, I assume,' laughs Cody. Ted, immediately realising his mistake, joins in with the laughter and soon all the men are laughing loudly. That is, all except Zack, who has his back turned to the group. He's looking down at his phone, which he holds close to his chest.

'It wasn't Pickles at all!' He thrusts his phone into his trouser pocket, then turns around to face the rest of the men, all red in the face now.

'Who wasn't Pickles?' asks Ted, as though the past three minutes had not happened at all.

'It was Eccles who said, "he's fallen in the water", in the Goon Show. Not Pickles. Actually, a few of the characters said it over several episodes. Bluebottle, in particular. It was said in the last ever broadcast of the show.' Zack takes a drink of Coke and smacks his lips together.

'He's right, Ted,' says Cody. Frank signals his agreement.

Ted raises his eyebrows and purses his lips.

'Well, I never, Zack. Walkin' bleedin' encyclopaedia you are, my son.'

Zack flushes with pride.

'I'm off for a pee before the second half,' says Frank, taking another long gulp of beer then slamming his glass down a little too hard on the counter. 'Sorry, Ted,' he says and begins the long, breathless journey across to the other side of the bar. As he is about to reach the passageway leading to the toilet, the front door opens and Jack is

42

standing there, his shirt sleeves rolled up to his elbows. The others look at Jack and then at each other.

Jack regains a little breath and shouts: 'He's fallen in the water!'

'Eccles!' shout the men, together. They burst out laughing.

'Eccles? What?' Jack takes a step nearer to the men. 'I'm not talking about Eccles. I'm talking about George. He's fallen in the water.'

'The water?' chorus the men at the bar.

'Yes!' There is urgency in Jack's voice.

'The brook at the back of the police station. George is up to his neck in it!'

'Does Stephen Miller know?'

'I banged on his door and shouted. He got to George as I ran to fetch you.'

'We thought you were doing your usual.'

'Christ Ted, this is serious. I think George is stuck. Let's get over there. Stephen's called Gary.'

'You didn't tell me it was tipping down, Jack.'

'Where have you been the last three hours?'

'Working in the pub, as usual, and watching the game with the lads.'

'It's a bloody monsoon out here, and the brook's flooding.'

From his flat in Green Crescent, PC Gary Carr responds in less than five minutes. He arrives to find his boss, Sergeant Miller, holding onto George who is not in a fit state to help himself.

'What can we do to help?' Ted bellows over the crashing rain.

'Get Clara! She'll be upset, but we'll need help to keep him calm.'

'Fire brigade on the way?'

'Yeah. Gary's called them, but response from Banfield can be over fifteen minutes. We haven't got that long.'

'Jack! Go and get the lads then call Doctor Roberts.'

'How's he doing, Sergeant?' Ted asks, joining the sergeant, PC Carr and George in the brook.

'Barely conscious and confused when he comes to.'

'Bloody hell, Steve, it's rising past his chin! Can't we get him out?'

'His foot's caught in a broken branch or something!'

'It's too dark to see clearly, Sarge. Can we get some lights down here?'

'I'll sort it Gary - I'll get the lads to drive the cars near the brook. Headlights should do it,' says Ted.

'Jeremy, thank God you're here.'

'I'll take over holding George, Stephen. You need to organise things.'

'He'll be under in a few minutes. We're going to lose him.'

'Stephen, I know this sounds crazy, but call Amanda. She's just got home. Tell her to bring our scuba gear.'

'You dive?'

'We've done it every holiday for the last five years.'

Sergeant Miller runs up the bank and grabs his mobile from Ted who has anticipated Jeremy's request.

'Yes, Amanda. Jeremy's with George. Please hurry.'

'Gary. How long will the Banfield fire crew be?'

'Just spoke to Control - ten minutes.'

'Amanda will be here in five.'

Back in The Cross, the match is abandoned by the pub regulars, but not by the players and match officials. No one cares that Chelsea were two-nil up at half-time and that Wolves pulled it back to two-each with ten minutes to go. Even their precious football takes a back seat when someone is in trouble. Particularly a Leeforder. Five cars line up by the brook, full beams bearing down on the scene, engines running to allow a quick retreat when the fire service arrives. Amanda Roberts sprints to the edge of the lapping water, carrying the masks. Two of the regulars follow her with the oxygen tanks.

'Thanks, darling. Put one on George and help me on with mine,' says Jeremy.

'I'll set up the tanks,' says Amanda.

As the masks are secured, the rain is streaming from the darkening sky and the brook is becoming unrecognisable from its state just a few hours ago. Water gushes against the men and smashes against the low bridge just ahead of them. George is the first to go under, once again losing consciousness. Jeremy Roberts screams at Gary Carr.

'Hold onto him, I'll see if I can free his feet!'

Gary, a good five inches taller than George, can just about hold his head above the surface. Sirens blast through the night air and two cars are moved. Amanda stands helpless at the side of the developing torrent as her husband dives down to the bed of the brook. The fire engine shudders to a halt, doors fly open and six firefighters sprint to the water's edge.

'My husband - Doctor Roberts - he's under there!' shouts Amanda.

'What's happening, Ted? Where's my George?' cries Clara.

As Ted takes Clara's hand and starts to explain, Jeremy rises to the surface like Excalibur and the firemen pull George free. Frank, Cody, Zack and now what seems like a pub full of regulars are all there, cheering like the football supporters they are - for a hero, and for George.

'Jeremy. Is he going to be alright?'

'We're working on him. We'll do everything we can. Hold in there, Clara.'

As his mask is removed, George splutters. His wife weeps.

'He's going to pull through, Clara! He's going to be okay!'

*

Ethel serves the first coffee of the day. She's grateful her cafe is located at the far end of the precinct.

'No, not the hairdressers! That's two things in twenty-four hours!'

'Looks like it, Sherry. Good job there was so much rain. Kept a lot of it at bay.'

The flames could be seen from The Cross's car park and the smoky stench picked up as far as the church in the opposite direction.

'Was anyone in there – how's Jessica?'

'I think it started in the early hours. Jessica was called out.'

'How do you know?'

'I've just seen Nick on his way to the Centre. She'll stay there with him while the firemen do their stuff. She's terribly upset.'

The flower shop, music emporium, Meredith's Cards and the sandwich shop were all closed as soon as the emergency services arrived. There is no apparent damage to any other properties, and the damage to the building itself is minimal. They appear to have caught it in time, but all the equipment and furniture lie in ruins. These are the occasions when, yes, we are relieved that the annual insurance premium has been paid, but as to the owner, they may well sit and reflect on a business built, developed and then possibly ruined. Jessica Townley, quite naturally, feels exactly that.

'Darling, we'll sort it out. Get the assessor in, everyone will help with the clean-up. A few weeks' disruption.'

'That's one thing I have got right, Nick, I've already called him. He'll be over later this morning.'

Cody Thornton, having a slow start to the day in the chip shop after the excitement of the football match and George's emergency, is drawn not only to the events unfolding less than thirty yards away on the other side of Market Street, but also to the owner of Meredith's Cards. Standing by the stalls, well clear of the ardent efforts of the firefighters, Miss Park cuts a forlorn figure. Cody wants to reassure her. For one infinitesimal moment, he wants to hold her as part of the consolation package he could offer. She hasn't suffered like George or Jessica, but her business is being disrupted. Convinced that Agnes is calculating the direction of his gaze, he makes a speedy attempt at distracting her thoughts.

'Batter ready, love?'

'What were you looking at?'

'It's a mess, isn't it, Jessica's place?'

'Well, yes, but nothing we can do.'

'Thought I'd go over tomorrow and help with the clean-up. Frank has already organised a whip-round.'

'Would they do it for us?'

'Course they would, you know they would.'

'What's for tea?'

'We don't get this excitement in North Banfield. If we didn't work in Leeford, we'd miss out.'

'Lin, what sort of answer is that?'

'Just saying. What did you want?'

'What's for tea?'

'We'll have to eat that spaghetti carbonara.'

'Why?' says Sherry, with a look that suggests she's practised exasperation at the School for Frustrated Sisters.

'Goes off at midnight.'

'Oh, for God's sake, Linda, we've had this conversation before. Does it say, "use by" or "best before"? Anyway, do you honestly believe that at two minutes past the witching hour, loads of food suddenly jumps up and says, "that's it, I'm off!"?'

'Dunno what's eating you, Shez.'

'You are, most of the time. If that spaghetti is alright now, it'll be alright in twelve hours' time. Okay?'

'If you say so. Anyway, it's your fault.'

'How do you make that out?'

'You're always scouring the ends of the aisles at Spendfields. You know they specialise in massive discounts on short-dated stuff. You're a Wally for the bargains.'

'I do the budgeting. You'd just spend it all as it comes in.'

'You make it sound so complicated.'

'Forget it, Linda. Gomez is coming. Wish you didn't gawp at him like you do.'

'Sherry...' but the door opening curtails the sisters' nonsense.

'Sherry, could I have a quiet word?' asks Gomez.

'You okay, Suptra?'

'No, Ethel.'

'Here's your coffee. You don't have to tell me, but it might help.'

'I told you I can't go to India.'

'I remember.'

'It was a long time ago, but I got involved with a gang in Kolkata. I was stupid. Took a loan from some gangster.'

'Why? How much?'

'Ten thousand dollars - to help my cousin in Birmingham. His business was in trouble.'

'What happened, Suptra?'

'They gave me the money, and then I transferred it from my bank in Kolkata to my cousin, Jamani.'

'And?'

'I haven't heard from him since. Disappeared. They called in the loan, and I had no way of paying it. Plus the fifteen percent interest.'

'So, did you leave India?'

'I had to. That's why I came to Leeford over twenty years ago, and I can't go back, Ethel. I don't know how I'm going to explain this to Nita. I feel so ashamed.'

'How's George, Clara? I heard he almost drowned.'

Ethel pours tea into a China teacup, reserved for Clara's exclusive use for as long as anyone can remember. The cafe is empty apart from the two old friends sitting at a table near the counter. Clara absent-mindedly stirs milk into her tea. Ethel spoons the froth off the cappuccino she has made for herself.

'You look like you could do with something to eat. Are you sure you won't have a piece of toast?'

'No, thank you, Ethel. I've lost my appetite. It was such a shock. Poor George had no idea what was happening to him.'

Ethel takes a sip of coffee. Perfectly made, she thinks. 'Did they take him to hospital?'

'Yes, they checked him out. He was physically okay. They discharged him a couple of hours after he arrived. Physically, he seems fine.'

'Physically? You've said that twice, Clara. But mentally? How is George mentally?'

Clara sighs. 'Well, not so good. He thinks he's still a headmaster and we seem to be reliving the days when we lived at the school.'

'You were the matron, right?'

'Yes. Matron, wife, head cook and bottle washer, surrogate mother, counsellor. It was a full-time job caring for those boys. But I did love it. And George was such a good headmaster. Strict, but very caring.'

'And now he thinks he's back there?'

Clara looks out of the window. It's a bright day and the precinct is beginning to fill with early shoppers on the way to the market. *Normal people, living normal lives,* thinks Clara. 'Yes, I believe he does, Ethel. I truly believe he does.'

'Cody. Good morning.'

'Good morning, Jessica. I thought I'd just come over, see if you need any more help.'

Jessica Townley looks around the smoke-damaged remains of her hairdressing business. She has called her customers to cancel their appointments and, with one or two exceptions, has received sympathy and offers of help. She is worried that however loyal her customers have been, they will migrate to the hairdresser in Banfield, and she will not get them back when she reopens. Whenever that will be.

'I'm just waiting for the insurance assessor's report. It might take a few days and I can't do anything until we have that.'

'Ah, bureaucracy, the curse of the modern age, eh?' Cody puffs out his chest, as he always does when making a pronouncement.

'I suppose so, Cody. But at least we're insured. Many businesses aren't.'

Cody is about to express his opinion on businesses that do not take out insurance when they are both distracted by Meredith Park, who has entered without either of them noticing.

'Hi, Meredith.' Jessica, beams at her neighbour, relieved at being spared a lecture from Cody.

'Hi, Jess. It's a bit dead in the shop. I thought I'd pop in and say hello.'

Cody clears his throat. 'Has the fire affected your business, Meredith?'

'Well, trading's been difficult for a while now, but the fire can only make things worse.'

'Oh, I'm sorry, Meredith.' Jessica gives Meredith a hug. Cody feels a pang of envy.

'It's not your fault, Jess. These things happen, don't they.'

'Ah, that's where you're wrong, Meredith!'

Jessica and Meredith turn to face Cody, who immediately regrets his outburst.

'Meaning?' The look on Jessica's face tells Cody he needs to tread carefully.

'Well, I'm just saying that everything has a cause. Nothing more than that, Jessica.' He looks from Jessica to Meredith then back to Jessica again. 'Things just don't happen by themselves, do they?' The two expressionless faces make no response. 'I mean, there's always something causes a fire, isn't there. Unless, of course, it's spontaneous combustion. There are instances when people have just…' Cody's exposition of spontaneous combustion, a phenomenon that he would welcome right now is interrupted by Meredith taking her leave. Cody watches her go through the door and turn towards her shop. He continues to look long after Meredith is no longer in view. 'Well, Jessica. I think I'll be off too, if you don't need me here.'

'No, I'll be fine, Cody.' There is an uncomfortable pause as Jessica tries to suppress her anger and Cody tries to suppress his regret, not so much at having upset Jessica, but having upset Jessica in front of Meredith. Once outside, Cody takes a deep breath that fills his lungs. He lets it go slowly and immediately feels calmer, though a little lightheaded. He begins to cross the road, then changes his mind and pushes the door into Meredith's shop. 'Hello again, Cody. What can I do for you?'

A lot, thinks Cody, then checks himself. He takes another deep breath.

'Meredith. There's something I've been wanting to ask you.'

Meredith cocks her head to one side. Cody wishes she hadn't. He feels the same sensation that coursed through his body when he first met Agnes, thirty-two years ago. He feels his throat tighten. He feels nervous. And a little guilty.

'Erm, do you have any birthday cards?'

Meredith frowns. 'We are a card shop, Cody.'

Cody feels his face redden. 'Yes, of course. Of course, you are.' He looks round at the rows of cards neatly displayed on plastic racks and carousels. On one side of the shop small gifts are arranged on shelves, each tagged with a buff-coloured label stamped Park Cards and Gifts.

'Cody? You wanted a birthday card?'

'Yes, yes. I did.'

'We have fifteen different ones. Which one would you like?'

Cody looks at the cards and then at Meredith. His mind goes back to forty-eight hours earlier when she was standing outside the shop, looking so forlorn. He could help her. Yes, he could help her, after all! 'One of each, Meredith. I'll take one of each!'

'Do you want another cup, Clara?'

'No, that'll do me. I'd better get back to George. He'll be wondering where I've got to.'

'Of course,' says Ethel, gathering the empty cups. 'Oh, before you go, I must tell you about Suptra.'

Clara, who has risen from her seat, smooths the back of her dress and sits down again. There is nothing she likes more than a titbit of news about Leeford's residents, particularly if it's something she is not supposed to have heard (as she suspects in this case, from the way Ethel had almost whispered 'I must tell you'). 'Oh? Go on!'

Ethel relays everything Suptra has told her about his huge debt (inflated by Ethel to one-hundred-and-fifty per cent of its original value) and the danger he is in if he returns to India. Clara had not expected such drama to unfold on such a normal morning as this. 'Yes, if he doesn't pay the money before he gets to India, he could be in real trouble. There are some not very nice people that want their debt paid back.' Clara is wide-eyed and leaning across the table, eagerly awaiting

Ethel's next sensational revelation.

'So, you can see his problem. He can't tell Nita, of course.'

'Of course. What would she think of him?'

'Exactly!'

'Clara, this is between you and me, mind. I don't think Suptra wanted anyone but me to know.'

Clara taps the side of her nose.

'Understood.'

'You've taken your time!' Agnes is wiping glasses, still hot having just come out of the washer.

'Have I?' Cody is surprised how small his voice sounds.

'And what's in that bag?'

Cody grips the bag, filled with fifteen assorted birthday cards.
'Nothing.'

'Let me see.' Agnes throws down her cloth and moves towards where Cody is standing.

'Stop!' he pushes out his hand, as if to halt traffic. Agnes stops, despite herself.

'It's something for you. A surprise. From Meredith's. I hoped you wouldn't be here. I'm going upstairs. No questions.' He lowers his hand, turns one hundred and eighty degrees, and runs upstairs. Agnes shrugs and picks up her cloth.

Poor Suptra, thinks Clara as she walks slowly back to her house. *Such a nice man too. And poor Nita, if she ever finds out, which she surely will as soon as they are in India.* The house is quiet. There is a space in the vestibule where George's hat and coat normally hang. She assumes he has gone for a walk. So far, this has not been a problem and he has always returned after about an hour. Still, she can't help worrying a little. She doesn't have to work until the afternoon, but whenever she thinks about being in the shop, she feels her stomach tighten. Why didn't she just say that she had found the ring and hand it to its owner? It is such a beautiful thing, so perfect. Now, the very thought of it hangs over her like the sword of Damocles. She goes to the bedroom and takes the ring out of the drawer. Twelve thousand pounds, right there in her hands. But if she sold it, what would she do with the money? She couldn't spend it. People would notice. And it would be stolen money. She could go to prison for it. She puts it back, as she has done every day since it first came into her hands, then shuts the drawer and closes her eyes. Suddenly, an idea hits her like a bolt of lightning. 'Of course! Of course!' she shouts. 'Of course!'

'Stephen, hold on a second.'

'Sorry, Doc. In a hurry. Trying to catch up with Allen Gomez. Difficult man to pin down, but it's the main market day. He'll be there.'

'Never mind your gnomes. What about our Swedish friend?'

'Nothing I can do Jeremy, sorry.'

'What do you mean, nothing you can do?'

'He's disappeared.'

'Disappeared?'

'You know, Jeremy, for a doctor with all those certificates, you have a terrible habit of repeating what people say.'

'Repeat... well, what do you expect? Is there no trace?'

'Nothing, apart from the sighting in the cafe. Now, that was strange.'

'What was?'

'When I popped in to talk to Ethel, she was bleating on about Suptra and that someone wanted to kill him. Crazy talk, I thought, but it was the new customer that intrigued me.'

'Man or woman?'

'Man – fits the description of our forgetful Swedish artist.'

'What was so strange?'

'He ordered a coffee and cream bun and paid cash, no problem.'

'What's so strange about that?'

'Ethel reckons he had a London accent.'

'Mr Gomez, do you have a minute?'

'Sergeant, good to see you.'

'About these gnomes – any more gone missing?'

'No, but they wouldn't, now she knows.'

'Who knows what, Mr Gomez?'

'That old bat, the Cleeve woman. She's being careful now.'

'Steady now. There seems to be a bit of history between you.'

'You could say that.'

'Is it true that you want to take over all the stalls?'

'Not exactly.'

'How exactly, Mr Gomez?'

'The old-timers are holding us back. We need a vibrant market, like the one in Brum. I'd have themes, like the German market.'

'Knackwurst, that sort of thing?'

'Unless you're being facetious, yes. German sausage and stuff like that.'

'Why did you have good old-fashioned British gnomes on your stall then?'

'Well...'

'Might I suggest we make it known that if the missing gnomes turn up, we'll say no more about it? Wouldn't want the expression "false accusation" to come into play would we, Allen?'

Allen's eye wanders to the passing figure of one of his launderette girls. Sergeant Miller recognises a leer when he sees one and Allen is distracted long enough to be caught off-guard.

'Deal, Mr Gomez?'

'Okay, if you insist.'

'Back again, my dear?'

'Ethel, you're the only person I can truthfully talk to.'

'Sit down, I'll do your usual.' Ethel gestures towards the stairs. The upstairs part of the cafe is more comfortable and, usually, more private. Most customers prefer to sit downstairs; only when the sun faces south to warm the precinct do they brave the outside tables for their morning cappuccino. Clara finds a spot near the window, hesitates then chooses the seat facing the precinct.

'What is it, Clara?'

'The baby.'

'The baby?'

'We'd only been married for two years. He was so delighted and proud that he was going to be a dad.'

'You miscarried?'

'Yes, but at seven months. I was bad enough, but George never ever got over it. Then we stopped talking about the baby, as if it never happened.'

'So why, after all this time, are you so upset? Sorry, that sounds unkind. You know what I mean, love.'

'No, it's okay Ethel. It's just George. You know the night of the flood?'

'George getting stuck and Jeremy saving him?'

'Yes. Well, before it happened, we chatted at home about this and that. George, bless him, asked me to make sure the boys stayed in their dorms. Then he went for a walk.'

'What happened, Clara?'

'He saw me crocheting, you know, that stuff I do for Oxfam, the baby clothes that we put on the dolls.'

'What did he say?'

'He asked me when the baby is due. Our baby.'

'Oh my God, Clara!' Tears are forming in Ethel's eyes.

'I told him there is no baby. He was so sad. It broke my heart.' Ethel sighs and reaches across, gently touching Clara's hand. Clara lets her tears flow and grips Ethel's arm with her other hand.

'I – I love him so much Ethel, and I feel that I'm losing him.'

Edward Palmer, Ethel's partner in life, mounts the last step to reach the upstairs section of Billy's Cafe, just as the two women embrace. 'Oh my, I'm sorry,' stutters Edward.

'It's alright love, we're just a bit upset about something.'

'I'll leave you to it. See you at home tonight. Nice to see you, Clara.'

The man grasps his second pint. 'No problem with having four or five tonight,' he mutters to himself. 'I've got a room for the night and the Scirocco is safely tucked away in the car park. People go on about company car drivers, but I love that car and it deserves to be looked after.'

'Another one after that?' enquires Cody.

'Don't mind if I do. The wife's not here so I'm off the leash. How's your little woman treating you?'

'She's wonderful. Sounds corny, but it's the stuff dreams are made of.'

'What, like Ross Poldark and Demelza, only a twenty-first-century version?'

'Goes a bit deeper than that, and I don't have the shape to go shirtless in a field of barley.'

'Almost poetic. But what's she like?'

'Oh, a smile that would melt the heart of a Russian oligarch. The way her bottom lip juts out ever so slightly and the thing she does, tilting her head when she looks at me, and in such a cheeky, saucy way.'

'Go on, tell me more.'

'Dark brown hair that tumbles onto her shoulders and wisps about as she talks or turns her head. She wears glasses – reminds me of a sexy librarian - but they bring out her lovely deep blue eyes that add to that cheeky smile. She thinks her nose is too big, or too long, but I think it gives her a royal appearance, you know, like Princess Di.'

'Sounds lovely.'

'She is, with a personality to match. I'm so lucky to know her.'

'You know, Cody, on reflection, I won't have that third pint. I'm off early in the morning. Next stop Crewe, then a new customer in Leeds. Never stops. Fascinating talking to you, mate, and it's been nice to meet someone new. I haven't stayed in this village for some years. Nice to hear the lovely things you've said about your wife...'

'Hang on. My wife?' Cody snaps back to accompany his double-take.

'Your little woman, the love of your life?'

'Oh no, mate, that's Agnes. I wasn't talking about... I was...' He leaves his sentence hanging. Even Cody is too sensible to completely open up to a fellow drinker - even a total stranger.

'Linda! Hi!'

'Hello Allen, always a pleasure.'

'Yes, well, is Sherry around?'

'Dental appointment. Remember?'

'Yeah – can you give her a message?'

'Course.'

'She's always wanted to go to the Botanical Gardens at Birmingham. Thought we'd make a day of it. Tell her I'll pick her up at your place at ten, Sunday morning.'

'No problem, Anything else?'

'No, that's it, thanks. See you, Linda.'

'Yes, you will,' she says as he walks away from the launderette. Linda has no intention of passing on any such message to her beloved sister. Within an hour she is on the phone to Gomez. 'Allen? It's Linda. Sherry couldn't call you. Dental thing. There's a slight change of plan - she'll meet you at ten on Sunday, but it will have to be here, at the launderette.'

'Why?' asks Allen.

Linda had anticipated the query. 'Our least favourite uncle is paying a visit. Coming here is perfect for getting out of the way. I'd do exactly the same in her position.'

'Okay, ten it is, at the launderette. Thanks Linda, you're a gem.'

'See you Allen...'

Sunday morning, and Sherry knows nothing of the arrangement. There is no visiting uncle, and she is having a well-deserved lie-in.

'Where are you off to, Lin?'

'Wouldn't you like to know?'
'Got to be a fella.'
'Could be, Shez, could be.'

'Oh, hello Nita, I didn't expect you to be at home.' Clara feels her face reddening.

'It's Sunday. My PPA time, which I never get at school. Would you like to come in?' Nita Sangra steps to one side, exposing a long hallway.

'PPI time? Are you claiming?'

'No, PPA. It's time they give us to plan and assess. Three hours a week. It's a joke! I spend at least that amount of time every night marking and planning lessons. On Sundays, I try to catch up with everything, though I never do.' Nita can see that Clara is determined to remain on the doorstep. 'Is there something I can do for you, Clara?'

'It's your uncle I've come to see. Is he in?'

Nita shakes her head. 'No. It's his day helping out at the Community Centre. He won't be back until teatime. You could pop down there if you like.'

If you like. Clara is not sure that she does *like* anymore and is beginning to think her idea of what to do with the ring is a stupid one. However, she thanks Nita and walks in the direction of the Community Centre.

Agnes is filling the fish fryer with fresh oil, ready for the lunchtime opening. Sunday, the quietest lunchtime of the week, but enough business to make opening worthwhile. *Thump. Thump. Thump.* She wonders if other residents who live in the flats above the shops can hear it. Her watch reads 10:30, too early for music. *Thump. Thump. Thump.* She shouts upstairs. 'Adam! Turn that music down!'

Since her son Adam moved back into the flat following the breakup of his latest long-term (for Adam) relationship with the girl from Banfield, he has become a teenager again, staying out until the early hours, leaving his clothes wherever they have fallen and the state of the bathroom after he has used it would have the health inspectors closing down the chip shop. Working with him is fine - living with him is becoming a nightmare. *Thump. Thump. Thump. Why isn't Cody telling him to turn it down?* thinks Agnes, knowing how her husband is usually ready with a sharp word for their son for the slightest misdemeanour. *Thump. Thump. Thump.* Then a sound like a klaxon, followed by more thumps in quick succession. 'Right, that's it! Adam!

Turn that music down!' *Thumpthumpthumpthump*. 'Now!' Agnes goes into the yard and returns with a hundredweight bag of potatoes. *Adam should be doing this,* she thinks. *Or Cody. Where is Cody?* The music is so loud that Agnes can't hear herself think. She runs up the stairs to Adam's room, but the music is not coming from there. The music is coming from the lounge. She opens the lounge door and is met by the sight of Cody punching the air, hopping from one foot to the other, almost in time with the music. 'Cody! What the…' Agnes reaches over to the music player perched on top of the television and switches it off. Cody punches the air one more time, then collapses in a heap on the sofa.

'What on earth are you doing, Cody? I thought the ceiling was going to come through!'

Cody throws his head back and spreads his arms wide. 'Ah, it's so good!'

'So good? So loud!'

Agnes picks up a CD case from the floor. 'Dance Anthems?'

'Yes, Agnes. Some of the best are on here.'

'Since when have you been interested in dance anthems? I've never seen you dance in all the years I've known you.'

'I've never found the right music, before. And now I have,' says Cody with a grin, before a fit of coughing takes him over.

'You okay?' asks Agnes, concerned for her husband's health, if only briefly.

Cody rises from the sofa. 'Ouch!' A pain in his lower back shoots through his body.

'See, that's what dance anthems do for you. Anyway, how do you know about this, this music, if it can be called music?'

'I heard it in a shop and fell in love with it, straight away.' Cody stretches towards the ceiling in an attempt to relieve the pain.

'Which shop? In Leeford? No one plays this stuff in Leeford.'

'I can't remember. Maybe in the pub.'

'Well, I can't imagine Ted or Sally playing this noise for one moment.'

Cody sits back on the sofa. 'It must have been a shop then. Perhaps Meredith's.'

'Meredith's? When were you in Meredith's?'

'I think I'll get some frozen peas on this muscle. Do we have any?'

'When, or more to the point, *why* were you in Meredith's?'

Cody feels queasy but cannot decide whether it's from the back pain, or his wife's interrogation. 'I can't say. But hasn't someone got a

60

birthday coming up soon?'

Agnes groans. 'I'll get you those peas. We need to open soon. Where's Adam?'

'Oh, he texted last night to say he wouldn't be home until this afternoon. With some fancy woman, no doubt.'

Agnes laughs. 'Fancy woman. I haven't heard that phrase for forty years. Maybe you should stick to dad-dancing – it's more appropriate for men of your age.'

Clara walks through the main hall of the Community Centre to the kitchen where Suptra Singh is washing a paint brush in the sink.

'What have you been painting, Suptra?'

'Oh, just touching up. Keeping the place looking nice, you know.' Suptra places the brush on a piece of kitchen roll and empties the sink. Clara watches milky water spin around the plughole. 'What can I do for you, my dear?' he asks, drying his hands on a towel.

Clara swallows hard. 'Suptra, I hope you don't think we've been gossiping, but Ethel has told me about your situation.' Suptra dries each finger in turn, then hangs the towel over a rail at the side of the sink.

'My situation? And what would that be?'

Clara swallows again. 'The money you owe. The trouble you are in if you go back to India.' Suptra walks out of the kitchen, into the main hall.

'So, does everyone in Leeford know my situation, Clara?' Suptra's voice echoes through the empty hall.

'Oh, no. Certainly not. It's just that Ethel was worried. She needed to tell someone. She takes hold of Suptra's arm. 'And I'm glad she did because I can help you.'

'Help me? How? By talking about me?'

'No. I really can help you. With the money you owe.'

Suptra feels Clara's grip on his arm tighten. He notices her bony hand, the fingers slightly bent with the onset of arthritis. 'Go on then, Clara. Tell me.'

Clara takes a deep breath. 'When my mother died, a few years ago now, she left her estate to me and my two sisters. The money, the house, and its contents were split three ways. However, she also left each one of us something to remember her by. Martha had her collection of Wedgwood figurines, Dorothy had all her books and I had...' Clara reaches into her handbag, '...this ring. 'She places the ring into Suptra's hand. He turns it around so it catches the light.

'It's beautiful, Clara, but how does it help me?'

'I believe it's worth quite a lot of money. More than you need to pay off your debt so you and Nita can go to India.'

Suptra takes the ring and holds it up to the light. 'But it's your ring. It was your mother's.'

'I know. But I have no use for it. It's been at the back of a draw for years. I'd almost forgotten about it and then when Ethel mentioned...'

'My situation?'

'Yes. Well, I thought it could do some good. You could sell it, pay off your debt and let me have any money that might be left over.'

Suptra shakes his head. 'I couldn't, Clara. You might need the money to pay for George's care at some point. Why don't you sell it?'

'I couldn't sell it. It would be wrong. But I can give it to you, as a gift. To help you.' Tears form in Suptra's eyes. 'But Suptra, please don't tell anyone. Even Ethel doesn't know about this.'

Suptra is taken aback. 'I don't know what to say, Clara. I really don't.'

Clara gives his arm a firm squeeze. 'Just say you'll take it, Suptra. That's all you need to say.'

Cody is lying on the sofa, a packet of frozen peas strapped to his back. Along with feeling the worsening pain, he feels guilt as he hears Agnes moving about downstairs. He reaches for his phone and sends a text to Adam, telling him he has had a slight accident and that his mother needs help quickly. Adam responds immediately to say that he can be there in fifteen minutes. Good, thinks Cody, it must be a local girl he's with. He lies back and closes his eyes. And thinks of Meredith Park.

'I have to go. Mum's on her own in the chip shop and it's nearly opening time. Dad's had an accident of some sort.' Adam pulls on his shirt and trousers.

Meredith sits up suddenly. 'Oh no, poor Cody. I hope he's okay.'

'It's probably nothing, but I'd better go. I'll see you later.'

'I hope so, love.'

Adam blows her a kiss and runs downstairs.

Chapter 13: Arson? Really?

'I'll now hand over to Mr Frank Watson, leader of our parish council and very well known in the village.' The head teacher sweeps her arm to the side and announces, 'Mr Frank Watson!'

The children, well-versed and rehearsed for these occasions, provide Frank with the appropriate welcome. Some of the children look across to their parents, who, seated amongst the staff, seem oddly out of place. Zack Peterson rarely attempts eye contact with his father who always supplies the blessing at morning prayer on Friday mornings, and, for some reason, Zack tends to look slightly embarrassed. His friends don't help, sometimes wearing their shirts back-to-front to imitate the presence of a dog collar. The Reverend John Peterson is a 'proper' parish priest according to Frank. He has never attempted to define 'proper', but Frank and many of his age group in Leeford appreciate a vicar who will visit the elderly in the local care home, who will visit Banfield General on a regular basis and a man who doesn't exclusively reserve his Christian ways for the Sunday morning pulpit.

Unable to look straight at his father, Zack does, however, share a glance with seventeen-year-old Clare Adams, whose parents, Steve and Mel, are also awkwardly perched on the decidedly uncomfortable wooden chairs usually provided only for staff at the side of the assembly hall. Frank steps forward. 'Thank you, Mrs Windrush. Thank you, children. I would like to welcome the parents who have taken time out of their busy schedules to attend this important occasion.' He beckons to someone at the side of the stage and continues. 'I would like to ask Doctor Jeremy Roberts to join me on stage.' As Jeremy makes his way up the five well-worn steps, both Nita Sangra and Mandy Cleeve, teachers in Spring Hill Junior and Senior respectively, appear from behind the curtain, Nita holding the award and Mandy carrying a huge bouquet.

'Welcome, Doctor Roberts. Everyone in the hall is aware of the bravery and dedication you demonstrated a few weeks ago when you saved the life of one of our respected village citizens, Mr George Dennis. Unfortunately, Mr Dennis is unable to attend today, but his wife, Clara, is with us.' Another round of applause and Frank concludes the presentation. 'Without further ado, I am proud to present Doctor Roberts with this special award – the Freedom of Leeford Village, the highest accolade we can bestow. Many congratulations, and thank you again on behalf of Mr and Mrs Dennis and the village of

Leeford.'

Frank, Jeremy, and Jenny Windrush complete their speeches, thanks and counter-thanks, while Zack and Clare continue their tennis match of glance and counter-glance. *Romance isn't dead*, thinks Steve Adams, grinning at his wife, but reserves a careful half-grimace for his daughter just to make sure she understands: *I'm your dad – watch yourself.* Zack also gets the message.

It's also Spring Hill School's prize-giving day. Ted and Sally Coleman are present and the proudest parents in the hall as their daughter Gayle, only six years old, receives a special award for 'perseverance and hard work'. Holly Cleeve, Vera's eight-year-old granddaughter, is called up to receive the 'Junior Writer of the Year Award'. Her 500-word short story about missing gnomes wowed the judges (the head of the English department and Jenny Windrush) but perplexed many who had the opportunity to read the text as it appeared to put Nanny Cleeve in the frame for many of the crimes for which she had recently been accused.

Festivities, awards and applause concluded, Jenny Windrush ushers the children from the hall, giving parents and teachers the opportunity to compare notes. Jeremy makes his escape, complete with his 'Freedom of Leeford' award and his wife, Amanda, but not before he makes it clear to the audience that a number of individuals deserve credit for what they did for George that night.

The conclusions of the draft report of the fire investigator are to say the least, inconclusive; 'Electrical Fault' being the essence of his findings. However, after more detailed forensic analysis and a correction to an incredible oversight by the fire department, Jessica Townley receives a letter clearly marked 'cc: Banfield Police, S&G Insurance'. The contents cause her to go straight to Nick's office at the Community Centre.

'We've only just reopened, and they send me this. The press is bound to get hold of it.'

'Try not to worry, Jess, but I have to say - arson? Really?'

'Look what it says, Nick. "A small incendiary device timed to take effect in the early hours of the morning. A crude device, the sort of thing that could be made in a school science lab or an enthusiast's shed." What is that supposed to mean? Kids?'

'Don't know, Jess. We'll have to wait till Tuesday. That's when they want to see you.'

Cody picks up the envelope, feeling a tingle down his spine. It had been pushed through the letterbox before they opened for business. His instinct draws him quickly to the conclusion that the note is from Meredith, most likely the cause of the tingle, although the fear of Agnes getting to the envelope first is as likely a reason as any for tingles, or any other sensation related to the fear of being caught in the act. Cody would love to be in an act in which to get caught and hopes that the contents of the envelope will initiate the duet he has been dreaming of.

> *Dear Cody,*
> *Just a quick note to see if you are ok. I was very worried about you when I heard you were injured. Hope it's not too serious. Give me a ring when you have a chance, or pop into the shop later. We need to talk anyway.*
> *M*

It doesn't occur to Cody, semi-blinded by romantic possibilities, how Meredith found out about his dance-related injury. He has only one thought in his mind: *She wants me.*

'Where's Sherry?'
 'I won't lie to you Allen. Listen, can we go somewhere and talk?'
 'Hope you're not messing me about Linda.'
 'I know you've got all day. You were expecting to go to the Botanical Gardens. I need to talk to you. What if we picked up some stuff to eat from Taylor's shop and make the morning of it?'
 'Okay, but...'
 'Allen, let's just get in the car.'
 At 23, six years Sherry's senior, Linda has dealt with men like Allen before. She knows that he has always fancied her younger sister, but she wants him. Not being a market day, the butcher's shop is closed, so the whole Taylor family are serving in a busy farm shop on the Kidderminster Road. Violet, not a woman to mince her words, approaches Linda in the fruit aisle. Completing the squeeze test on a kiwi, her favourite fruit, Linda pauses for the inevitable question.
 'Are you and Allen seeing each other then?'
 'Not really Vi.'
 'I'll take your word for it.'

Allen, oblivious to the exchange between the women, is studying the array of English and Australian wines on display. 'Somerset Vine, last year's. Nice and fruity,' offers Ken.

'Eh?'

'The bottle you're holding. You're miles away, aren't you?'

'Sorry Ken, I'll have this one.'

'Do you want to wait till your friend has got the food for your picnic?'

'What do you know about that?'

'I don't call my dear wife 'Radar Vi' for nothing,' says Ken, grinning and winking towards his son who is talking a great interest in developments.

'Got the food Allen - drinks sorted?' asks Linda.

'Yes, I'll pay.' Doug can barely contain a muffled snort that had originated as a giggle. He's seen Allen in action at The Cross, but this, he thinks, is different. She's got him on the hook. Of course, the Taylors have no idea about the scheme Linda has concocted.

'I'm off to the wholesalers. I'll leave you to open up, Cody.'

Agnes's voice trails off as she bustles down the hallway, through the kitchen to the backyard.

'Okay, dear!' shouts Cody, but Agnes is already driving out of the yard.

The wholesalers. A fifteen-minute drive, fifteen minutes to buy stock and load the car, maybe twenty if she decides to have a look around, then fifteen to drive back. Forty-five to fifty minutes - plenty of time to see Meredith and get back in time to fire up the chip fryers before Agnes returns.

'Have you seen my uncle today, Ethel?' Nita sips froth off the top of her coffee, leaving a foamy moustache above her bright red lipstick. Ethel offloads a second heaped spoonful of sugar into her tea. She is about to tell Nita about her moustache when Nita contorts her bottom lip to clear it away.

'No, love. He hasn't been in at all today. Strange for him.'

'Hmm, that's not the only thing that's strange. This morning, he was up at the crack of dawn, singing his head off. He made breakfast, which he never does, and talked about going to India as soon as he has sorted out some business. Has he spoken to you about this?'

Ethel waves to Clara, passing by the window. 'No, he was his usual reserved self yesterday.'

'I don't know, then. But he's been so miserable lately. Seeing him happy is something, I suppose.'

Cody peers out of the bedroom window. Meredith's shop is open. He takes the note out of his back pocket and unfolds it for the fifth time that day. The paper smells of her perfume and he inhales the scent deeply. *We need to talk.* It says it, as clear as day. There is no doubt in Cody's mind - this is a turning point in his life. He has considered the implications of leaving Agnes, Adam and the fish and chip shop but when you are hopelessly in love, what can you do? Agnes will just have to accept their marriage is over. It's been a good one, mostly, but all good things come to an end, don't they? And Adam, well, he has little to do with him now, apart from providing board and lodging when one of his many relationships has broken down. No, it's time to move on and this is the first step.

Nita takes out her purse and hands a five-pound note over to Ethel.

'If you see my uncle, can you try to find out why he's so happy? I know that sounds strange, but happy is not his natural state!' They both laugh. Ethel takes the change out of the till and goes to hand it to Nita, just as Nita's phone rings.

'Ah, it's my uncle. I can ask him myself.' Nita greets Suptra in Urdu. Then, her expression changes and she holds her hand up to her face. 'You've been...how?...why?...a ring?...where did you get?...what are they saying?...yes, yes, uncle. I'll be there as soon as I can!' Nita drops her phone onto the counter and looks wide-eyed at Ethel.

'What on earth's happened, Nita?' asks Ethel, worried that Nita might collapse.

'It's my uncle. He's at the police station. They've arrested him!'

Ethel is now as wide-eyed as Nita. 'He's been arrested? What's he done?'

Nita shakes her head. 'It can't be true, it can't be. There has to be a mistake.'

Ethel grabs Nita's shaking hand. 'Whatever it is, we can sort it out. What's he done?'

'He's been arrested for trying to sell a stolen ring!'

Cody, his sizeable stomach churning, crosses the road to Meredith's shop. He pauses outside, takes a deep breath and pushes open the door. Meredith is serving a customer, wrapping their purchase in pink tissue paper, around which she ties a red ribbon.

'That's lovely, Meredith. You are so good, thank you.' The customer pays Meredith and leaves the shop. Meredith tidies the counter.

'How are you, Cody? I heard you've had a bit of an accident?'

Cody feels a twinge in his lower back. 'Oh, it's nothing. Just exercising, you know. I like to keep in shape.' Meredith resists the temptation to look down at Cody's prominent gut, the result of years of drinking beer and eating the day's fish and chip shop leftovers. Cody wants to get straight to the point. 'What is it you wanted to see me about, Meredith?'

Meredith steps from behind the counter. Cody feels a tightness in his chest. He puts out an arm, but Meredith walks straight past him and turns the OPEN sign around. 'This won't take long, but it's best no one comes in for a few minutes,' says Meredith. Cody gulps and feels a trickle of sweat coursing down his forehead. He pulls out a handkerchief and wipes it across his head and face.

'Yes, it is hot in here, isn't it?' says Meredith. 'Let's go through to the back room.' Cody's head is spinning. He struggles to put one foot in front of the other as he follows Meredith through a narrow passageway into a large airy room, which Meredith uses as both a stock room and a kitchen. 'Are you okay Cody?' She asks, pulling out a chair.

'Yes, yes, yes. It's just back pain, you know. It makes me, well, you know.' He pulls out his handkerchief and wipes away more sweat.

Meredith opens a window. 'Cody. I have a delicate question to ask you and I want an honest answer.'

Cody composes himself and sits upright. *Yes*! he thinks. *Whatever the question, the answer is 'yes'!*

Meredith leans towards him. 'Do you think an age gap is a problem in a relationship?'

Cody clears his throat. 'Well, I, I suppose, it depends if, well, no Meredith, no. No, if two people are in love, then the age gap does not matter at all.'

Meredith agrees. 'I'm glad you think that way, Cody. I have always thought of you as a wise man.'

Cody will take 'wise man', for now, though something a little more romantic would have been preferable.

Meredith continues. 'You see, Cody. I have fallen hopelessly in love. It's come straight out of the blue. In the past couple of weeks, to be precise.'

'Oh, Meredith. I've done the same.'

'You have?' *A long while ago*, thinks Meredith. 'So, you'll know what a wonderful, yet confusing thing it is?'

'Yes. But it's something that cannot be resisted. You have to give in to it Meredith. Give in to it!'

Meredith touches Cody's arm, sending a shockwave through his body. 'The trouble is, Cody, I worry what Agnes will say.'

Cody thinks about this. *What will Agnes say? A lot, probably. Yes, she'll have a lot to say, and he must make sure all the windows are closed when she says it*. The prospect of facing Agnes produces more sweat. 'Well, my dear. Agnes is a practical woman. No, that's not the word. Though she *is* practical. Pragmatic. That's the word. Anyway, she'll understand. Eventually.'

Meredith walks over to the sink and gazes wistfully out of the window. 'But I can't ignore the age difference. I'm so much older and I think that might be a problem, not now, but later on.'

'Older? Sorry, did you say older?' Cody furrows his brow. A drop of sweat drips onto the table in front of him.

'Yes, Adam is, what, ten years younger?'

'Adam?'

'Yes. How old is he exactly?'

'Adam? My Adam?'

'Yes. Who did you think I was talking about? I thought he'd told you we are seeing each other.'

Cody rises from the chair, but feels faint and sits down again, heavily. Meredith turns from the window. 'Oh my God, Cody. Are you okay?'

He stands again, turns and walks slowly back into the shop, holding onto the wall and an assortment of shop fittings, Meredith guiding him with her hand on his back.

'Do you want me to call Agnes? Or Adam?

Cody places one foot heavily in front of the other. After a few more steps, he is standing by the front door. 'I'm sorry, Mere...I just have to...the fish fryer, you know...Agnes...'

Meredith opens the door and Cody staggers into the street, shielding his eyes from the blinding sunlight.

'So, let me get this straight, Sergeant. You think someone deliberately set fire to Jessica's hairdressers. With a bomb?'

'Well, a small incendiary device, Nick, rather than a bomb, *per se*.'

'A bomb by another name,' says Jessica.

Sergeant Miller taps his pen on the table. 'So, the questions are how did it get there and who put it there?'

Jessica and Nick look at each other. Ever since they received the letter, they have been wracking their brains thinking who would have done such a thing. 'We don't know,' says Nick. Jessica gives a confirmatory shake of the head.

'Does anyone have a grudge against you? Do you owe any debts?' Sergeant Miller is beginning to feel uncomfortable asking his friends such personal questions.

Nick and Jessica chorus, 'no'.

Sergeant Miller turns to Jessica. 'Have you had anyone in acting strangely, or out of character?'

Jessica thinks. 'No, not that I can think of.'

Sergeant Miller's colleague, PC Gary Carr, who has not spoken until now asks, 'any disgruntled employees? Have you sacked anyone, recently?'

'No, the girls have been there for a couple of years now. Perfectly happy, I think.'

'And before them?'

'Before them, there was … oh, no, it couldn't be her. It couldn't be.'

'Who, Jessica?' asks Sergeant Miller, leaning forward. Nick looks at Jessica.

'No, it couldn't be. Oh my God, Nick!'

'Don't you remember, Nick?'

'Not with you yet, love.'

'That girl, the one with the big hair.'

'Big hair?'

'That's what you used to say, you know, sixties-style, beehive.'

'Good God, Jess, you mean...'

'Gail.'

Sergeant Miller feels honour-bound to regain control of the interview. *This is the problem dealing with friends and neighbours,* he thinks.

'I only know one Gail in this village – Gail Perkins who works at Burry's?'

'That's her,' says Jessica.

PC Carr, taking notes and trying to be the efficient policeman, attempts a way in, ignoring the Morse-like glare from his boss. It isn't the first time that PC Carr has misjudged the tone of an interview and his superior's grip on proceedings.

'What's she got to do with you?'

'She worked for me for a while – started about three years ago, part-time.'

'Hairdresser?' Stephen jumps back in, with a wave of his right hand to PC Carr, who reluctantly slumps back into note-taking. *It's not like this in the movies,* he thinks.

'No. More on the till, but we did let her wash clients' hair occasionally and we discussed an apprenticeship. I told her she'd have to sweep up, make the tea and be prepared to go to Banfield College for at least two years.'

'Did you fall out over this?' asks Sergeant Miller.

'Christ, Jess, I remember now,' interrupts Nick.

'You might as well tell Sergeant Miller and PC Carr the story, Nick. I'll make us all a cup of tea.'

'If you know the details, Nick, start from the beginning,' says Sergeant Miller.

Nick relays what he remembers about Gail Perkins. 'She seemed a nice enough girl. Early thirties. In fact, whenever I pop into Burry's, she's always polite with me – as recent as last week.'

'Go on.'

'She's worked at Burry's chemists for two years – since she left the salon.'

'She left under a cloud, would you say?'

'Well, yes.'

'Dispute about the work, or the pay?'

'Not at all – nothing to do with her work. Staff at Jessica's salon get a discount when they get their hair done. Twenty-five per cent is the standard discount. Half-price if you let an apprentice work on you.'

'Carry on,' says Sergeant Miller.

'Jessica had done Gail's hair a couple of times. Gail goes to sixties-style dances, and she likes her hair done up, you know, a bit like Cilla did in the Beatles era, or maybe that singer, er, Dusty Springfield?'

'Got it. Complicated hairdo, got to get it right,' interjects PC Carr, trying to be helpful, but another stare from Sergeant Miller sends him back to his notetaking.

'Anyway,' continues Nick, 'on this occasion, Jess was away from the shop for some reason. One of the girls was in charge, and Gail wanted her hair done. This time she wanted it bleached blond with blue streaks for some reason. One of the apprentices, second year at Banfield College, quite a promising hairdresser, started on Gail's hair.'

'What happened?'

'Here's the thing. Jess wasn't there. Her deputy had popped out for half an hour, and the young kid started mixing the stuff to colour Gail's hair.'

'I think I can see what's coming.'

'Well, yes, there was a mix-up with the bleach. It's a combination of hydrogen peroxide and ammonia, then they apply the dye.'

'Did it burn her, or what?'

'Sort of. The thing is it not only ruined her hair, she lost most of it from the back of her head.'

'Crikey! Was it fixable?'

'No, she ended up in hospital – skin grafts, all sorts.'

'Is she okay now?'

'If you can call wearing a wig, "okay"'.

'How come I haven't heard about this?' asks Sergeant Miller.

'It was kept quiet, and it wasn't a police matter. She was understandably embarrassed by having a huge bald patch at the back of her head.'

'Right. What did she do? Was she angry, did she make threats?'

'That's the strange thing – no. She just handed in her notice. Then we had a solicitor's letter claiming compensation against Jessica's business insurance.'

'How much?'

'Three thousand.'

'Bloody hell – did Jessica pay it?'

'Yes, I did,' says Jessica, handing mugs of tea to Sergeant Miller and PC Carr. 'It was our responsibility. My responsibility. The poor kid. I would have asked for more.'

'But you think she's the one who might have caused the fire?'

'I wouldn't have done,' replies Jessica, taking over the conversation from her partner, 'but she's well qualified for where she works now.'

'Why?' queries Sergeant Miller.

'Gail had been to university but came to us because she couldn't find a job locally at the time that suited her qualifications.'

'What was her degree in?'

Jessica hesitates, looks straight into Sergeant Miller's eyes and replies: 'chemistry.'

'You're enjoying yourself, aren't you?'

'I suppose...'

Linda reaches over, touching his knee. A light touch that, if Allen was travelling on the bus or the metro, he would not have noticed. Not an accidental touch, a brush of the knee, so slight, so delicate, a tingle courses through him. 'You were saying, Allen?'

'Linda, what do you expect of me?'

'You've not mentioned Sherry once.'

'I ... well, it's all so unexpected.'

This time, Linda knows she can take it further. She places her hand on his chest, pushing him to the ground. They both ignore the stray sandwich that is wedged between his back and the damp grass that has escaped the cover of the blanket Linda had covertly smuggled into the car. She caresses his face with both hands, slowly, agonizingly slowly, running her fingers down his cheeks and then kisses her own index finger and places it onto his lips. She moves closer. Allen is completely submissive, totally under her spell. Her lips meet his, and for the first time he makes his own move, grasping her shoulders and pulling her down towards him, sealing the embrace.

'No further Allen, just kiss me.'

'Linda, I never realised.'

'I knew you fancied my kid sister, but I've always wanted you.'

'Oh God, Linda, I can't believe this is happening.'

'Just hold me. Just hold me.'

*

'I have the feeling, Gary, that we're going to be busy the next few days.'

'You mean following up the Gail Perkins thing?'

'And we've got Suptra Singh in the cells at Banfield.'

'Are they taking it on, Sarge?'

'No, it's our case. I think he'll talk to me. Not said a lot so far, apart from a garbled call to his niece.'

'Shall I come with you?'

'No, you get off to the chemists and ask Gail to meet both of us at the station tomorrow morning.'

'Banfield?'

'No. Keep it local, Gary. We'll see her in Leeford.'

Sergeant Miller immediately sets off for Banfield. No more than a ten-minute drive, even in traffic. He uses the time to formulate his questions. At the station, he finds Suptra in a more talkative mood than Sergeant Miller's Banfield colleagues had described.

'Are you going to tell me what happened?'

'I don't want to get anyone in trouble.'

'Do you trust me Suptra? We've been friends for a few years now.'

'I do, but I'm finding this all very confusing.'

'Frightening as well, I imagine.'

'Yes, and I feel ashamed. But what have I actually done wrong?'

'Let me be the judge of that Suptra, but you must tell me everything – from the start.'

Suptra recounts the day when Clara went to see him at the Community Centre.

'So, she knew about your problem with the gang in India, the money you owe and all that?'

'Yes. I think Ethel and Clara confide in each other about everything.'

'Never mind that, let's focus. Tell me exactly what she said about where the ring came from. Word for word, if you can remember.'

'She said, "when my mother died, she left the estate to me and my two sisters. It was all split three ways, but she also left us all something to remember her by. Martha had her Wedgwood figurines, Dorothy her books, and Mother left me this ring".'

'So, she claims that the ring came from her mother?'

'That's what she said.'

'Okay, Suptra, you can go home now, but there are strict conditions - talk to no one about this and have no contact with Clara.'

Chapter 16: Double Trouble

'Where have you been? I'm starving!'

Sherry is standing at the end of the hallway as Linda enters, brushing a stray piece of grass from her dress.

'Starving? Don't you eat if I'm not around to feed you?' Linda hangs her jacket on a coat peg, knocking off a couple of scarves in the process. She curses and wraps them angrily around the coat hook.

'Ooh, someone's got a mood on them,' says Sherry, rearranging the scarves.

'Leave me alone. I'm tired.' Linda brushes past Sherry and goes into the kitchen. Sherry follows her. Linda opens the fridge, grabs a carton of orange juice, and takes a long drink.

'And *I'm* hungry! Where have you been?'

'Oh my God! Do I have to tell you everything?' Linda sits down and leans across the table. Sherry sits opposite her sister.

'No,' she says, quietly. 'You've been a long time though. I was worried.'

Linda groans. 'Okay. If you must know, I've been...oh, don't cry.' She stands and walks round to Sherry, throwing her arms around her. 'I'm sorry. I'm being a cow, aren't I?' Sherry nods. Linda kisses her on top of the head. 'I'll make us some tea. Burgers and chips alright?'

Sherry nods again. Linda goes to the fridge and takes out a packet of burgers and a bag of oven chips. Sherry sniffs, then blows her nose loudly. 'So, where have you been?' she asks.

Linda takes a deep breath. Then she notices the calendar on the back of the kitchen door with one date circled in red. 'I've been...shopping. In Birmingham, if you must know.'

'Birmingham? I could have gone with you. Why didn't you tell me?'

'Because, dear sister, it's your birthday very soon and I wanted to get you something very special!'

Sherry blows her nose, again. 'And did you?'

'Did I? You bet I did! You'll love it!' Linda separates two frozen burgers.

'So, where is it?'

'Eh?'

'You didn't come in carrying any bags.'

Linda turns to face the sink. 'I've hidden it.'

'Where?'

'If I told you that, it wouldn't be hidden, would it? Just be prepared to be very surprised, though you've almost ruined it!'

Sergeant Miller is about to put the phone down when he hears a voice on the other end.

'George. It's Stephen Miller. How are you?'

'I'm as well as can be expected, Stephen, thank you. What can I do for you?'

'Actually, it's Clara I need to speak to. Is she there?'

George shouts upstairs.

The next voice Stephen hears is Clara's. 'Hello, Stephen. This is a surprise.'

'Hello, Clara. It's not a social call, I'm afraid.'

'Oh?' Clara signals for George to leave the room. When he has left, she whispers, 'what has George done now?'

'George. Nothing. And, I'm hoping, neither have you.'

'Me?'

'I'll get straight to the point. Did you at any time give a diamond ring to Suptra Singh?'

There's a long silence on the other end of the phone. 'Clara? Are you there?' Clara sits on the chair next to the phone table. 'Clara? I think there's been some misunderstanding and I'm afraid Suptra...' Stephen is interrupted by a barely audible Clara.

'I want to hand myself in.'

'I'm sorry, Clara? Did you say you...'

'Yes, Stephen. I want to hand myself in. How do I do that?'

Linda is watching a film on TV, while Sherry is watching her work her way through a family-sized packet of cheese and onion crisps. 'What happened to the diet?' she asks, as Linda grabs another handful.

Linda waves a crisp in the air.

'You know what, Sherry? I don't care about my body anymore. This is how I am. Some people, naming no names, find me very attractive.' Something catches Sherry's eye on the TV, and she lets Linda's comment pass. Her concentration is broken by the flashing of her phone perched on the chair arm. A text message:

Hi Sherry. This is Allen. Would u like 2 go out with me 1 eve? Your choice where 2 go. Will understand if u don't. Get back 2 me. IMPORTANT:

'Who's that?' asks Linda, through a mouthful of crisps.

Sherry rests the phone on the arm of the chair. 'Oh, it's just...ah, I love this bit!' She points to the TV and claps her hands. Linda gives her a bewildered look. Before she can ask the question again, her phone beeps. A text message:

Hi Lin. Thanks for today. I loved being with you, although it was not what I expected! I want to see you again. Your choice where 2 go. Will understand if u don't. Get back 2 me. IMPORTANT: don't tell sis. Keep 2 ourselves. Allen xox

Linda sighs. 'Phone company. Damn nuisance, always asking me if I want an upgrade!'

PC Carr knocks on Sergeant Miller's door and enters his office.

'She's here, Sarge.'

'Gail Perkins? Take her down to the interrogation room. I'll be there in a few minutes. Clara is on her way, and I want to make sure she's okay when she arrives.'

'Right, Sarge. I'll sort Gail out.'

PC Carr is almost out the door when Sergeant Miller calls him back. 'Clara says she wants to hand herself in. Do you think she stole the ring?'

'Dunno, Sarge. Doesn't sound like Clara. But it is the ring that's on the jewellers' list of lost and stolen items.'

'Well, let's hope there's a reasonable explanation. I can't imagine arresting Clara!'

'Want a cuppa?'

Linda looks at her sister in disbelief. 'You're asking me if I want a cup of tea? Do you even know how to make a cup of tea?' Sherry sticks her tongue out at Linda and goes into the kitchen, picking up her phone on the way. As soon as the kettle begins to make a noise, she begins texting:

```
Hi Allen. Car park back of library. 6.00
Tuesday. Won't tell Linda. Sherry xoxoxo
```

Linda listens for the kettle to make a noise, then begins texting:

```
Hi Allen. I loooveeedd today. Meet me in car
park back of library. 6.00 Wednesday. Won't tell
Shez. Lin xoxoxoxo
```

Five minutes later, Sherry walks into the lounge carrying two cups. She puts them down on the coffee table and sits back in her chair.

'What's happened?' she asks.

'Happened?'

'The film. What's happened?'

Clara sits opposite Sergeant Miller, her hands resting on her lap.

'So, Clara, you want to hand yourself in. Do you know what that means?'

'Yes, Stephen. Of course, I do.'

'Are you saying you have committed a crime?'

'Yes. I wouldn't be handing myself in, otherwise, would I?'

'No, of course not. I'm presuming this is something to do with Suptra and your mother's ring?'

'Yes. Except the ring was not my mother's. I found it.'

'Found it?'

'Yes. In a handbag. A handbag someone handed into the shop.'

Sergeant Miller sits back. 'Go on, Clara. Tell me the whole story.'

It has been a quiet lunchtime in the chip shop and Cody is draining the last of the chip oil into a large metal can. He sighs heavily, just as Agnes appears carrying a mop and bucket. 'Oh dear. Someone's not happy,' she says, dragging the mop over the entrance. 'What's up?' Cody twists the lid on the metal can and tucks it away under the counter. He holds his back and grimaces as he bends.

'Nothing, love. I'm fine. Just a bit down.' He half-smiles at Agnes, but she is busy swishing the mop to and fro across the floor.

'Maybe you need to go upstairs and play some more dance music. You seemed very happy when you were doing that.'

Cody feels another twinge shooting down his leg. 'I think my dancing days are over, Agnes. I have to face the facts. I'm getting old.'

Agnes laughs. 'Getting? I thought you'd already got there!' Cody does not respond. He stands in the doorway looking out at Meredith's shop.

'Oi! I've just mopped there!' says Agnes, running the mop into the back of his leg. As Cody passes Agnes, she drops the mop and holds his hand. 'Look, love. We can't help getting old. The thing is, I love you even more the older you get!'

Cody hangs his head. 'I don't deserve you. I'm being very stupid.'

'You're not stupid, Cody. You're a good man.' She cups Cody's face in her hands. 'Now, how about you and I get dressed up and go to the pictures in Banfield? There's that new film with whatshername in. You know, the one off that programme.' Cody shakes his head. 'She's married to him; the one with the eyes,' continues Agnes.

Cody laughs. 'Going out with you tonight, Agnes, will make me the happiest man in the world!'

Sergeant Miller opens the door of the interrogation room. PC Carr is sitting at a table opposite Gail Perkins. 'A word, Gary.'
Gary steps into the corridor. 'I'm developing a rapport with Gail, Sarge. I think there's chemistry between us.'

'Not funny, PC Carr. Not funny at all!'

'Sorry, Sarge.'

Sergeant Miller lowers his voice. 'Suptra Singh is totally innocent. Clara Dennis has got herself into one hell of a mess. I'll tell you the whole story later, but she's saying she has stolen the ring she gave to Suptra to sell.'

'Her mother's ring?'

'Yes, except it's not her mother's. She found it and didn't give it back. The best thing we can do is contact the ring's owner, explain the situation, particularly Clara's difficulties with George and try to stop her pressing charges. If she agrees, we can let the matter drop. But first, let's deal with Gail Perkins.'

'Nick, glad I caught you.'

'What is it, Frank? I've got a meeting in half an hour.'

'A few weeks ago, we talked about grasping the nettle by the horns. You never got back to me.'

'Eh?'

'The village fête. Jessica was quite rude to me. Talked about beating a hasty retreat.'

'Yes, I remember you being sarcastic.'

'I was not.'

'Look, Frank, we've never seen eye-to-eye, but I've always thought of you as an honest chap. It may have been sarcasm, but you did say that we should stay out of the way when the committee meets.'

'Okay, okay, let's call a truce,' offers Frank.

'Well, do you still want the room?'

'Fourteenth of next month. 10.00 a.m. to 3.00 p.m.'

'Suits me. Diary's clear that day.'

'By the way, Nick, what is wrong with your girlfriend? Not the business of the fire, is it?'

'Gloating, Frank?'

'Don't start that again. No, seriously, is she alright? She's been sniffy with me a couple of times this week.'

'If you must know, we think it was arson.'

'Can't be, can it?'

'Looks like it.'

'Any suspects?'

'It's being looked into and it's for the police to decide what happens next. Please don't repeat any of this. I know what you're like.'

'You've insulted me now, Nick, but I'll let it go. We have to work together, don't we?'

'You mean you want me on the committee?'

'Oh no, sorry, you misunderstood. You still don't qualify, do you? Your role is to provide the room and refreshments.'

Zack is ready this time. *Jack Simmons and his Pound Challenge,* he thinks. *Who's he kidding? Let's see if we can make it more interesting.*

'Hi Zack, who's this then?' enquires George Owens.

'This is Clare, a friend from school.'

'Playing truant then?'

'No, study period. We're supposed to be in the library.'

'What brings you to the market then? Looking for a bike?'

'You looking after Jack's stall as well? Didn't know you were into clothes and toys.'

'Cheeky monkey. Dental appointment. Covering while he's away.'

'Look George, any chance of a quick chat with you and the lads?'

'What about?'

'Jack's Pound Challenge is tonight. I thought we might spice it up a bit.'

'Sounds interesting. I'll give Ken a shout. Cody is around here somewhere. Buying cards, I think.'

Clare gazes at Zack, impressed that he can deal with anyone. *Even Mom and Dad like him*, she thinks. *It's his eyes, clear and blue – they sparkle when he talks. I'm so lucky…*

'Penny for them love,' says Ken, unwittingly breaking the spell.

'Oh, I'm admiring this Raleigh Pioneer on George's stall.'

'The Hybrid?' jumps in the stallholder.

'How much?'

'To you, darling, £260 – normally £295'

Clare has no intention of buying a bike but tries to clear her thoughts.

'What's up?' says Cody, leaning on Ken's shoulder.

'Young Zack wants a few words.'

'Thanks for your time lads. You all know about tonight at The Cross. We could do one over Jack, if you're interested.'

'I'm always interested,' quips Cody.

'Why don't we throw the challenge back at our friend Mr Simmons?'

'Tell us more, Zack.'

'We up the ante. Say we offer him a stake of £3 each and get him to pay out £6 for each winning answer.'

'What's the point in that?'

'That's just the start. He's a gambler is Jack. I reckon there'll be at least fifteen to twenty people in the pub tonight who will have a go. That's at least £45 in Jack's kitty to start with. Why don't we tell him he can make ten quid clear profit, minimum, if he offers a prize of £35 for anyone who gets all four answers right?'

'How do you know it's four quotes?'

'I asked him, yesterday.'

'What's the split then?' asks George.

'Me and Clare are both in, aren't we?' says Zack, looking to his girlfriend for support.

He continues. 'That's five of us – me, Clare, you George, Cody, and Ken. Five-way split, £7 each.'

'Not much in it for us, is there? And, anyway, we've got to get the answers right. We've never done that well before,' declares Ken, puffing his chest out as if to emphasize his seniority.

'That's where I come in. I can find anything on my smartphone in seconds. The money's not the thing, and don't forget, we get Jack to commit to £6 for each correct answer as well. That's £59 in total. He'll be out of pocket, and we'll have a bit of fun.'

Clare giggles at Zack's ingenuity and the way he can control men twice, three times his age - *and those eyes. Can't wait to get back home with him,* she muses. *Mom and Dad are out.*

'She's off again – love's young dream. Thinking about that hybrid again, young Clare?' jokes George.

'Are you all in lads?' asks Zack.

'Should be a giggle,' answers George.

'I'm in,' from Ken.

Just a 'yep' from Cody and they disperse as they spot Jack turning the corner by The Cross, holding his mouth with a grimace that can be seen from thirty yards.

'Right. Everybody ready?'

Zack's forecast was correct – the pub is packed. Always a buzz on Pound Challenge night.

'How many tonight, Jack?' enquires Ted.

'Two – got a sore mouth. Want to keep it basic and short tonight.'

'What? You can't do that – you promised four. Do you know four quotes or are you losing the plot?'

'Yeah, a promise is a promise,' shouts George, from the back of the room.

'Okay, okay, four it is.'

Ken, Cody and George approach Jack, putting Zack's proposition to him, leaving Zack and Clare out of it. They are his mates – he listens to them. 'It's a deal. Sounds great. I like a challenge – and the chance to make a few quid.'

'Order, order!' shouts Ted. Someone mutters to Zack about underage drinkers. 'Yes, she's seventeen and drinking J2O, alright?' The complainant silenced, Ted sets the ground rules and prepares the quotation gladiators for battle.

'Let's have some hush. Pound Challenge, folks. Three pounds each at the counter and don't forget to order more drinks after, to either celebrate or drown your sorrows! Thank you.'

'Typical publican,' mutters someone in the crowd, probably Frank Watson.

Jack begins. 'Right lads and, erm, lasses, let's get started. I'll give you all four quotes. You can write them down then you've got two minutes.' The meeting at the market had concluded with the agreement that Zack would give George all the answers, but Cody, George, Clare and Zack would each go forward with their individual solutions.

'Here we go – Number One, an easy one to start:'

"It's freezing and snowing in New York – we need global warming." Number Two: "The way to get started is to quit talking and begin doing." Number Three: "The greatest glory in living lies not in never falling, but in rising every time we fall." Number Four: "Didn't I help it? I just took it back, is all. Awful tired now, boss. Dog tired."'

Zack has the answers in under ninety seconds.

'George – go and get your six quid. It's Donald Trump. Clare, number two is Walt Disney. Cody, you have number three – Nelson Mandela. I'll take four.'

'What the hell was four?'

'The character John Coffey, in the film The Green Mile. I knew it anyway.'

The first two individual prizes are taken, then Frank Watson calls for attention.

'What's going on, Frank?' demands Ted.

'Cheating, that's what's going on.'

'Cheating? How?'

'Ask young Zack to bring his smartphone to the front. I remember Ian Beale doing this scam in Eastenders years ago. Sorry, Jack, but you've been stitched up.'

Tuesday, 4.30 p.m.

One thing you can say about Sherry – she's rarely late. Linda will claim that her sister possesses many attributes, tardiness not being one of them. They have an early tea together, both offering the other their own spurious version of their plans for the evening. Sherry wants to make sure that her older sister is nowhere near Leeford Library at the time she's meeting Allen.

'I'm meeting some old college mates in East Banfield. Where are you off to?'

'Me? Oh, popping into Wolverhampton – the club shop has a sale. They're open till eight.'

'Good. Get me one of those tee shirts.'

'Which one?'

'You know, the one with the Mexican flag and the number nine. No more than a tenner.'

'If they've got them.'

'Ta.'

'Who are these mates?'

'You never got to know my friends at Banfield College, did you?'

'S'pose not. Anyway, got to get ready.'

'And me.'

'Bags me the bathroom first.'

Tuesday, 5.45 p.m.

Linda is on her way. Sherry had left the house fifteen minutes before her and is in position, aware of the camera. They've had a lot of vandalism in the car park shared with the doctor's surgery. She knows where to stand, just out of the camera's line of sight, but she can't see the entrance to the car park from there. *He won't be here till after six, she thinks. I'll hear the car passing down the side of the library. Oh my God, Allen Gomez. He's gorgeous and he fancies me. He picked me, not Linda. She hears the car. It's 5.55 p.m. He's early.* It stops at the corner of the building, a few yards before the right turn. The door slams. Footsteps. He's coming. The evening shadow is thrown across the corner into the centre of the camera's invisible beam. Sherry catches her breath, expectant. She looks up.

Linda.

Sherry can't contain herself. 'What the hell are you doing here?'

Linda has a sudden thought and checks her phone. *Should be Wednesday 6.00 p.m.*

Chapter 18: Ted, the Magician

An eerie silence descends on The Cross as Zack makes his way to the bar. George, Ken and Cody cast glances at each other. Jack looks bewildered. Clare has her eyes fixed on Zack, as she has done throughout the whole evening.

'Give that phone here, my lad!' Zack deposits his phone in Frank Watson's outstretched hand. 'Now, let's see what you have been looking at while this challenge has been going on.' Frank taps the screen, frowns, taps the screen again.

'It's password-protected,' says Cody, winking at Zack. Frank hands the phone back to Zack.

'Well, unprotect it, then!' Zack taps in four numbers and is about to give the phone back to Frank, when Ted intervenes.

'Hang on Zack. You're not obliged to do that. There might be personal stuff on there, Frank. I suggest he gives the phone to me, so it's out of his reach.' Zack gives the phone to Ted, who puts it in his pocket.

'I'm sorry, Ted. That's not good enough. There's money at stake here. And the reputations of those involved. And, if I may say, the integrity of the Pound Challenge, which attracts a sizeable crowd of paying customers.' Frank points around the room at the customers enthralled by the situation unfolding in front of them.

'Frank, you're right,' says Ted. 'Mind if I tap in your passcode, Zack? I saw what it was. You can change it when you get the phone back.'

Zack shrugs. Ted taps in a code and hands the phone to Frank. 'Right. This will confirm my suspicions, mark my words.' Frank gives the phone a few taps and scrolls down the page. He stares at the screen for a while, his face turning redder and redder. A few beads of sweat form on his brow.

'Something wrong, Frank?' asks Ted.

'It appears I might have made a slight error of judgement, Ted.'

'Oh, what makes you think that?'

Frank swallows hard. He hands the phone to Ted. 'Hmm. It seems that Zack's recent browsing history points to him searching for weekend breaks in London. Hardly something that would lead to him being able to pass on the answers, is it Frank?'

George, Ken and Cody shake their heads. Clare continues to look at Zack, marvelling at how calm he remains in the face of a crisis.

'I, I, I don't understand...he, I'm sure...but I thought...', mutters

Frank.

'I think an apology is in order, Frank,' says Ted.

Frank straightens his tie and coughs. 'Of course. I apologise unreservedly, Zack. I made a terrible error of judgement. I beg your forgiveness.' He offers his hand to Zack, who takes it, reluctantly.

'S'okay,' he says.

Frank glances at his watch. 'It that the time? Well, I'd better be off. Goodnight, all.' He marches across the room and pushes through the double doors that open onto the street.

'Okay, everyone. Normal service is resumed!' shouts Ted.

Gradually, the customers pick up their drinks and soon there is the normal buzz of a pub on a busy Tuesday evening. George, Ken, Cody and Jack look confused. Zack is about to join them, when Ted beckons him.

'Zack! A word!'

At the police station, PC Carr and Sergeant Miller are standing outside the interview room. Sitting inside is Gail Perkins, waiting to be questioned.

'Just to fill you in, Gary, the owner of the ring has agreed not to press charges against Clara. I explained how she has been quite distressed lately and that what she did was totally out of character.'

'Yes, I was surprised when I heard about it, Sarge.'

'Also, she didn't exactly steal the ring, she just didn't give it back when it was reported lost, so it would be difficult to charge her with theft.'

'I suppose so,' says Gary.

'Anyway, it's all done and dusted. I'll call and see Suptra in the morning. The poor man has had such a fright!'

They look through the one-way mirror at Gail Perkins, sitting motionless as she has done since arriving at the station.

'Right, Gary. Let's get on with it!'

They enter the room and sit opposite Gail, who continues to stare straight ahead. Sergeant Miller begins. 'Miss Perkins. Thank you for being patient. We'd like to ask you a few questions.'

Ted escorts Zack into a small room behind the bar, stacked with crates of soft drinks and boxes of crisps.

'Thanks for that, Ted. You've saved my life! How did you do that

87

stuff with the phone? You must be a magician. Can I have it back?'

Ted puts his hand firmly on Zack's shoulder. 'Don't you ever do that in my pub again! Do you hear?'

Zack immediately feels two feet smaller.

'You *did* cheat. *I* know that and so do you.'

Zack looks down at his trainers. 'Yes, I did. I'm sorry. We were trying to stitch Jack up.'

Ted releases his grip. 'Well, I'm disappointed in you. But I'm more disappointed in those that agreed to go along with it and I'll be having words with them too.'

'I won't do it again, Ted.'

'I know you won't, Zack.' Zack turns to go back to the bar.

'Hang on,' says Ted, reaching into his pocket. 'Your phone.' He hands the phone to Zack. 'Wait. Just let me check it's the right one.' He pulls a phone from his other pocket. Zack looks at the phone in his hand and then the one in Ted's.

'They're identical!'

Ted winks. 'I know. I have no idea what your passcode is. I had been searching for a City Break for me and Sally, later in the year. The phone Frank Watson was looking at was mine.'

'Ted, you're a genius.' Zack laughs and Ted cannot help smiling. 'Thanks for doing this for me.'

'You? I didn't do it for you! You see how popular the Pound Challenge is. I can't afford to lose my punters because of your cheating!' Zack walks away sheepishly.

'Anyway,' Ted shouts. 'You're not off the hook, entirely, my boy.' Zack stops and turns.

'What d'ya mean?'

'Your Clare will be expecting you to take her on one of those City Breaks she thinks you've been looking at!' Ted bursts into fits of laughter as Zack skulks back to the bar.

'Gail. This is not helping. If you know something about the fire at the hairdressers, and we've every reason to believe you might, then it's best you say so.'

Gail Perkins continues to look straight ahead, ignoring Sergeant Miller's words.

'Sergeant Miller is right, Gail. You will have to speak if this goes to court.' She briefly looks at PC Carr and then straight ahead again.

'I'll ask you one more time, Gail. Do you know anything about the recent fire at Jessica's?' At the sound of Jessica's name, Sergeant Miller notices Gail clench her hand into a fist.

'Jessica Townley. I believe you and she have a bit of history.'

'What did she tell you?' Gail suddenly becomes animated and thumps her fist down on the table. 'Eh? What did she tell you?' she repeats, thumping her fist down again.

Sergeant Miller asks, 'what do you think she might have told us, Gail?' Gail relaxes her hands and stares straight ahead.

Sergeant Miller sighs. 'Look, Gail. We've had enough. If you're refusing to cooperate, then I'm going to have to arrest you on suspicion of arson. Of course, you can call your solicitor, but I suggest we keep it to a chat at this point, until the facts can be established.'

Gail leans back in her chair. 'You're right. I know something about the fire at the hairdressers.'

'Now, we're getting somewhere,' says Sergeant Miller, trying to keep the conversation friendly, despite his obvious irritation.

'Yeah, I know something about it. But it wasn't me that caused it.'

'What am *I* doing here? What are *you* doing here? You said you were meeting your friends in East Banfield.'

'And you said you were going to Wolverhampton.'

The two sisters glare at each other, rapidly thinking of an excuse for being in the car park. It's Sherry who speaks first.

'If you must know, I'm meeting a fellah.'

'A fellah? Who?'

'I'm not saying.'

'Anyone I know?'

Sherry fiddles with a long string of beads she is wearing around her neck.'Maybe. Maybe not.'

'Oh, come on, Sherry. You're not ten years old!'

'If you must know, I'm meeting Allen Gomez.' Linda's eyes widen.

'Sorry. Did you say, Allen Gomez?'

'Yeah. He texted me. Says he wants to go on a date.'

Linda looks up to the sky, then down at the floor. 'Well, would you believe it?'

'Yeah. Actually. I've always thought he fancied me,' says Sherry, with a wide grin.

'So, why the secrecy?'

'What?'

'Why didn't you tell me?'

Sherry wraps her necklace around her fingers. 'Because...'

'Because he told you not to tell your sister? Is that it?'

Sherry shakes her head. 'Sorry, how do you know that?'

'Because he told me the same thing!'

'Oh my God! He wants to date both of us? On the same night?' Sherry lets go of the necklace and the beads rattle as they fall back into position.

'What a creep!'

'Yes,' agrees Linda, 'what a creep!'

'I didn't know he fancied you, Linda. He hardly ever speaks to you when he comes in the laundrette.'

Linda feels a chill run down her spine. 'Er, no. I didn't know, either.'

'Well, he's going to have such a surprise when he finds us both here!'

'Yeah,' says Linda, in a very small voice, 'he is.'

Chapter 19: Frank

Frank Watson – father, businessman, parish council leader, demands respect, earning it most of the time. On his way out of the Community Centre, Frank finds another victim.

'Jeremy – there you are!'

'Oh, Frank, nice to see you. I was just on my way to see Nick about… something.'

'Never mind, I need a quick word. Could you run the tombola at the fête this year?'

'Who's run it in the past?'

'No one.'

'So, you've not had a tombola before?'

'No, Jeremy, we've never had a fête before.'

'I see. Anyway, when is it?'

'The fête sub-committee will finalize the date. Can I press-gang you onto the committee? We meet here on the fourteenth, next month.'

'Look, Frank…'

'Doctor, I know you're a busy man. All those patients to see and looking after your lovely wife. Tell you what, just take on one of the roles. What do you say, tombola or committee?'

'Well…'

'Let's make it easier - I'll put you down for the tombola. Less responsibility. Can't have our esteemed GP burning out, can we?'

'Frank…'

'That's settled then. Have a word with Nick – he's got all the tombola stuff. The WI run one at their Bring 'n Buy.'

'I'm very busy…'

'That's why I picked you - you know, give a job to a busy man, woman, er, person.'

'Okay, I give in.'

'Good man. Knew you wouldn't let me down.'

'Goodbye, Frank. I'll get back to you.'

'See you Doc… oh, by the way, have you decided when you're herding the sheep through the village?'

'What?'

'It's your right. You are the first person since the millennium to have the Freedom of Leeford bestowed upon your person. It's an ancient right, back to when Leeford was just a church and six houses. The old River Lee, now just a stream mostly, except when we had the flood,

George and all – but of course you know that – '

'Frank!'

'What's wrong?'

'I must get on. There will be no sheep herding, no committee, but I will do your damn tombola if it keeps you happy. Now I must go in and see Nick.'

Must be under a lot of pressure, Frank thinks to himself. 'Bye, Doc.'

'Come on Frank, it has to be your round sometime,' suggests Jack Simmons.

'Listen, Shakespeare, when I want your opinion, I'll ask for it!' Frank fires back.

'Opinion, a sovereign mistress of effects - now that's Shakespeare. Othello, Act One, Scene Three.'

'Good God, it wasn't like this when I first came to The Cross,' says Frank.

It was the summer of 1972 when Frank first walked into The Cross. As far as he is aware it had always been called 'The Cross' and he has often considered doing some research at the Black Country Museum to find out. The sixty-three-year-old Frank Watson doesn't 'do' the internet, apart from business emails and his daily check on his Santander 1-2-3 account. Social media is definitely a no-go area.

Barely seventeen years old, looking like a tired twenty-one-year-old, he drank alone. Successful in his 'O' levels the previous year - three grade A and five grade B – he was the only pupil at Banfield Grammar passing more than five 'O' levels to leave at the age of sixteen.

'Help me in the business, Francis,' his dad pleaded.

'Dad, I told you, I don't want to work in asbestos.'

'It's not dangerous - it's all treated stuff anyway.'

'It's not that, Dad. I've had five years being pushed around, people telling me what to do. I want to do my own thing.'

'Son, do what you like, but it's your mother. She wants the best for you.'

Doreen Watson, a well-meaning and loving mother, had not prepared her son for the perils of grammar school life. As the only successful eleven-plus entrant from East Banfield Junior, Frank arrived at Banfield Grammar on a dismal morning in September 1966. Alone, clad in worsted shorts, while ankle socks and a school cap. Doreen insisted.

'Do I have to wear the cap, Mom?'

'It's part of the set uniform.'

'Bet I'm the only one.' He was right. Not the only student issued with a cap, but the only boy actually wearing one as he arrived at the school entrance. It triggered Frank's first experience of bullying and it was not to be his last. The shorts and ankle socks didn't help either.

He started life in a two-bed terrace in East Banfield. His mom and dad owned the house - unusual in those days - but Cecil was doing quite well in the business, cutting and supplying seals and gaskets for the motor industry. As the business expanded, the family moved to a three-bed detached in Spring Hill, Leeford, one of four houses sited directly opposite the shopping precinct and market area; Frank's first experience of Leeford Village. However, schooldays had a lasting effect on young Francis. Nobody calls him that these days.

That first day, he tried to engage the other lads in conversation about Bobby Moore, Nobby Stiles, Geoff Hurst *et al*, but to no effect. The cap had to go and when they knew his name was Francis, the screaming and gurgling, 'it's Frank, actually', didn't cut it. The screaming you might expect and understand; the gurgling, well, that was just cruel. Frank could not fight off two burly fifth formers who had decided that his head would fit inside the toilet bowl.

Retribution for the two burly fifth formers never came. Within two years, one was off to Oxford to eventually become a lawyer of some repute, the other sent up to Cambridge and trained to be 'something in the city'. Frank, however, did what a proportion of victims were tempted to do - he became a bully himself. By the end of his third year at Banfield Grammar, he had his own gang and meted out a variety of punishments to the unwary, the unaware and, in his opinion, the underclass. He wasn't being completely truthful with his dad when claiming to have been 'pushed around for five years'. Maybe the first year, but you have to give him some credit – he survived.

Many people in the village look at Frank today – his military bearing, his officer-style approach to meetings or indeed any discussion, and they don't realise that the nearest he got to the military was two years in the Boys' Brigade. But boy, could he march! Toughened up at school, he eventually did join Cecil in the business. Even his dad started to call him Frank.

*

Frank often relives the significant events in his life. Childhood, school, of course, but the true pattern of his life was formed when he joined the business. He had no idea that the partnership with his dad would be short-lived. In less than two years working alongside Cecil he had proved to be a quick learner, as adept at sizing and cutting a head gasket as he was drafting a set of accounts. His dad insisted that he start a business studies course at Banfield College, but on his eighteenth birthday, the potential struggles of the next few years were brought sharply into focus.

'Francis, it's Mom.'

'You never call me at work.'

'Your dad stopped at home today. He probably didn't tell you, but he hasn't been well lately.'

'What's happened, Mom?'

'Dad's in hospital. Oh, Francis.' Doreen started to cry.

'It's okay, Mom. Is he in Banfield General?'

'Yes, Darling. Ward C4, the Cancer Unit.'

'I had no idea – shall I pick you up from home?'

'No, I'm already here love. They let me use their phone.'

Cecil had reduced the hours he worked at the office, sometimes only doing two days a week. 'I'll do the accounts at home over the next few days, Francis. I can keep your mom company at the same time - alright?' Not that he needed Frank's approval, but he was the first adult to truly respect the young man and demonstrate that respect on a daily basis. Frank has never forgotten that.

Frank had coped remarkably well, and Cecil had developed a good team around him. Only Doreen knew that her husband had been undergoing chemotherapy as an out-patient. The treatment for the prostate cancer had not worked. It had spread to the pancreas, and he had become anaemic. Cecil died at four o'clock the following morning.

Eighteen years of age, and Frank was effectively in control of the business. He was lucky that Cecil had carefully selected and trained his team to cope without him. His manager, Steve Coplan, was fond of Frank and knew the only chance the business had of survival was for Frank to develop and succeed personally. He made it his mission to support the young man who was now grieving the loss of his father.

Frank met Sally at college. They went out a few times and grew close very quickly. They were engaged within the year. As he was taking his final exams, Sally had some news for him.

'This is going to come as a bit of a shock - I'm pregnant.'

They hadn't planned a short engagement, but he needed to review his objectives. Doreen felt she could not stay in the house. After a few months she went to live with a cousin in North Banfield. Doreen died ten years later after a long battle with breast cancer. The business was ticking over, but not thriving, and he would not be able to afford to keep his parents' house. He decided to move into the middle of the village. A smaller three-bedroom house became available in Green Crescent, with a significant difference in value between the two houses. Mature beyond his years, Frank put an offer in for the house and the deposit was paid before he and Sally had a beautiful baby girl – Megan. Years later, she asks Frank about her mother, Sally.

'Dad, can I ask you something?'

'What's that love?'

'Did Mom ever get to see me when I was born?'

'For a few minutes, Megan, just a few minutes.'

'But the fête's not for ages yet,' exclaims Simon Brown. 'And who's to say that they'll want us to play?'

'We might as well form the band anyway. Be a laugh, and it's something to do.'

'You're bound to say that, Zack. My money's on you being lead singer,' jumps in Adam.

'I'm the one with the sound-proofed music room at the vicarage; a perk of being the vicar's son. Plenty of room – could you match that at your dad's chip shop?'

'Well...'

'Exactly.'

'He is the oldest, Zack, and he is the best lead guitarist we know,' says Simon.

'Don't worry, I'm happy to play guitar and follow instructions,' says Adam. 'I haven't got time to lead a band and organise stuff anyway.'

'That's settled then,' says Zack, 'Anyone object to Clare on drums?'

'What?' shouts Simon, a bit louder than he intended. They have been close friends at school for nearly five years and he always knows when Zack is manipulating him. This is one of those occasions.

'You know she's good. Please don't tell me you want an all-male band.'

'Okay,' says Simon, 'but we still need a bass player.'

'Got some ideas, and I think Clare knows someone.'

'Who's going to write our songs?' asks Simon.

'Don't you worry about that. I've written one already,' answers Zack.

Sergeant Miller draws his chair closer, fixing his gaze on Gail, not wanting to miss the slightest hesitation, a careless word, even the tightening of her mouth as the stress levels increase. 'What have you got against Jessica Townley?'

'Nothing.'

'Come on Gail, we've seen your reaction. You hate her, don't you? You helped somebody set fire to the salon.'

'It wasn't me!'

'PC Carr, get Gail a cup of tea, will you?'

'Sugar, Gail?'

'Never mind the sugar,' snaps Sergeant Miller, nodding towards the door.

As PC Carr leaves the room, Sergeant Miller places his hand on Gail's right arm. 'Now, Gail, you know me well enough. I'm not letting this go. Whatever you did, we'll find out. If you helped somebody, you will have to tell us. It can only help your situation.'

'I can't tell you who it is.'

'Okay, let's step back. What has Jessica done to you? She wasn't at the salon when the accident happened, was she?'

'She was responsible.'

'Maybe, but you didn't make a big fuss at the time. You just put the claim in, and you won. End of story.'

'Wasn't just the accident.'

'Ah, we're getting somewhere. You have a grudge against Jessica. Right?'

'Not her. Him.'

'Who do you mean?'

'Nick.'

'Nick Allthorpe?'

'Yes.'

'What's he got to do with it?'

'We were together for a while, until SHE came along.'

Tuesday, 6.10 p.m.

'He's here. What shall we do, Lin?'

'Leave the talking to me – I know his type.'

The sun decides to fall slightly in the sky, hiding behind a collection of cumulonimbi. The occupant of the car indicating right into the short driveway has no control over the movements of the heavenly bodies, but the timing is perfect. Shadows cast by the library building creep forward just enough to conceal the two sisters. Allen Gomez switches off the ignition, knowing full well that he is fashionably late. He likes the idea of trying out the younger sister. Linda intrigued him, possibly beguiled him, but he likes both of them; Sherry's fresh youth against something in Linda. Yes, that something that drove him into a mental somersault. Maybe I'll plump for Linda after tomorrow night, he thinks. For tonight, let's have some fun with Sherry. Spotting a flicker in the security light's beam, he senses movement by the wall.

'Who is it? That you, Sherry?'

'Two for the price of one, Allen!' snaps Linda.

'What? You're supposed...'

'Yeh, supposed to be here tomorrow. That right?'

'What's going on?'

'That's what we'd like to know,' says Sherry, unable to conceal the metaphorical scratching in her voice.

'Listen girls, I'm sorry, but this is a bit of a mix-up.'

'Damn right it is!' Sherry bites back.

'Shez, leave this to me. Go home! I'll see you later.'

'Sure?'

'Yes. I've dealt with worse than our Mr Gomez.'

Sherry avoids eye contact with her six o'clock date as she exits the car park, dragging her feet as if the effort is too great.

'She's gone. Alright, Mr Gomez. A word,' she says, pointing to his car. 'Move it into the corner. We don't want to be disturbed, do we, Allen?'

'What, you mean...?'

Steve Adams and Nick Allthorpe share one passion – football. More specifically, Banfield Town, currently languishing in 22nd place in the Southern Region Division Five.

'You used to play, didn't you, Nick?'

'I didn't give myself a chance. Three games with Town's reserve side, that was it.'

'How come?'

'Simple really - football, the rock band and girls. Guess which two came out on top!'

'This is different though. Even Cody and George are applying.'

'Which George?'

'Oh, come on. George Owens. He's pretty fit for fifty-five.'

'S'pose.'

'How about it then? Shall we both apply?'

'Go on then. Not a bad way of keeping fit, and it's about time Leeford had their own team.'

'Hey, Nick, guess who the head coach is?'

'No, don't tell me, not Frank!'

'Well, sort of, but don't panic, it's Frank Reed. Even *he* thinks he's too old - even for six-a-side walking football.'

'Of course, Steve. He played for the Town back in the sixties and seventies.'

'Played until 1983 – cracking midfielder – looked after himself.'

'Nice bloke as well,' says Nick.

'It'll be interesting to see who else applies. Come to think about it, where do we apply? To the Centre?'

'No. Ted's taken on the role of club secretary. The list's behind the bar. Ted reckons we might be able to play in the Banfield and District Division Eight by next season.'

'Wonder if there's a Division Nine?'

'Hello Clara. Tea?'

'I'll have a bun, Ethel. And a cuppa of course.'

'Celebrating?'

'I should be, but I don't feel like it.'

'Do you want to talk about it?'

As Ethel pours the boiling water into two mugs, she knows, of course, that Clara wants to talk about it. Ethel's role in the village is much more than cafe owner. She has carried on the tradition started by Billy, her late husband. He was a great listener, not nosey, but he had a knack of saying just the right thing. Ethel appears to have taken on the mantle.

'Thanks Ethel.'

'Now, my dear, is everything okay?'

'No different with George, but he's not going to get any better.'

'The ring?'

'Back with its owner. Suptra is in the clear, thank goodness, and I'm not being charged. I will have to take a break from the shop, though. Not sure how long it will take Sheri to forgive me, or to trust me again. Mind you, she did tell me to concentrate on George.'

'My dear Clara, have a break. Sheri will come round. She knows that you are basically a very honest person. Otherwise, it's great news, isn't it?'

'Of course, weight off my mind, and I need more time at home anyway. But the shame...'

The tinkle of the small bell signifying a movement of the front door makes both women look up. Suptra and Nita enter the cafe.

'We don't see you two in here together very often. Tea and chat?' Ethel offers a table in the corner, but Suptra has no secrets now – not from his friends.

'No, can we sit with you ladies?'

'Of course,' says Clara, pleased to have completed her business.

'We've come to a decision. Oh, and before I carry on – Clara, please forget about the ring. You meant well, and I forgive you for what happened.'

'Oh Suptra,' says Clara, touching his hand.

'We're friends, Clara, and we wanted to tell you and Ethel together - we're never going to India.'

'What about your ambitions, Nita?'

'It's too complicated and too dangerous. My Uncle Suptra's safety is my priority, and he cannot go back – ever. And if he can't go, then I won't.' Suptra grasps her hand and kisses her lightly on the cheek. Tears form in Ethel's eyes.

'Oh, I'm so pleased for you. You are our dear friends and we have been so worried.'

'Right, Gail, we'll get back to your motivation, but you must tell me what part you played in the fire.'

'I…I have knowledge of chemicals.'

'We know.'

'Before I left the salon, I took a copy of the set of keys. It was quite a while before the opportunity presented itself. I had almost decided to throw away the keys and forget it, until I met him for the first time a few months ago.'

'Who?'

Chapter 21: One, Two, Three, Four

Allen's hands are shaking as he selects reverse gear, at the same time tapping the 'down' button for the driver's window. He catches Linda's eye as he carefully inches back towards the rear wall of the library, now drowned in shadow. 'Are you getting in, Linda?'

'No, you come out here. There're a few things I need to say.'

Closing his door and trying to steady himself, Allen takes a deep breath, then notices a smear on the central embellisher. He turns his hand, so the cuff of his jacket faces the offending mark and gently rubs it away. Then he turns to face her.

'A bit of a Romeo aren't we, Mr Gomez?' Linda stands with her hands on her hips. Allen Gomez's usual confident manner had deserted him the moment he saw Linda and Sherry standing in the dim glow of the security light. 'What do you have to say for yourself?' Linda is not going to let him leave without an explanation, but Allen's mouth is so dry he can hardly speak. He smiles instead. 'And you can wipe that smile off your face!' Linda can hear in her own voice that of her mother scolding her whenever she had misbehaved. This amuses her slightly, but she remains straight-faced.

Allen spreads his arms wide. 'I'm sorry, Linda. I just thought...'

'You just thought that it would be cool to have both of us on the go at the same time, eh?'

Allen looks down at the floor. He hasn't felt this humiliated since he was made to stand up in front of the whole regional sales team to explain it was his poor sales figures that had prevented the whole team achieving their bonus for the year. He had resigned shortly afterwards and made a vow to himself that he was never going to work for anyone again. Right now, with Linda Cross moving ever closer to him in a threatening manner, it's difficult to see how he can resign from this situation. 'Linda, I'm, I feel...' he stutters. She is so close to him now that he can feel her breath on his face. He gulps.

'If you ever, EVER, go anywhere near my sister again, then I will make you pay dearly!'

Another gulp.

'I will tell everyone, what a sleazy, selfish character you really are. You understand?'

Allen nods, his forehead almost touching Linda's.

'Say it, then.'

He licks his lips which are so dry they are stuck together. 'I understand.'

'Yes, I think you do,' says Linda, moving closer.

'I do. I understand,' says Allen.

'Good. Now kiss me!'

'Wha...'

A person walking past the vicarage might feel a pang of nostalgia for a gentler way of life as they hear the strains of a Vaughan Williams song coming through Reverend Peterson's open study window. Or, they might feel uplifted by a Handel oratorio, or even pause to question the deeper meaning of life after a few bars of a Mahler symphony. But not today. Today, the sounds coming from the vicarage are such as have never been heard before in Leeford Village. The sounds of guitars tuning, the opening riff of Times Like These, played through every effects pedal known to man in such a way that would be completely unrecognisable to the Foo Fighters, the writers of the song. And then there is the bass, which, if the volume were to be turned up half a notch, would dislodge masonry that had weathered many a storm over centuries.

Zack was correct in assuming Clare would know a bass player and Ziggy has turned up and tuned up and is adjusting his strap, so his bass is just above his knees. Unbeknown to Zack, his soundproofed room is effective to the extent that no one in the house can hear him practising his violin (which none of his friends knows anything about), or his father tinkering on the piano, preparing for an upcoming service. It is not so effective for an onslaught of amplification. Luckily, Zack and his friends are the only ones in the house and are blissfully unaware of the quizzical looks on the faces of passers-by.

'Where's Clare?' shouts Simon, eyeing the empty drum stool at the back of the room.

'She's on her way!'

Simon tries to lip-read Zack but fails and shrugs his shoulders.

'She's on her way!'

Zack shouts again. Another shrug. Zack goes over to Adam's amplifier and pulls out the lead. Silence.

'What the...' says Adam, looking down at his guitar switches.

'Give it a rest, Adam. I can't hear myself shout,' says Zack.

Ziggy goes to pluck another deep note but receives a look from Adam that causes him to rethink his move.

'Now, I can speak.'

The others put down their instruments, in case the temptation to play gets the better of them.

'Clare's on the way. Before she comes, I want us to work out this song I wrote a couple of weeks ago.' He pulls a folded sheet of paper out of his back pocket and spreads it on top of Adam's amplifier.

'It's a love song…'

Immediately, there is a collective groan from the others.

'Is it called "Clare" by any chance?'

Zack ignores Adam's comment. 'It goes like this.' Zack proceeds to sing a couple of verses of the song.

'Well, it's got something, mate, even if it is a love song,' says Simon. 'Have you got the chords, so we can have a go?'

'I have. But here's the killer chorus.' Zack belts out the chorus. When he finishes the others look at each other, quizzically. Then at Zack.

'Mate. You're not actually going to sing that are you?' says Adam.

Zack looks bemused. 'Of course, it's the best bit of the song.'

Adam and Simon both look away. Ziggy shakes his head and plucks a low D that sends a framed Peterson family photo crashing to the floor.

'Who, Gail? Who did you meet?'

The name almost escapes from Gail Perkins' lips, but she checks herself and leans back in the chair. 'What's in it for me?'

Sergeant Miller does a double take. 'What do you mean "what's in it for me"?'

'If I tell you who it is, what do I get out of it?'

Sergeant Miller throws his hands up in the air. 'Unbelievable!' He draws out the word.

Gail continues. 'I'm serious. If I'm going to give you vital information, information that would have taken you years to find out for yourself, then there has to be something in it for me.'

PC Carr walks back into the room carrying three cups of tea on a tray. He places the tray on the table and passes one cup to Gail, one to Sergeant Miller, then sits down with his own cup in front of him.

'Oh, thank you, Gary.' Gail takes a sip of tea. 'No biscuits?'

PC Carr stands,' Oh, I'm sorry, I didn't…'

'SIT DOWN!' Sergeant Miller slams both hands on the table. There's an uncomfortable silence before he speaks again.

'PC Carr. Miss Perkins here thinks that we should be rewarding her for the information she holds that will enable us to solve the crime.'

PC Carr takes a long drink of tea and smacks his lips. 'Fair enough, Sarge.'

'Fair enough? FAIR ENOUGH? Give me strength!'

Sergeant Miller spends the next silent minute trying to quell his anger and frustration. He takes a couple of deep breaths and, when he next speaks, it is with his usual composure. 'Look Gail. This is the situation. If you tell us who actually planted the device, whose idea it was, then it will help your case when you come to court to defend yourself against whatever we decide to charge you with. If you don't, then we will have to assume that you carried out the whole operation and that could mean a long prison term.'

PC Carr drains his teacup. 'Fair enough, Sarge.'

Sergeant Miller sighs. 'So, what is it to be, Gail?'

Clare walks into the music room just as the rest of the band are finishing Zack's song.

'Hi! Perfect timing! Well, you are a drummer!' Zack laughs at his own joke then hugs Clare. They embrace for what to the others is an extraordinarily long and unnecessary time before Clare sits behind her kit. She makes a few minor adjustments, plays a couple of rolls across the toms and then waits.

'What are we doing then?' she asks, drumsticks poised.

'A song I wrote a couple of weeks ago. You'll love it. It's very easy, isn't it?' Zack looks around at the others, who are looking glumly at their instruments. 'Just play a straight four-four beat, but rock it up in the chorus.'

'Okay, I'll count you in,' says Clare. She clicks her sticks together four times and the band launch into the song. There are two verses, followed by a short guitar solo from Adam, before a rising sequence of chords leads into the chorus:

And I'm so glad that I met you
And I'll never forget you, Aman----da.

It's a well-known fact, even to those with little musical knowledge, that once a drummer unexpectedly stops drumming, much of the power in the song is lost. Gradually, the others follow Clare's lead and what follows can only be described as an awkward moment.

'Why have we stopped?' asks Zack. 'It was sounding great!'

Clare puts down her sticks. 'Who's Amanda?'

'What?'

'Who is Amanda? The girl you wrote the song for.'

'It's no one. It's just something I wrote.'

'A couple of weeks ago!' Clare stands behind the kit.

'Yeah. But it's not about anyone.' The penny drops. 'Oh, I can see why you...' He is unable to finish the sentence before Clare rushes out of the room. Adam bites his bottom lip. Simon scratches the back of his head.

'I had to use Amanda. I needed a name with three syllables,' offers Zack.

It's Ziggy who speaks next. 'I think you've just lost your girlfriend, mate.'

Zack's face reddens.

'It's worse than that,' says Adam, 'we've lost our drummer.'

Chapter 22: Clara

'A cup of tea, Ethel, please. And are those scones fresh?'

'They certainly are. Made them this morning.'

'I'll have one then. Just butter.' Clara sits down heavily at her usual table. A couple of minutes later, Ethel brings over two scones and a large pot of tea.

'You look like you could use a little company, dear,' says Ethel, sitting down opposite.

'Can you tell, Ethel?'

Ethel pours the tea into two cups. 'Of course, I can tell. How long have I known you?'

'You're making us sound like a couple of old biddies!'

'We are, aren't we?' They both laugh. 'So, go on then. Is it George?' Ethel's tone is serious, as it always is when she talks about George.

Clara sighs. 'Isn't it always?'

'What's he done now?'

Clara takes a sip of tea and a bite of her scone.

'It's not what he's done. It's what he's said.'

'Oh?' Ethel raises her eyebrows. She sees Frank Watson walking towards the window. *Not now, Frank*, she thinks. He taps on the window. Clara and Ethel look up. Frank waves at them and moves on. Ethel breathes a sigh of relief. 'So, what's George said, then?'

'Well, on Sunday night, we were watching a film on the telly. When the ad break came on, George looked at me and said, "fancy a cup of tea, Chloe?"'

'Chloe? That's your dog's name, isn't it?'

'It is. It's also the name of George's ex-wife.'

'He named your dog after his ex-wife?'

'Yes. I know it sounds odd, but that's how it is. Then, he carried on talking to me, as if I were her. He brought the tea and asked me if I'd had a good day at the hospital.'

'The hospital?'

'Yes. Chloe was a nurse. She had an affair with one of the surgeons. That's why she and George got divorced.'

Ethel scrapes up the crumbs from her scone into the middle of the plate. She pours herself another cup of tea.

'So, what did you say?'

'Well, I went along with it for a while. I knew this was George becoming confused. He's got a lot worse lately, so I'm used to him getting things mixed up.'

Ethel reaches out for Clara's hand. She takes it in her own and gives it a gentle squeeze.

'The next night, we were clearing up after tea. I'd made George a steak and kidney pie. It's always been his favourite. He always said he would not have married me if I couldn't make a steak and kidney pie. Anyway, after we finished, he kissed me on the cheek and said, "that was lovely, Doris. You always make the best steak and kidney pie".'

'Doris? Who's Doris?'

'Doris was George's wife, before he married Chloe. Doris ran off with a butcher.'

'Well, in all the years I've known you, Clara Dennis, I never knew any of this.'

'It was a long time ago, Ethel.'

'It must have been. I mean, how long have you and George been married?'

'Forty-seven years, this year. We were in our twenties.'

'How did you meet? I don't think you've ever told me.'

'There's a lot I haven't told you, Ethel. A lot I haven't told anyone.'

Ethel stands up and begins to clear the table.

'Sit down, Ethel,' says Clara. 'I want to tell you now.'

Ethel sits.

'George was housemaster at a boys' public school in Herefordshire. I was at college in the same town, training to be a legal secretary. It's not what I wanted to do, but my mother had very firm ideas.'

'What did you want to do?'

Clara flushes a little. 'I wanted to be an air hostess.'

'Air hostess?' Ethel laughs.

'Yes. I think it was the uniform. And the idea of travel. The furthest I'd ever been was a week in Scotland. My parents were very reserved. They never liked to go out of their comfort zone and talked about the week in Scotland for years afterwards. Like it had been an expedition.'

'So, you were at college.'

'Yes. There was a pub in the town and the college girls and the teachers from the school used to meet up. It was all very civilised.'

Ethel winks at Clara.

'Well, most of the time,' says Clara, blushing again.

'George was a regular at the pub and we got to know one another, as friends. He was very clever and a bit old-fashioned. I liked that. He was a real gentleman and had a very peculiar way of talking.'

'Still does,' says Ethel.

'Well, yes. I suppose he does.'

Clara is about to continue when Ethel puts up a hand to stop her.
'What about Doris and Chloe? Were either of them part of the pub group?'

'No. George had married and divorced them by then. It all happened when he was very young. He was quite bitter. Particularly about Chloe.'

'Yet, he named his dog after her?'

'Yes. Maybe there's some symbolism there, come to think of it. I mean, she is a female dog.'

'Ah, I see,' says Ethel.

Clara continues. 'George and I got to know each other well and this eventually led to clandestine visits to his room at the school. We would sit and listen to music, classical mostly and some jazz. We'd never had music in our house. I used to switch on the radio sometimes, to listen to pop music, but my mother would switch it off.'

'Why did she do that?'

'She was a very strict Methodist and seemed to object to any form of enjoyment, actually.'

'You were religious then?'

'No, not at all. She was and I'm sure my father only went along with it to keep the peace. I used to go to chapel with her, until I eventually rebelled. I can't say I hated going, though, and the people were lovely. My mother seemed to have her own version of Methodism, which was far stricter than that practised by the others at the church.'

'So, when you went to George's room you did more than play music.'
Ethel winks again.

'Not at first. At first, we sat and talked long into the night. I remember having to run past the bursar's office in the early morning, so George wouldn't be found out. I think George was afraid of entering into another relationship, given that he had already been twice divorced.'

'Oh, Clara!' laughs Ethel. 'Listening to music, talking into the night. I mean, you, an ex-Methodist and a man of experience! There must have been more.'

'There was. And a few weeks later I found out I was pregnant.'
Ethel puts her hand to her mouth.

'Oh, I'm sorry, love. Was that the baby you lost?'

'Yes. I kept it quiet at first, even from George. But when it began to show I told him. He was over the moon and within a month we were married. It was a registry office in Hereford. Just the two of us and a couple of friends as witnesses. We rented a little house near the school, and I left college. It was idyllic and George was wonderful, so attentive. And then…' Clara swallows a lump that has risen into her throat.

'Oh, Clara. Don't get upset. Let's have another cup of tea.' Ethel stands again and puts the plates onto a tray.

'I want to continue, Ethel. There's something I need to say. Something I've never said to anyone.'

Ethel sits down slowly.

'Go on.'

'I lost the baby, as you know, after seven months. George was devastated. For a while he went into a deep depression. The school let him take time off, but they eventually gave his job to someone else. We packed up and moved to Birmingham, to George's parents.'

'Not your parents?'

'No. My mother worked out that the baby would have been conceived out of wedlock and I was no longer welcome in her house. I never saw her again, though I did write letters to my father. I sent them to him at his office and he used to reply. Sometimes.'

'Wow,' says Ethel. 'And you've never told this to anyone?'

'That's not the part I have never told anyone.' Clara looks straight at Ethel. 'The part I have never told anyone is that it was not George's baby.'

Ethel is speechless and sits open-mouthed.

'It was the lecturer at college. We had a fling for a few weeks, at the same time I was seeing George. The baby could not have been George's, because the dates were all wrong.'

Ethel clears her throat. 'Well, you are a dark horse, Clara Dennis.' She stands and walks around to Clara's side of the table. She puts her arm around her. Clara begins to cry.

'Come on, girl,' says Ethel. 'You'll have me at it if you're not careful!' She picks up a serviette and offers it to Clara, who wipes her eyes.

'You know, Ethel. I feel like a great weight has been lifted.'

'Well, that's funny, Clara. Because I feel like a great weight has been dropped upon me!'

They both laugh.

'Another pot of tea? A piece of Victoria sponge?' asks Ethel.

'Only if it's three days old. Like the scones!' says Clara with a wink.

'Will you just listen to me for a minute?'

'I've nothing to say to you, Zack.'

'Oh, so you are speaking to me then?' This precipitates a stony silence of the Clare variety.

'Look, there is no girl called Amanda. She doesn't exist.'

'Really?'

'Of course. I'm not going to be corny like the Oldies and say you're the only girl for me, but you are.'

'Zack, I do love you.'

'Come here and prove it.'

'Oh, Zack, how did Ziggy get on?'

He leaves his hands on her shoulders but hesitates.

'Hang on, Clare, forgot to ask. How do you know Ziggy?'

'Didn't I say? He's my ex.'

'Listen Gail, you can see what Stephen, er, Sergeant Miller, is like. He won't give up. You might as well give him what he wants.'

'Will it really help me?'

'Of course. You will be charged at the very least with being an accessory. If you don't cooperate, you might be classed as a co-principal.'

'What does that mean, Gary?'

'PC Carr to you.'

'Okay, but what does it mean?'

'If you are charged with arson, you could get life.'

She doesn't need to speak. Gary has no need to push. She will tell Sergeant Miller what he wants to know, even though it will hurt her.

'She's ready then, Gary?'

'How do you know?'

'You can be as thick as pudding, sometimes mate. The double-sided mirror?'

'Oh, you were listening, boss?'

'You do catch on quickly, but I have to say PC Carr, you've come up trumps this time with your little chat. I thought you were going to ask her out at one stage.'

'Give me some credit...'

'Never mind that, I'll see Miss Perkins in a minute. But you do realise you were talking a lot of legal crap back there, don't you?'

'I was?'

'Principal? What the hell was that?'

'The main, y'know, criminal?'

'Gary, you really have been watching too many old episodes of Starsky and Hutch.'

'Fargo.'

'Pardon?'

'Fargo – the American crime series. Brilliant.'

'Whatever Gary, but "principal" in the UK is not the main criminal. In this country, the principal is a person who gives another party the authority to act on their behalf.'

'Okay, I've learned something. But it seems to be working, doesn't it, boss?'

'I'll give you this one, Gary, I'll give you this one.' *He'll never get through his sergeants' exams*, he thinks to himself.

'Gail.'

'Sergeant Miller.'

'That's better. Now, this is being recorded and can be used as evidence in court. I am starting the tape now. For the tape, what is your name?'

'Gail Perkins.'

'Why did you have a grudge against Jessica Townley?'

'Two things – first, she came along and ruined what I had going with Nick Allthorpe.'

'We've spoken to Nick. He says it was a casual fling; two or three dates.'

'I slept with him.'

'I'm not sure that's relevant to the case, but I will accept that you became infatuated with him. Is that true?'

'If you want to put it that way, yes.'

'And then he met Jessica.'

'Dumped me like a brick in a canal.'

'Then why target his girlfriend? *He* was the one that hurt you.'

'Don't know, I just did.'

'Then there was the hairdressing incident.'

'Yes, but she paid for that. The money came in useful.'

'You don't seem so bothered about that.'

'I was, until a few months ago. Then I met him.'

'Who?'

'Martin Frobisher.'

'How does he fit into this?'

'I fell in love with him.'

'How? Where?'

'Don't judge me, Sergeant, but there is a scheme for single women to write to prisoners in jail.'

'I've heard of that. So, you became a pen pal to Martin. What was he in for?'

'Arson.'

'I see. What's his background?'

'Born in London. His dad worked at the fish market. His mom's Swedish.'

'What?'

'The fish market.'

'No, about his mom!'

'Swedish.'

'What happened next?'

'We'd written to each other for nearly nine months, and he was due for early release. I met him in a pub in Banfield and I fell in love with him.'

'Speaks Swedish, does he?'

'Well yes. Why?'

'No reason, Gail, no reason.'

'Tea, Sarge?' interrupts PC Carr.

'For God's sake, PC Carr, this is not the time.'

'Sorry Sarge, I'll do it later.'

'Gail, who initiated the idea of the fire at the salon?'

'He did - it's strange this, but he'd had a run-in with Jessica over some work he did for her.'

'What work?'

'He's a trained plumber and he worked on the toilets at the back of the salon. She claimed they kept overflowing after he'd finished the work, got somebody else to fix the problem and didn't pay Martin.'

'So, he'd got a grudge against her, and your grudge was with Nick, essentially.'

'That's right.'

'We're getting somewhere now.'

112

'Can I have a break?'

'Toilet?'

'No, I'm tired.'

'Sorry, Gail, I want to finish this. What happened next?'

'I have knowledge of chemicals. It was a joke at first, over a few drinks. I suggested that we make a timed incendiary device that would fuse two chemicals together, causing a reaction and, well, a fire.'

'Go on.'

'He jumped at the idea. I wasn't sure at first. I'd already had the money from Jessica – that was easy. She never argued about it, but he goaded me about Nick and finally persuaded me to help.'

'What did you actually do?'

'I didn't make anything. I listed the relevant chemicals, told him how to mix them, and we both researched incendiary devices on the Net. He took control, and I would have done anything for him. Gave him a set of keys for the salon as well.'

'Do you have an address for him?'

'Only his mom's flat. His dad died, and it was never clear where Martin lived. I could never work him out. He was strange, but had a way of drawing you in.'

'Did you know about the drawings and the Swedish phrases?'

'I heard about them, but Martin never mentioned it.'

'Where is Martin now, Gail?'

'I've no idea, Sergeant – honestly.'

'Okay, Gail, you will be charged as an accessory, but I'm grateful that you have finally been honest. Thank you. PC Carr, that cup of tea would be welcome, wouldn't it, Gail?'

'What's his full name?'

'Ziggy Zagger.'

'You're kidding.'

'Changed it by deed poll.'

'What was his real name?'

'Cedric Arbuckle.'

'Right. I can see why he changed it. Bowie fan, is he?'

The conversation continues, and Zack is feeling increasingly uncomfortable. They both have exes, but she has brought Ziggy into his band. *Does she want him back?*

'Hi Ted, exciting news about the new footy team.'

'George, I can't wait to see you in your shorts.'

'Shucks Ted, bet you say that to all the girls.'

'I must say I love your enthusiasm, if not the sight of your legs.'

'What about you, Ted? Are you playing?'

'Not with my knee. I'll stick to being club secretary and bucket and sponge man.'

'Hey, Ted,' shouts Cody, 'what formation do you think Frank will plump for?'

'Eh?'

'Four-four-two? Four-two-four? Three at the back with wingbacks...?'

'Hang on Cody, hang on a minute, that would be impossible.'

'Why?'

'It's blummin' six-a-side walking football!'

'So?'

'Crikey, Cody - help me out here, George – SIX-A-SIDE.'

'Oh, sorry, Ted. Agnes says I was at the back of the queue when the brains were handed out.'

Ted responds with a muttered 'hmm'.

'Mind you, George, we'll need a squad. People always drop out at the last minute. Anyway, here's the man himself.'

'Hi Ted, George, Cody.'

'Hi Frank!' the three men respond in unison.

'Pint please, Ted.'

'Have you seen the latest list?' Ted tries to get the head just right on Frank's pint.

'Let's have a look then,' says Frank Reed, reaching out for the clipboard that Ted keeps on the bar.

'Now, let's see – well done George, Cody, Nick Allthorpe, Steve Adams – good, a bit of youth...'

'Youth?' jumps in George.

'Steve's only fifty – not exactly in his dotage – and Nick's only thirty. He'll be one of the younger players, unless we get some of the students involved.'

'Frank?'

'Yes, Cody?'

'Any women?'

'What do you mean, women?'

'Are women allowed to play?'

'Not thought about it. But if they apply, we'll encourage them to start a ladies' team.'

114

'Don't know about that,' says Ted, 'Sally is thinking about applying. Only a question of sorting out dressing rooms. The school has offered its outdoor five-a-side pitch and the school facilities outside school hours. No problem there.'

'Oh, I don't know,' says a worried-looking Frank, as George and Cody nod their heads in agreement - whether that is with Ted or Frank, no one is quite sure, and Frank continues to grimace. 'I just don't know.'

Chapter 24: Taking the Biscuit

It's late. Sherry has been calling Linda for the past two hours. She is about to report her missing when she hears a key turning in the front door. She breathes a sigh of relief and steps into the hallway.

'I thought you'd been mugged, or something. Where've you been?'

Linda hangs her coat behind the door. 'I needed to clear my head, Sis.'

'For four hours? Your head must be empty by now.' Sherry laughs at her own quip, but Linda walks quickly past her into the lounge where she flops down on the sofa. Sherry sits next to her. 'So, did you give it to him, Lin?'

A surge of blood rushes to Linda's head. 'What?'

'Did you tell him what we think of him?'

'Oh. Yeah. Yeah, I did.'

Linda's phone vibrates in her pocket. Luckily, Sherry is in the midst of her rant and does not hear it.

'What a sleazebag! He wanted both of us. Can you believe it?!'

Linda shakes her head.

'I never ever want to see him again!'

'We have to see him again, Shez. He's our boss.'

Sherry sighs. 'Yeah. Shame. Still, I bet you frightened him off.'

Linda rises from the sofa. 'I'm off to bed.'

Sherry lunges forward and surprises Linda by throwing her arms around her. 'Thanks, Sis. I'm so glad you saved me from that idiot.'

Linda pulls herself away. 'Yeah. G'night.' At the top of the stairs, Linda reads a text:

```
Hi. What a fantastic night. Can't wait to see
you again. Tomorrow? Call me. Al xx
```

Clare raises her sticks high in the air. The band wait for her to give the signal and then, give or take a semi-quaver or two, they strike the final power chord together. Zack imagines himself running to the front of the stage, foot on monitor, his adoring fans baying for more. He imagines Clare looking from behind her drum kit, jealous at the adulation he is receiving from girls in the front row of the arena, who will later gather backstage, only to be told by Zack's entourage that he has left the building. He is brought back to reality by his mother

116

entering the room.

'I've brought some lemon squash and biscuits.'

Zack mumbles a very quiet, 'thanks', which is echoed more loudly by the rest of the band.

'Well, you're all working so hard. I thought you need a little break. Give me a shout if you'd like some more.'

Zack is aware of Simon and Adam smirking and his face reddens. 'Bye, Mom,' he says ushering his mother towards the door.

Mrs Peterson is about to leave when she notices a couple of empty Coke cans on the floor. 'Oh, my goodness. You don't have a rubbish bin down here, do you? I'll bring one next time I come down.' Simon has his back to the rest of the room and Zack can see his shoulders moving up and down.

'Thanks, Mrs P,' says Adam, his smirk now a wide grin.

'My pleasure, love,' says Mrs Peterson.

Adam and Simon burst into fits of laughter as soon as Zack's mother closes the door.

'What?' shouts Zack, his voice a mix of anger and embarrassment.

'Lemon squash and biscuits! Very rock and roll, Zack.' Simon fails to stifle his laughter.

'Just get on with the next song,' says Zack.

'Right, everyone,' shouts Adam. 'You all know our primary school favourite, *The Wheels on the Bus,* do you?'

At this, Simon collapses onto the floor. While Zack is focusing on the antics of Simon and Adam, he does not see Ziggy take a glass of lemonade and a handful of biscuits from the tray. Neither does he see him take a second glass and pass it to Clare.

'Football? At your age? Are you mad?' Agnes pours a bucket of oil into the chip fryer. 'You'll have a heart attack!'

Cody puffs out his chest. 'I'm as fit as I was twenty years ago. Fitter, because I used to smoke then.'

Agnes looks him up and down, focusing on his not inconsiderable middle-age paunch.

'I admit I might need to shed a few pounds,' says Cody, patting his stomach. 'Underneath here, Agnes, is a six-pack waiting to get out.'

Agnes shakes her head.

'A Watney's Party Seven, more like!'

'Good grief, Agnes. Now who's showing their age?'

Jack Simmons is scanning the six-a-side sign-up list at the end of the bar.

'Usual, Jack?' calls Ted.

'Yes, please, Ted. It's a fine team you're forming here. A little on the mature side, perhaps, but a fine team, nonetheless.'

'Ah, but age has no bearing here, Jack. This is walking football. It's like normal football, but everyone has to walk.'

'Never heard of it,' says Jack, walking to the other end of the bar to greet a pint of mild.

'It's becoming a big thing, Jack. There's lots of men, and women for that matter, who want to play football, but whose legs no longer carry them along like they used to. Walking football is the perfect sport.'

Jack sips the froth from the top of his pint. 'Sounds daft to me.'

Ted grunts. 'I bet you have some football quotes, Jack.'

Jack puts down his glass and leans towards Ted. 'In football, everything is complicated by the presence of the opposite team.'

Ted puts his finger in the air. 'Wait, don't tell me. I know that one.' The contortions on Ted's face would certainly not be out of place in a gurning competition. However, he has to admit defeat. 'Can't remember, Jack. Who was it?'

'Jean Paul Sartre.'

'Oh, I see. No, I didn't know that. Who did he play for?'

'You off out again?' Sherry is scraping chocolate chip cookie ice cream from the bottom of the tub as her sister comes into the lounge to look at herself in the mirror. 'I thought we were having a girly night in?'

'Yeah, me too, Sis. Kelly just called. She wants an urgent heart-to-heart.'

Linda tries her best to sound disappointed. 'Kelly Bale? From the surgery?'

'Yeah. She sounded very upset.' Linda dabs gloss onto her lips and pouts at the mirror. *Girl, you look great*, she thinks.

'I didn't know you knew her that well.' The ice cream tub is now completely clean. Sherry gives the spoon a final lick.

'I don't.'

'But she wants a heart-to-heart? With someone she hardly knows?'

'Well, sometimes it's better to discuss things with someone that's not too close to you, don't you think?'

Sherry crushes the empty tub on the coffee table and a dribble of trapped ice cream escapes from the bottom. She scrapes it up and licks her finger. 'I tell you everything. I don't need no one else.'

'Well, you're you, aren't you? People are different,' says Linda. She hates lying to her sister, but the thought of her knowing the truth is too terrible to contemplate. Kelly Bale lives far enough away for her sister not to encounter her anytime soon.

'Won't be late,' she says, giving a wave as she leaves the room.

Sherry sighs and slumps in her chair.

The band has three songs ready to perform at the fête and Zack is pleased with the progress they have made. Lemonade has been drunk, biscuits have been eaten and they are packing their equipment.

'What are we called?' asks Adam, wiping a cloth over his strings.

'I haven't thought about that,' says Zack.

'We need a name,' says Clare, 'anyone got any ideas?'

Numerous band names are briefly considered and rejected.

'I know,' says Simon, 'The Lemonade Drinkers!' He laughs out loud, but the running joke has already worn thin. 'Sorry,' he says, sheepishly, 'I thought it was funny.'

A long silence follows.

'Difficult, isn't it?' says Clare, unscrewing her hi-hat cymbals.

The others agree.

'The Leefords,' suggests Zack, hopefully, but the blank looks he receives from the others tell him what they think of his idea.

'The Villagers,' offers Adam.

'It's good, but there's already a band called The Villagers,' says Simon.

'Why don't we go away and come up with ten names each? We can decide at the next practice,' suggests Zack.

They agree this is a sensible option and are about to leave when Ziggy says, 'Fait accompli.'

'Sorry?' says Zack. This is the first time he has spoken to Ziggy since Clare revealed their past relationship.

'Fait accompli' repeats Ziggy.

'Fait accompli?' says Simon. 'We haven't decided the name. How can it be a fait accompli?'

Ziggy laughs. 'It's not. But it's a good name for the band.'

'Go on,' urges Adam.

'Our first gig is the village fête, right?'

'If they want us to play,' chips in Simon.

'So,' continues Ziggy, 'I thought a name that had fête in it, would be good.' He looks around the room for support.

'It makes no sense,' says Zack, 'it's even spelt differently.'

'It doesn't matter. And it doesn't have to make sense. It's just a name.' The lack of opposition from everyone apart from Zack gives Ziggy a surge of confidence. 'Fait Accompli', he repeats.

'Yeah, definitely has a ring to it,' says Simon.

'Definitely,' concurs Adam.

'What about you, Clare?' asks Ziggy.

Clare zips up her stick bag. It's a while before she says, 'I think it's a great name.'

'That's that, then!' says Adam, clapping his hands, 'Fait Accompli. It's a fait accompli!'

Adam and Simon congratulate Ziggy, shaking his hand and slapping him on the back. Clare continues to pack up her sizeable kit, aware of Zack backing out of the room without saying a word.

Chapter 25: Over the Hedge

'She's done it again!' grumbles the over-worked police sergeant.

'Who has?' asks PC Carr.

'Vera.'

'What's she done now?'

'Seems that most of the gnomes in the village have gone missing. I suspect we'll find them in the Cleeve garden.'

'How do you know?'

'Vicar's wife. Doesn't sound very Christian, but she's ratted on Vera.'

'What you gonna do, Sarge?'

'Very professionally put, PC Carr. You'll go far. As for Vera, I suppose we should go and have a look.'

They don't need to bother with the car, as the station is located less than thirty paces from the East Banfield Road, just past the shallow brook (that famously flooded in the deluge) and The Cross pub, frequented by most of the inhabitants of Leeford Village at some time or other. The two men, trying to look official (and even the smart uniforms don't help), narrowly avoid a tragic end, failing to stop at the bright red pelican stop light, the equivalent of the American 'Don't Walk' sign. Well, they DO walk, and the esteemed parish council leader, Mr F. Watson, engineers a manoeuvre that many would think impossible. Lewis Hamilton-esque, he swerves one way and then the other, appearing to aim for the two officers of the law. Fortunately, their nimble feet and youthful gait propel them from certain death to the safety of the pavement.

'I'll have him one day, Gary, I swear.'

'Who?'

'What do you mean, "who"? Didn't you see him?'

'You mean Frank? Yeah, he waved at me as he went past.'

'Went past? Give me strength. Did I interview you for this job, Gary?'

'Yes, with ACC Garfield from Banfield. In fact, it was at Banfield Station. Alice in accounts makes a nice brew there.'

'For God's sake, Gary, get a grip. Let's get up to Vera's.'

'Hi, is that Paul Simon?'

'Eh, is that you, Linda?' stutters Allen, almost dropping his phone.

'Answer my question.'

'Paul Simon? Put me out of my misery.'

'Your last text. You said, "call me Al".'

'Got you. Sorry, I'm all over the place right now. Can I see you later?'

'You can see as much of me as you like, Mr Gomez.'

'Are you messing me about, Linda?'

'Allen, I haven't seen your flat yet. I think we need some time alone, don't you?'

Allen's mouth dries, his lips sticking together as he struggles to find the words he needs.

'You there, Allen? Are you ready for this?'

'Of course, I am. You know how I feel about you, Linda. You're driving me crazy.'

'Meet you in the usual place at six. Then it's back to your flat.'

'Here's your post, Ted. Why they don't bring it to you in the bar beats me.'

'Thanks, Frank.'

'You're not here at lunchtime very often. Any reason?'

'I don't get mistaken for a football coach very often either.'

'Sorry, I'm not with you,' asks Ted, looking puzzled.

'You know I have little or no interest in sport, apart from the Ashes. A certain tradition that I adopted from my father. He always used to say, "Frank Watson, we cannot afford the humiliation of losing to the Australians. Most of them were deported from England years ago. The shame…"'

'Frank, sorry to interrupt your late father in full flow, but what's that got to do with what you just said?'

'The football coach thing?'

'Yes,' says Ted.

'Oh, some of the school kids got the idea that I was the coach of the new team. One of them had the cheek to say he wouldn't even sit on the subs bench for me.'

'But it's Frank Reed that's... oh, I see.'

'Yes, I know what people think of me, particularly the youngsters after the Zack mobile affair. Maybe you could put them straight?'

Ted starts to open the first envelope, murmuring to himself as he does so while doing his best to take in Frank's rambling. 'Banfield and

District Football League... you were saying, Frank?'

'Tell them it's Frank Reed, not me. They'll stop pestering me and I realise they'd rather play for him. They listen to you, Ted.'

'Okay, Frank,' mutters Ted, losing concentration.

'Something important in the post?'

'From the league – hang on – aah, they've accepted my application, blah blah, can't be doing with the small print, great, we're in!'

'Well done, lad. I've no interest in football, but I'm pleased for you.'

'Thanks, Frank, I appreciate it.'

'Sarge?'

'What is it, Gary?'

'Why are we going round the back?'

'For one thing, I know Vera's out. This is her keep-fit day at the Community Centre. Nick tipped me the wink.'

'Oh, very Maigret.'

'Eh?'

'Nothing, Sarge.'

'And, Clouseau, if we're using fictional detectives for pet names - and yes, I did hear you – Vera lives opposite the vicarage. You know what Hilda is like, AND she's a gnome fanatic. I simply don't want her involved. Okay?'

'I've never been round the back of these houses,' muses PC Carr.

'Well, you'll have your chance in a minute,' the exasperated sergeant replies.

'Brill.'

'Here we are then.'

'What do we do now, Sarge?'

'See that hedge?'

'Yeah, the eight-foot thing?'

'That's the one.'

'What do we do then?'

'Not we, you. Climb up and have a look in the garden.'

'It's always flamin' me,' mutters PC Carr.

'What was that, PC Carr?'

'Nothing Sarge, nearly there.'

'What can you see?'

'Hang on, bit prickly this. Hang on a minute, what's this?'

'Yes, Gary, what is it?'

'You've got to see this, Sarge!'

'I'll climb up – give me a hand.'

He joins PC Carr at the top of the hedge, only to be confronted with the most amazing sight he has witnessed since moving to Leeford. It would be fair to say, however, that in terms of the sights and scenes to be experienced in a small village like Leeford, there is not a great deal of competition. Sergeant Miller reaches the top and peers over, hanging onto PC Carr's arm for support. 'It's a bloody gnome convention!'

'There must be three hundred of the blighters in her garden,' exclaims PC Carr.

'But we've only had reports of a few dozen missing - the entire gnome population of Leeford can't be more than fifty. Where the hell has this lot come from?'

'When is it, anyway?' queries Sheri.

'What?' replies Ethel.

'You were just talking about it – Leeford Day.'

'Oh, I'm not sure of the exact date.'

'How can we find out? I don't honestly know anything about it.'

'When did you first hear about the celebrations, Sheri?'

'Well, Clara was chatting to Vera and a couple of others in the...'

'Clara? Is she back working?'

'Yes, we've got over our problems, Ethel. I knew at the time she was under such tremendous strain. It must be a relief that poor old George is getting proper treatment now.'

'I'm so pleased – about Clara I mean – and George as well, if he's a little better.'

'Apparently, Leeford Day originates between the wars – 1930s probably. Leeford was such a small village, or hamlet, going back to the sixteenth century so they say, with only twenty or thirty people living here as recently as ninety years ago. The county council, as it was then, created the town of Banfield which became a metropolitan borough, with all the various regions within the town. Even back then, people had started moving out of the centre of the town towards the countryside to the west.'

'Those that could afford it,' interjects Ethel.

'Exactly, plus a few tradesmen, and then the market developed. Brought a few people in.'

'Sorry to butt in, ladies' says Cody, who has somehow managed to escape the fish and chip shop for a quick coffee and bun at lunchtime.

'How did you get past your Agnes?' asks Ethel.

'Got a tunnel,' he quips.

'Got one into the card shop as well,' shouts George Owens, sitting in the window with his special mug as he keeps an eye on the stall.

'Belt up, George!' snaps Cody.

'Anyway,' he continues, ignoring his friend, 'I might be able to help.'

'How?' chime the two ladies, almost in unison.

'As you say, we're pretty sure that the origin of Leeford Day is in the 1930s, and I happen to know there's only one person still alive in the whole of Leeford who lived here at the time.'

'Who's that?' asks Ethel.

'Howard Smithson. He's at least ninety-six and he lives in Rosewood Nursing Home on the Banfield Road, just before the General. On the left-hand side. Ironically, opposite a chip shop. No competition for us as it's two miles out of the village, but...'

'Sorry, Cody, could we stick to the point?' jumps in Sheri. 'Tell us more about Howard. I vaguely remember him. Wasn't he a postman?'

'Yes, and he first did that job on a push-bike in about 1935. They started 'em young in those days. If you'd got a job, you could leave school.'

'Has anyone spoken to him recently?'

'Frank Watson knows him quite well, but he says that Howard's concentration and memory come and go. On any given day, he might not recognise you, and Leeford Day wouldn't mean anything to him.'

'We need to know more. Let's go and see him,' says Ethel.

'What, now?'

This time Cody and Sheri are in unison.

'Can't shut the cafe now, and you've got a chip shop to run. We'll have to organise something.'

Chapter 26: No Guarantee

'Free beer is it then, Ted?' asks Cody, looking at the others gathered around the largest table in the lounge of The Cross.

'How do you make that out?' There is a slight tremor in Ted's voice as he contemplates the cost of providing eight pints, *gratis*.

'Well, we wouldn't be here if you hadn't told us to come, so you can't expect us to have to pay for something we wouldn't have wanted under normal circumstances.'

The others mutter their agreement.

'But most of you are in here every night.'

Cody winks at Nick.

'Yes, but that's through our own volition. We've been press-ganged here tonight.'

Ted sighs. 'Okay, half-a-pint each. But only after I have said what I am going to say.'

'I'm having you on Ted, but thanks for offering,' says Cody.

Ted grunts and produces the letter he has received from the Banfield and District Football League. He waves it jubilantly in the air.

'I have the great pleasure of informing you all that we have been accepted!'

'Into the League?' asks Frank Reed.

'Yes, Frank. We'll be in Division Eight, of course, but every team must start somewhere.'

George Owens looks quizzically at Ted. 'There are eight divisions of walking football teams? The same as the eleven-a-side?'

Ted re-reads the letter. 'Must be. It clearly says we have been accepted into Division Eight.' He prods the piece of paper in his hand.

'Walking football is very popular these days,' says Nick. 'I am surprised there are eight leagues, though.'

'Well, that's as maybe, but not only have we been accepted into the league, we have our first game a week on Sunday!'

'Who are we playing?' asks Nick.

'North Banfield Social. Away,' says Ted.

There is a collective intake of breath. 'North Banfield Social? The police are there most nights,' says George.

'I know it's a bit rough, but that's the youngsters causing trouble. This is walking football, George. I'm sure it'll be played in the right spirit,' says Ted, unconvincingly.

Sherry Cross flicks through a magazine, imagining how she would look wearing each celebrity's outfit. An article about how to meditate yourself slim holds her concentration, before it is broken by her name being called over the waiting room's speaker. She stuffs the magazine into her bag and takes a short walk along a corridor to the nurse's room. She knocks on the door.

'Come in,' calls the nurse, not a voice with which Sherry is familiar.

Nurse Kelly Bale greets Sherry with a wide red-lipped smile, exposing a row of perfectly straight white teeth.

'Oh. Hi, Kelly. I wasn't expecting you.'

Kelly walks over to a drawer and takes out a couple of needles and a phial of orange liquid. 'No, it's my day off usually, but Angela has childcare issues. So, I'm covering.' She checks Sherry's notes on the computer screen. 'You know the drill, I suppose?' she asks.

'Yeah, every three months. A good dose of B12 to keep me going.'

Kelly jabs the top of Sherry's arm and in a couple of seconds the procedure is complete. 'That's it, then. See you in three months' time.'

'Thanks Kelly.' Sherry picks up her bag and blushes a little when she sees that Kelly has spotted the magazine sticking out of the top, with a 'Leeford Surgery – Do Not Remove' label stuck to the front cover. 'Oh, I hope you and Linda managed to have a good chat,' she says as she is about to leave the room.

Kelly is disposing of the needle and preparing for the next patient. 'Sorry?' she says, looking up at Sherry.

'The other night. You and Linda? She went to see you.'

'Your sister, Linda? I haven't seen her for over a year. Let me think…'

Before Kelly can think, Sherry is spitting the words 'she lied to me, my own sister lied to me,' as she rushes past a line of waiting patients.

Sergeant Miller and PC Carr, now furnished with a car for added gravitas, are situated at the end of Vera's road.

'How much longer are we going to sit here, Sarge?' PC Carr crosses and uncrosses his legs for the third time in a minute.

'As long as it takes,' is the unwelcome reply from Sergeant Miller.

'I don't think my bladder can hold out for as long as it takes!' PC Carr unfastens the belt on his trousers, which gives him some relief.

Sergeant Miller is looking out of the driver's window, as he has been for the past two hours. Of all the cases he has had to deal with, the mystery of Vera's gnomes is the one that has perplexed him most and he is determined to get to the bottom of it, even if it means waiting in the car at the end of her road all night.

'Sarge, I'm going to have to find a bush, or something.'

Sergeant Miller is about to explain the law about urinating in public when he spots Vera. 'There she is, getting off the bus!'

PC Carr looks to the end of the road and sees Vera Cleeve laden with a shopping bag in each hand, ambling up the street. 'I wish she'd walk quicker,' he says, shifting his position. 'Shall I go and help her?'

'No. We have to maintain an element of surprise. Catch her off guard.' PC Carr wonders how many episodes of Starsky and Hutch his sergeant has seen. Eventually, Vera reaches her front door and turns the key. 'Right, here we go,' says Sergeant Miller, excitedly, jumping out of the car. He is about to apprehend Vera before she steps into the house, when PC Carr calls out to him. 'Hang on, Sarge!' Sergeant Miller turns and is faced with the sight of PC Carr standing next to the police car pulling up his trousers from around his knees.

'What are you doing?'

'The belt, Sarge. I forgot.'

Vera Cleeve has slipped into her house. Sergeant Miller and PC Carr knock on the door. It's a while before she answers, in which time PC Carr has clocked a large yellow bush which would provide adequate cover from the road if needed. Eventually, Vera answers the door.

'Oh, hello Stephen. And Gary.'

'Good evening, Vera. Mind if we come in?' PC Carr hops from foot to foot. Vera frowns at him then realises why they might be standing on her doorstep.

'I'm just about to have my supper, actually. Could you come back another time?' PC Carr shakes his head.

'No, Vera. We need to talk to you now,' says Sergeant Miller, calmly.

'Right now,' interjects PC Carr, much less calmly.

'What about?' asks Vera.

'Let us in and we'll tell you.'

Vera thinks about this. 'I don't have to let you in, do I?'

'No. You don't have to. But it would not be good for you if you refuse us entry. We'd like to ask you about the rather large collection of gnomes you have in your garden. Could we take a look?'

Vera bites on her bottom lip. 'Gnomes? I don't know what you are talking about, Sergeant. I truly don't.'

PC Carr has decided that deep breathing might help him, and he is walking up and down the driveway sucking in air and exhaling it slowly. Vera and Sergeant Miller watch him for a while in disbelief.

'Well, if you're not going to cooperate, we will just have to search your property for what we believe to be stolen gnomes.'

'You can't,' says Vera, emphatically, folding her arms.

'We can't?'

'You don't have a warranty.'

Sergeant Miller suppresses a smirk. 'A warranty, Vera?'

'Yes. I've seen it on the telly. You must have a warranty to enter private premises.'

Sergeant Miller is about to explain Vera's error when PC Carr rushes past, pushing Vera to one side and dashes up the stairs. He opens doors into Vera's bedroom, then a small box room before finding the bathroom. A shout of 'Alleluia!' can be heard throughout the house.

'Hmm,' says Vera, 'entering an elderly lady's house without a warranty. That's not good is it, Stephen? Not good at all.'

Meredith Park is cashing up at the end of a profitable day. The new range of stationery has been a success and she is pleased with herself for having taken the risk in buying it. She takes the float from the till and locks it in a desk drawer. She has closed a little earlier than usual, to make sure she is ready for Adam when he arrives to take her to the cinema. At first, she had been very secretive about her relationship with Adam, partly because of what the gossips might say about the age difference and partly because of his reputation for being a womaniser; she did not want to make herself look a fool. However, it has been a few weeks now and Adam has been very attentive, running across from the chip shop to see her each day as soon as the lunchtime rush is over. She has been to dinner a couple of times at Adam's house and gets on well with Cody and Agnes, Adam's parents, although she always feels Cody is uncomfortable in her presence.

She looks around the shop and congratulates herself on her achievement. The past few years have been a nightmare, but she is beginning to think she can finally put it all behind her now. That was another life, totally different from the life she has now. She is Meredith Park and though she can never speak about it to anyone, not even to Adam, perhaps it's time to bury the past and the dark shadow of Meredith Evans, for ever.

A free spirit. A wild child. A hippy-chick - there have been many epithets used to describe Meredith Park's attributes over the years. But, sitting in her shop sipping a cup of hot chocolate, she would no longer admit to identifying with any of them; they belong to another time. To Meredith Evans, a ghost from the past with a habit of haunting the present in unexpected ways. Such as today, when the phone rang, just before lunch.

'Hello, Park Cards and Gifts,' said Meredith, cheerily. Silence on the other end. 'Hello? Can I help you?' There was the sound of someone whispering to someone else. Meredith knew better than to continue the call and hung up.

It's probably nothing, she thinks, taking a bite out of a piece of shortcake. A wrong number. A prank. She berates herself for getting so worked up about it. Meredith Evans would have forgotten about the call the minute it ended. She would have uttered an expletive and carried on with the rest of her day.

Sometimes, late at night when the only sound in North Banfield is the occasional drunk veering off the pavement into the bins waiting for collection in front of the shops, she remembers Meredith Evans. Or, like right now, sitting in her shop, drinking hot chocolate. She remembers the little girl from the small mining village in South Wales, where generations of her family had lived for centuries. First, they worked the land, then the coal pits and then joined the long queue of miners collecting their weekly dole money. Meredith Evans' father had managed to find work driving around the country delivering carpet tiles, manufactured in the nearby town. He could be away for days and paid little attention to the child conceived after a drunken evening celebrating a Welsh victory on the rugby field. Meredith's much older brothers saw her as an inconvenience, someone to be dragged to school every morning and dragged home again each evening. She was loved, there was no doubt in her mind about that, but she was certainly an inconvenience.

From a very early age, when no one was looking (which was most of the time) Meredith would run down her street of terraced houses and course her way through a maze of alleyways until she reached the main road leading to the town. Here, she would pause and look to the top of the hill that overshadowed the village, bright and verdant in the summer, dull and grey in the winter, and imagine what was over the other side. She often attempted to climb the hill, but at the point where the gentle grassy incline gave way to jagged rock, she always had to turn back. *One day*, she thought. *One day*.

She was an avid reader and a regular visitor to the village library, where she was allowed to sit and read any book she wanted, though she never took any home with her. The books told of secret worlds, fantastic creatures, incredible journeys, and she did not want to share these with her family. They wouldn't understand. As she grew into her teenage years, her reading became more esoteric, and the world of the mind and spirit became her dwelling place. She would spend hours in meditation, or chanting endless mantras in her bedroom, much to the annoyance of her mother who liked to listen to the radio. Every now and then, she would announce to the family that she was entering a period of silence (much to the relief of her mother), or that she was going to fast every Tuesday, or become vegetarian, then vegan. She shaved her head, grew her hair long, wore dreadlocks. She joined several campaign groups and would stand in the village centre, handing out leaflets and stickers, which she would later find littering the streets.

One day, she was about to leave the house to go to school in the town, when she overheard her mother and father talking.

'She's an embarrassment, Bronwyn,' said her father.

'That's an awful thing to say about your daughter, Hugh.'

'Well, she is. Look at the way she dresses. Why can't she dress like the other girls in the village? They look so pretty.'

'Oh, pretty, eh? You been looking at them, then?'

'Not like that, no. But they make an effort. They look like proper women.'

'Well, she's different, I'll give you that. But it's only a phase, I'm sure.'

'Well, I hope it is. Because, Bronwyn, I have to say that I'm ashamed to admit she's my daughter.'

Meredith ran out of the house, tears streaming down her face. There was a queue at the bus stop, and she decided that she was not going to school. She turned down an alleyway and ran to the bottom of the hill. She sat on the grass with her head in her hands.

'What's the matter?'

The voice was deep and calm. She felt like she had known it all her life. When she looked up, a man,was standing over her. He was smiling. She shook her head. He sat down on the grass next to her.

'You are one sad girl, aren't you? I can help you.' He took her hand and she immediately felt safe. She also felt, well, she didn't know what she felt, but it was something beautiful. 'You don't belong here, do you?' he said. She shook her head. 'Come on,' he said, 'I'll take you somewhere you can be free.'

Two years later, Meredith Evans was perfectly happy. The new life into which she had entered took some adjusting to at first, but the people around her were supportive and loving. For the first time in her life, she had real friendships. She could be who she always wanted to be. *This is what's over the other side of the mountain*, she thought.

'They were never your family. Not in the same way as we are,' said Paul, the leadership team member assigned to Meredith, one day. And Meredith believed him. She believed everything he said. Why would she not? He loved her, he said. It didn't matter that she would never see her family again. Her life was better without them. Paul told her she was beautiful and that she would be able to go out one day and collect lost souls, just like her, that needed nurturing, that needed to be given wings.

That day came a couple of years later. She went into the city for the first time since arriving at the commune. Paul accompanied her. He still loved her, she was sure of this, though he spent most of his time looking after the new women. She was instructed to stand at the entrance to the shopping centre and hand out leaflets. Not to everyone, of course, just to those who looked like they needed to be saved.

'How will I know?' she asked.

'You'll know,' said Paul, 'you'll know.'

It was a Saturday, and the city was busy. This city was very different to the run-down and broken town next to her village. It was vibrant, new, shiny, exciting. The sounds, the smells, the people; all wonderful. She looked hard for people who needed saving, but they were difficult to spot. Paul had approached a few. Obviously, he was more perceptive than she was, but they had declined his advances politely and walked on. She watched the hordes of people coming towards her, looking at their faces, some smiling, some more serious, none looking as if they needed saving. Then, in the middle of a group of women, she spotted a face she recognised.

'Paul, it's my mother,' she said.

'Where?'

'In that crowd of women, going into that shop.'

Paul took her by the arm and led her out of the shopping centre. When they had walked for about ten minutes, he sat her down on a bench. 'That lady you saw. Who was she?' he asked.

'My mother,' said Meredith, looking perplexed.

'Who was she?' Paul asked again.

'My mother,' repeated Meredith.

Paul sighed. 'Who was she, Meredith?'

Meredith lowered her head.

'I don't know,' she said.

'That's good. Let's go home.'

Meredith was confined to the commune for the next four years. She watched other women going to the town with Paul and managed to convince herself that what she felt was not jealousy. Paul still slept with her occasionally, but he became ever more distant. She became increasingly isolated, and, despite their shortcomings, she longed to return to the village and her family, though she dared not mention this to anyone. Then, one day, when she was helping to prepare food for the evening meal, an Irish girl called Siobhán, who had only been at the commune for a couple of years asked Meredith if she was unhappy.

'Of course not,' said Meredith.

'Yes, you are,' said Siobhán, 'and so am I.'

The plot to escape the commune was hatched quickly. They were to leave that night, once all the lights had been turned out. They had no money and only the gowns that the commune provided, but Siobhán remembered the way to the town where they could find help. What they had not accounted for was the night guard standing at the entrance to the commune. A chase ensued and Meredith and Siobhán ran in different directions, so that only one of them could be caught. The sight of the night guard standing over Siobhán in the pale light of the moon is one that Meredith will never forget.

The police were not interested in anything Meredith told them. The commune had been established for many years and caused them no trouble. After questioning Siobhán, they concluded that no crime had been committed. They called Meredith's father who collected her and took her back to the village. It was a couple of weeks after Meredith had returned that one of her brothers saw a man he did not recognise standing at the end of the street. When he saw the brother, he walked away. The same thing happened a couple of days later and, after a meeting of the whole family, it was decided that for everyone's safety it would be better if Meredith left the area.

The hot chocolate has gone cold. A milky skin has formed across the top of the cup. Meredith walks to the front door and turns the sign to closed. She looks around the shop. It's wonderful. North Banfield is wonderful. She utters a silent 'thank you', to whoever it is that might be looking down on her. She is thankful that she is no longer Meredith Evans, wild child, free spirit. Lost soul. She left her behind in the commune. She is thankful that she is Meredith Park, proud owner of her own business and in love with a man who does not want her to look for lost souls. Thankful until the next time the phone rings and there is silence at the other end.

Chapter 28: Loving You Crazy, All six of You

'But are we ready, Zack?' asks Simon, plugging in his keyboard.

'Ready? We could have a two-hour set ready by the time the fête arrives.'

Of course, we're not ready, Zack thinks. *We haven't finished writing any songs yet.* He's not the only one thinking along those lines.

'I've got a song we could use,' pipes up Ziggy.

'What is it? They're not going to allow cover songs,' says Zack, not entirely sure this is true, but he wants his own songs, whenever they are written, to take priority.

'It's not a cover - it's my dad's'

'Your dad's?' questions Zack, with the incredulous look he favours whenever Ziggy has anything to say.

'Yeah, it's a straightforward pop song.'

'What's it about,' asks Simon, showing considerably more interest than the group leader, 'and what's it called?'

'It's a bit corny. "Love me Crazy".'

'Let's hear it then,' concedes Zack.

'He was about nineteen at the time, you know, late seventies. He was seeing this bird every Sunday night at the Spring Hill Hotel.'

'What?' exclaims Zack.

'No, not in a hotel room, you wazzock! They had discos at the hotel in those days. Dad loved 'em. Claimed he could dance a bit as well.'

'Dad dancing?'

'Not then. He wasn't even married.'

'Get on with it,' pleads Simon.

'Anyway, he totally fell for this girl. Jacqui, I think her name was. She seemed keen, apparently, and said she would never leave him.'

'Aah, shucks,' interjects Zack again, not wanting to give Ziggy a chance.

'They were dancing, and she told him she loved him - all that sort of stuff.'

'And?'

'She dumped him at the end of the night.'

'Why?'

'He never knew.'

'Somebody else involved?'

'He didn't know, but when he got home just before midnight...'

'Midnight?' snorts Zack, 'midnight? Bit early, wasn't it? Clubs go on till four in the morning these days.'

'Not in 1978. Not in Leeford you berk. Licensing laws were different then.'

'For pity's sake, Ziggy, finish your story and get to the song before I grow a beard and join ZZ Top,' pleads Simon, becoming increasingly irritated.

'Well, just after twelve o' clock the phone rang. It had to be Jacqui. Had to be.'

'What did she say?'

'We'll never know what she intended to say. He didn't pick up.'

'Answer phone?'

'They didn't have one in those days. Just a bog-standard telephone.'

'What did your dad feel about it the next day?'

'He used it in the song. The last line.'

'Which is?'

'I wish I'd answered the phone.'

'Let's hear it,' says Simon.

Ziggy plugs in his Ibanez Electro-Acoustic and starts to pick out a harmonious tune with his favourite chords - Am, G, Dm and C. No one knew he could play and sing so sweetly, and with such emotion. *This is the flamin' bass player*, thinks Zack.

I could not be happy without you
Knowing how much I care
You said that you'd never leave me
But that was all you could say.

And I said love, love me crazy
All I could do was run to you baby
And I said love, love me crazy
All I could do was run to you baby.

I took you dancing on Sunday
And held you tight in my arms
You danced as though you were happy
But then you gave back my love.

Ziggy repeats the chorus, '*And I said love, love...*' and onto the final verse, followed by the chorus three times:

136

You left me standing the same night
Crying, unhappy, alone
You called me just after midnight
I wish I'd answered the phone.

No one notices Clare standing at the back of the room.

'Oh, Ziggy, that's beautiful.'

'Thanks Babe.'

'Babe?' spits Zack.

'Zack!' shouts Simon.

'I'm not sure about it, but it's a pop song and it's the best we've got,' admits Zack, reluctantly.

'There we go, then,' says Ziggy. 'My dad will be over the moon!'

'Vera, how long have I known you?'

'Well, a good while, Stephen. I can call you Stephen, can't I? You're almost part of the family.'

'Then you know I've always looked after you. Remember when Hilda sent me over here a couple of years ago? Then there was Allen Gomez.'

'Stopped him dead in his tracks, didn't we?'

'Exactly. You trust me, don't you? No need for a warranty, um, warrant, is there?'

'I suppose so. Cup of tea?'

'I want to see what my young assistant was shouting about first, Vera.'

'He looked quite desperate for the toilet. Does he often pull his trousers down in broad daylight?'

'No, no, not usually... He'd loosened his...never mind, he's coming back down now.'

'Vera.'

'Mrs Cleeve to you, young whippersnapper.'

'Mrs Cleeve,' says PC Carr, in his I'm-an-officer-of-the-law voice, 'we're not going to find all the gnomes in the garden, are we?'

Vera looks sheepishly across at Sergeant Miller, ignoring the now relieved PC Carr.

'You won't find all of them in the garden, only a few. Some of them are mine.'

'Why do you do it, Vera?'

'I take them on gnome holidays, you know that.'

'Yes, the odd one. But hundreds?'

'There are loads packed away in the spare room and even in Vera's bedroom. Up to the ceiling, Sarge. I even found two behind the loo.'

'Sorry, Vera, we're going to have to take you down the station.'

Crestfallen, Vera holds out her hands, ready to be handcuffed.

'No need for that, Vera. This isn't The Bill, and you're not going to get very far if you make a run for it, are you?'

'We're here then, Ted.'

'George,' replies Ted, 'that's what I love about you - stating the blummin' obvious.'

Laughter rocks the minibus Frank Reed has hired, with George joining in, as they pull into the long driveway leading to the North Banfield Social Club.

'Do you want to see their secretary, Frank?'

'No, Ted. I'll concentrate on preparing the lads. You focus on the admin side of things.'

'Fine, Ted. I've got his name. John Smart, general manager and club secretary.'

'Think that's him approaching now. We'll find the changing room.'

'Catch up with you in a bit, Frank. We've got an hour before kick-off.'

'Mr Coleman? John Smart.'

'Ted, please. Good, to meet you, John.'

'Do you have your bar-coded document?'

'Yes, here you are.'

'I'm sure it's all in order. I've been to your pub, Ted. Nice pint, and I have to say, lovely place, Leeford.'

'Thank you.'

'Now, you can join your team, and, basically, we'll see you on the pitch.'

'Cheers, John. See you later.'

'In the bar – my treat!'

The minutes tick by. The boys are beginning to show pre-match nerves, with Frank doing his bit to build up confidence.

'I've seen some of their lads. They're even younger than me, and I'm the baby of the team,' says Nick.

'Pity we didn't have enough for substitutes,' pipes up George, 'if somebody gets injured.'

'In walking football?' says Steve Adams.

'Never mind all this negative talk,' interrupts Frank, 'in my day, we had much worse to put up with.'

'What formation are we playing?' queries Cody.

At that, the referee knocks on the door.

'Got your team sheet, Mr Reed?'

'Yes, here it is.'

'Are you sure?'

'Why?'

'Bit short, aren't you?'

'I suppose, but we're not professionals. They may be short, my lads, but they're stout-hearted.'

'Okay, let me confirm their IDs.'

'What you mean, like a school register?'

'If you like. Now, Nick Allthorpe?'

'Yes.'

'Steve Adams?'

'Yes.'

'George Owens?'

'Yes.'

'Cody Thornton?'

'Yes.'

'Justin Wilkins?'

'Present. Sir!'

'Er, Daniel Windrush?'

'Absolutely, your honour.'

Down the corridor, their studs click and clack on the freshly laid linoleum. They can see the light at the end of the tunnel. Literally. They eventually reach the pitch.

'Bit big, isn't it, Cody?' says Nick, looking concerned.

'What is?'

'The pitch. Thought it was three-quarter size.'

'Whatever.'

'Hang on,' shouts Steve from his left-wing position. 'Their subs haven't left the field. There's eleven in their half warming-up. I've counted 'em.'

'I'll have a word with the ref,' asserts Nick, taking control, although Frank has omitted to appoint a captain.

'Sir, a word, please?' calls out Nick to the man in black.

'Problem?'

'When are their subs going to leave the field? You've just blown for the kick-off.'

'Subs? They've only got one. Come on, let's get started.'

'But...,' stammers Nick,' they've got eleven players, we've only got six.'

'Thought you had a recruitment problem.'

The referee blows his whistle, and eleven young, fit, footballers bear down on the Leeford Six, running at a pace that even the thirty-year-old Nick Allthorpe struggles with.

'Hang on ref!' screams Frank from the touchline.

The ball runs out of play near Frank and Ted. They confront the ref.

'They're running!'

'So?'

'It's supposed to be walking football,' pleads Ted.

'No, this is Football Association rules football, Category A.'

'But we're Category B – walking football.'

'Not according to your registration document you're not,' says the ref, 'give me the damn ball so we can get on with the game.'

Chapter 29: The Same Old Song

'Great song isn't it?' says Simon, vigorously polishing his shiny keyboard with a soft cloth.

Zack is sitting at Clare's drum kit, tapping out a beat on the snare. 'What is?'

'Ziggy's dad's song. It's perfect for us.'

Zack hits the snare hard and the drumstick bounces into the air, landing on the floor by his feet.

'Perfect, is it? It would be, wouldn't it? Ziggy brought it.'

'Ego a little battered is it, mate?' says Simon. Zack scowls then lets out a long sigh. Simon stops his keyboard polishing and sits on the top of his amplifier. 'What's up, Zack? That's the best rehearsal we've had. And it is a great song.'

'It's not that.'

'What is it then?'

Zack scoots from behind the drum kit on the drum stool and sits in front of Simon. 'It's Clare.'

'Clare? I know she's behind the beat sometimes, but she does some nice fills. Did you hear when she...'

Zack cuts him off. 'Not her drumming.'

'Sorry, mate. I'm not with you.'

'I think I'm losing her. To Ziggy. To Mr Perfect.'

Simon laughs. 'You're joking, mate. The way she looks at you, she's totally smitten.'

Zack looks down at the floor. 'He called her "Babe"!'

Simon shrugs.

'I wonder if she used to call him "Babe"?'

Simon shrugs again.

'She never calls me "Babe"', mumbles Zack.

'Sorry, what was that?' asks Simon, cupping his ear.

'She never calls me "Babe"!' repeats Zack, louder this time and with a look of anguish that Simon has never seen before.

'Wow, he has upset you, hasn't he?'

Simon shifts uncomfortably as he notices Zack's eyes filling with tears.

'I think you're imagining things, Zack. She's over Ziggy. They finished ages ago.'

'Is that right? Well, you don't call someone "Babe" unless they mean

141

something to you.'

Simon bites his bottom lip. 'You might have a point there.'

Zack breaks into what Simon will later describe to his friends as a 'roar'.

'Take it easy, mate,' he says, wishing he had left the rehearsal with the others. He has been Zack's best friend for as long as he can remember, but dealing with a crying, roaring Zack is something he is not prepared for.

'If only I could write a song for her. Show her how much I love her,' sniffs Zack.

Simon turns off his amplifier and stands by the door, so he can make a swift exit should Zack become too emotional. 'You did write a song, Zack. I thought it was great.'

'Yeah, it was a great song...about another girl!'

'Oh, yes. "Amanda".' Simon grins broadly. 'So, it was about a real girl!'

Zack blushes. 'Kind of. It was a holiday thing. I was with my parents. She was staying in the chalet next door, with her friend.'

'Wow.' This is more like the Zack that Simon had known all these years. 'And did you and her, well, you know...'

'No! We never even spoke. But I was obsessed with her for a whole week. And for a few weeks after we got home.'

Simon laughs. 'So, you wrote a song about her? Maybe you should track her down. She'd be impressed. She might even speak to you!'

'It's not Amanda I'm trying to impress, stupid. It's Clare. Anyway, I'm not even sure her name was Amanda.' They both laugh and Simon breathes a sigh of relief.

'It was still a good song. I'm sure you can write one for Clare.'

Zack shakes his head. 'Yes, but it won't be anywhere near as good as Ziggy's.'

'Don't be so defeatist!' says Simon standing up, ready to leave. 'Anyway, it wasn't Ziggy's song, was it? It was his dad's.'

It's Zack who is now wearing a grin. 'You're right, mate!' he stands up and goes to hug Simon, who backs into the doorway.

'I *am* going to write a song for Clare. I'm going to write the best song she's ever heard!'

The group of men standing at the bar in The Cross could not look more crestfallen if one of them had accidentally thrown away the jackpot-winning lottery ticket.

'What'll it be then, lads?' asks Sally, Ted's wife and lunchtime barmaid. 'Champagne all round?'

'Just a pint for each of the lads, love,' says Ted, 'on the house.'

In silence, Sally places a foaming pint of beer in front of each of them. 'Dare I ask who won?' she asks, pouring a bottle of Diet Coke for Ted. The men stare into their glasses. 'Nick? Cody?'

Nick looks at Ted. 'Ask Matt Busby over there,' he says, not without a little contempt. Sally looks at her husband, who has picked up his glass and is walking over to a table in the corner.

'Annihilated we were,' says Cody. 'Annihilated.' He picks up his drink and takes a sip.

'Annihilated,' repeats Nick. 'I was trying to think of a word I could use to describe the experience to Jessica. "Annihilated" sums it up.'

Ted is sitting in the corner, his head in his hands. 'What was the score?' asks Sally.

The men look at each other. Justin shrugs his shoulders. 'We don't know, Sally.'

'You don't know?'

'No. They scored a lot and we didn't score any. The referee said he lost count after seventeen and came into our dressing room at half-time to see if we knew how many it was.'

'At half-time? Seventeen? At half-time?' Sally looks over at Ted who is lowering his head.

'Could have been more, but they took pity on us,' says Steve.

'Well, I won't ask you about the second half. What went wrong?' Everyone turns towards Ted.

'They had a five men advantage,' says George, 'a five, huge, young, fit men advantage.'

Sally shakes her head. 'You mean, they had eleven players? You mean, this wasn't a six-a-side walking football game? Oh, Ted. What did you do?'

Nick picks up his pint and drinks half of it in one gulp. 'Not only were we annihilated. We were humiliated, Sally.'

'Yes,' says George, 'there was a group of young lads, about seven or eight years old playing behind the goals. They asked if we wanted them on our team!'

Ted rises and walks over to the bar, places his empty glass on a beer towel and turns to the line of men. 'Sorry, lads,' he says, quietly. 'I'm truly sorry.'

Nick is about to speak when Jack Simmons, Leeford's walking book of quotations bursts through the door. 'Right, lads. Here's one for you. "We didn't underestimate them. They were just a lot better than we thought". Who said that?' The men turn in unison towards Jack. 'What? You need a clue?' he asks.

'Not now, Jack,' says Sally, fearing for his safety. 'Not now.'

The band have tuned their instruments and spent five minutes warming up, the guitarists playing snippets of well-known rock songs and Clare perfecting a paradiddle she has been practising on cushions at home.

Zack calls for silence. It takes a while, but eventually he has the floor. 'Before we start, I have a new song.'

Simon gives him the thumbs up.

'Who's it by, Zack?' asks Adam.

Zack takes a couple of deep breaths. He looks over at Clare, sitting behind her drum kit. 'Me.'

'Wow. In a couple of days? That was quick,' says Ziggy.

'Yeah, well, it just came to me.'

'Like "Yesterday"?' asks Adam.

'No, the day before yesterday,' says Zack. The others groan.

'Oh, I see, you mean how Paul McCartney wrote...anyway, I'll play it to you.'

'What's it called?' asks Clare.

Zack feels his face reddening. 'It's called, "Clare".' There's much mocking of Zack from Simon and Adam and Clare looks down at her drumkit. Zack plays the song. It's a simple structure, three verses and a chorus, expressing his undying love for Clare, the girl he dreams about every night, the girl he wants to be with forever. When he has finished, there is stony silence, broken eventually by a 'wow' from Ziggy.

'Oh, Babe. Thank you!' whispers Clare.

Simon mouths the word 'Babe' at Zack, who punches the air.

'Shall we give it a go then?' Zack calls out the chords to the band as they run through the song a couple of times. When they reach the chorus for the second time, the band stops playing, except Zack who is not aware of his mother standing in the doorway. Eventually, realising he's the only one playing, he turns around. 'Mom! I've told you...'

Mrs Peterson clasps her hands. 'Zack. That was wonderful. I haven't heard that song since...'

'A couple of days ago,' interrupts Zack, waving his mother away.

'Oh, no, love. Not since, oh, it must have been thirty years ago. Your father used to sing it to me when we were courting. He loves that song.'

'Mom. Go!'

'I can't remember the band. They were pretty obscure. It's one of their album tracks, so not many people know it...'

'Mom!'

'...oh, I wish I could remember. We've still got the record somewhere. I'll dig it out.'

Zack wishes he could dig himself out of the hole that is becoming deeper with every word his mother utters. She turns to leave then pauses in the doorway.

'And I love the way you've changed some of the lyrics. "Clare" fits so well.'

There is a stunned silence in the room.

'That's it,' says Zack, throwing his guitar down on the floor. 'I quit!'

Chapter 30: The Truth About Vera

'Bobby Robson.'

'Bobby Robson?'

'That quote from Jack, you know, the other team were better than us and all that rubbish.'

'I worry about you sometimes, Cody. Anyway, my shout – pint, was it?'

'Please. Did you notice those three empty units in the precinct, George?'

'Couldn't miss it mate. The workmen made hell of a racket the first day.'

'Any idea what's going on?'

'For once, I do. The one at the end is a new estate agent, and the unit two down from Billy's Cafe is going to be an optician. You will never guess what the name is.'

'How do you know the name if the workmen have only just started?'

'Saw them carry the sign through to the back. It'll go up when they've finished. Had a chat with the lads.'

'Put me out of my misery then, George.'

'Wait for it, Cody. It's a lady optician, apparently, and her name is Clare Una Clearly.'

'So?' says Cody, having already downed half of his pint.

'The sign that will be over the door will have, in large letters, her surname preceded by her initials. Got it, Cody?'

'Not with you, mate. "Clearly", preceded by "C U".'

'There you go,' says George as he sees the light switch on in Cody's eyes.

'You're joking, aren't you? C U Clearly?'

'You're hard work you are, Cody. And it's your round.'

'Sorry mate, got to go. Agnes has an appointment.'

'Not with the new optician?' quips George.

Cody makes it back in time for Agnes to brush past him, coat in hand.

'Just three for you to serve.'

Next in line, Mike Charles is waiting relatively patiently. He turns to Lee Morgan. 'A new fish and chip shop is opening on our estate, which is more convenient, so you might not see me for a while. I have to give it a try.'

'Of course, you do. This place is handy for me as it's on my way home from work.'

Lee looks beyond Mike to address the owner of Leeford Plaice who has heard every word.

'Can you put a haddock on for me, Cody?'

'Where is she, Sergeant?'

'Interview room.'

'Which one?'

'We've only got two, and the other one's full of that delivery of toilet rolls.'

'Can I see her?'

'Nigel, she was a bit agitated when we took her in, but I need to get to the bottom of all this.'

'What's your problem with a few gnomes?'

'A few? Anyway, Nigel, it's your house and she's your mom. What do you know about it?'

'Not my business. I keep well out of it.'

'As I say, it's your house, your garden. If a crime has been committed, you're implicated.'

'Up here on the left. Rosewood Nursing Home.'

'Cody, will they let us all in, or are there visiting restrictions?'

'No idea, Ethel, but we're about to find out.'

Sheri, sitting in the back of Cody's 2005 Corsa, taps him on the shoulder and points to the Mercedes pulling into the car park ahead of them. Unfortunately for Cody, it's Frank Watson, who takes the only remaining space. The frustrated Corsa driver mutters something unrepeatable under his breath. He also muses over the way Frank seems to turn up at places in a different car every time. 'Bully for him,' Cody mutters, 'you might have three cars, but I'm happy with mine.'

'I'll drop you here and find a space up the road.'

As Cody drives away, Frank beckons to Ethel and Sheri to follow him to the main entrance. 'They usually let me straight through. Don't even have to sign the book.'

'What's the benefit in that?' Ethel whispers to Sheri. 'Next thing you know, he won't be carrying any money and he'll be taking holidays at Balmoral.' Sheri giggles as Frank ushers his co-visitors into the lift.

All but one of the residents have reservations on the next available room on the ground floor. Most of them want a room on the ground floor, but much of the space is taken up by the dining room, offices and the TV room. Nonetheless, they would prefer not to be upstairs. The exception is Howard Smithson, described by F Watson esq as their 'visitee', yielding a pained expression from Ethel and a movement of the shoulders from Sheri.

Not only does Howard like the view from his second-floor vantage point, a panorama sweeping majestically across the West Banfield Trading Estate, the scene jostling with day-to-day images of dustcarts, dog-walkers (thankfully picking up what has been left behind, so to speak), and a legion of other ineffable vistas, but also, he rarely ventures downstairs. His meals are taken to his room. There is a second TV room on his floor, and, in the event of fire (the main reason for the predilection of the majority towards the lowest floor), the staff are well-drilled, and the fire escape is accessible at both ends of the building. Most of the guests are fairly mobile and, in the last test, everyone was out in a record time of four minutes, twenty-eight seconds. Frank Watson, for some reason, has all this information at his fingertips. They enter the room. Howard is awake, and, luckily, in good form.

'Hello, Frank. Lovely to see you. Brought some friends?'

'We've got some questions for you, Howard.'

The visit concludes within thirty minutes, and the four villagers (Cody managed to park eventually) have extracted what they need to know. They now have the official date for 'Leeford Day'. Their diaries and notebooks, and in Frank's case a PDA (Personal Digital Assistant, set up by his daughter who actually knows how to operate one) are suddenly kept busy. However, Frank's best Parker is soon thrust into action onto a standard notepad. 'We'll inform everyone, and I'll get Nick Allthorpe to book the Community Centre for the day.'

'Couldn't it be combined with the fête, Frank?' enquires Cody.

'No, it's a separate event, and I want to see the activities being weather-proofed, safely under cover.' This time, there are surreptitious glances between Ethel and Cody, but Sheri's shoulders are still kept busy with a slight movement, both hands palm upwards.

'Your son's waiting for you outside, Vera.'.

'Why have you brought him here?'

'It's Nigel's house. You live there, and he must know what you've been up to, but he denies knowing anything.'

'Your point, Stephen?'

He forgives the use of his first name. This is too important to focus on formalities. 'My point, Vera, is that whatever you have been doing, your son could be held responsible.'

'Leave him alone. It's all down to me.'

'Go on.'

'I set up a Gnome Exchange.'

'A what?'

'We use eBay to buy and sell gnomes, but some people like to swap them - change the image of their garden to a specific style, and I topped up the stock from gardens in Leeford and the surrounding areas.'

'Good grief, Vera. So, all that about Allen Gomez! He was right all along, and I warned him off.'

'Yes, but I still don't like him.'

'Not the point. I'll have to take advice about this, but you will be charged with something. You've stolen gnomes to order, haven't you?'

'I'm so sorry, Stephen. You've always tried to help me, and I've let you down.'

'What I don't understand is why Nigel and Mandy did nothing to stop you.'

'You really should leave Mandy out of this. She's got enough problems.'

'At school?'

'No, her husband from her first marriage is back on the scene. He's trouble.'

'Alright, but what about Nigel? It makes no sense that he hasn't intervened. Gnomes all over the house and the garden - hundreds of the damn things.'

'I, er, sort of blackmailed him.'

'Your own son?'

'I was desperate.'

'What's he done that's so serious he would give in? Or at least look the other way.'

'I threatened him with the Food Safety Agency. Let's just say not all of the meat he buys is from certified sources. Not good for a butcher's reputation.'

'I don't believe this. It gets worse. You're going to need a solicitor. I'm busy in court tomorrow, so I'm going to trust both of you. Go home and stay put in the house. I'll organise the duty solicitor and call you in a couple of days.'

A knock at the door causes him to pause. Sally, Sergeant Miller's wife, opens the door carefully and beckons him into the hallway. 'What is it, Sal? I'm busy with Vera.'

'You do realise I've taken the day off work to help you with phones and admin while Gary is sorting out the Gail Perkins case for tomorrow's trial?'

'I appreciate that, love, but what's the problem?'

'I can't find him.'

'You can't find him?'

'You asked me to phone him for an update on Gail's case. You know he took some things for Gail to the prison, don't you?'

'Er, no, I don't. But so what?'

'The last time anyone remembers seeing him, Gary was leaving the prison with a woman who was wearing a female warden's uniform.'

'He's been out with a few of the girls who work there. What are you saying, Sally?'

'He's gone missing. Not only that, Gail has escaped. They found a female prison warden in her underwear, bound and gagged. Gail used her uniform, helped by Gary, it seems.'

'My God!' shouts Sergeant Miller. 'They've eloped, haven't they, Sal?'

Chapter 31: Wherefore Art Thou…PC Carr?

'Gail Perkins? Gary Carr and Gail Perkins? I'd never put them together. She's not his type,' says Vera, stepping into the hallway, feeling not a little relieved that the attention has been momentarily diverted from her misdemeanours. Sergeant Miller rolls his eyes, knowing Vera will tell the whole of Leeford about the elopement before he arrives back at the station.

'Not a word, Vera! Okay?'

Vera shrugs her shoulders.

'Yes, Vera,' adds Sally, 'this is a highly confidential police matter.'

Vera sucks her teeth. 'I see. In other words, you want me to keep schtum about what I have just overheard.'

Sally and Sergeant Miller chorus 'yes'.

'And not tell anyone. Not even my Nigel.'

'Not even your Nigel,' says Sergeant Miller, putting away his notebook.

'Of course,' says Vera, slowly, 'there might be a price for my silence.'

'And might I guess what that price might be, Vera?' Sergeant Miller says, sensing the direction the conversation is heading.

'Well, the price might involve turning a bit of a blind eye to some of my little friends outside who, shall we say, might have found their own way here?'

'Are you trying to pervert the course of justice, Vera?' asks Sally.

'I'd say it's more a case of tit for tat, Sally. Wouldn't you agree Stephen?'

Sergeant Miller sighs. 'Alright, Vera. You agree to repatriate your, er, little friends within the next two days and we'll consider the matter closed.'

After Zack announced he was quitting the band, Adam, Simon, Ziggy and Clare gathered up their instruments and left the vicarage. From his bedroom window, Zack watched them hurry down the driveway. To add to his humiliation, Clare was walking with Ziggy who put his arm around her.

Zack sits forlornly on the edge of his bed. The band is over, his relationship with Clare is over. At first, he'd cursed his mother for exposing him as a fraud, but since then he has realised his own stupidity in thinking he could claim a thirty-year-old song as his own. How stupid he must seem in front of Clare, particularly with Ziggy, her ex-boyfriend being in the same room; cool, calm, older Ziggy.

'What an idiot,' he mutters, throwing himself forwards onto his bed, beating his fists into the duvet. 'What an idiot!'

'What are you doing?' asks Sherry, seeing her sister sitting cross-legged on the table they use for sorting laundry into whites, colours, and delicates, with her eyes closed, palms turned upwards, index finger and thumb forming the letter 'O'.

At first, Linda pretends to ignore her sister but then she takes in a deep breath, letting it slowly out with a soft 'whoosh.' 'Meditating,' she says, almost whispering.

'And why are you meditating?'

Linda takes another deep breath. 'I'm trying to empty my mind of all thoughts.'

'That shouldn't take long then.' Sherry switches on the iron, ready to press a suit that Frank Watson has asked to be cleaned urgently.

'I shall ignore that remark, darling sister.'

Sherry lays a pair of pinstripe trousers along the ironing board, thinking how much longer they seem than Frank's legs, not that she has paid that much attention to Frank's legs.

'You should try this Sher, it's fantastic.'

'Oh, yeah?' Sherry runs the hot iron to and fro, pressing a sharp crease into each trouser leg.

'So, is your mind empty now? As empty as the machines you should have loaded with the service washes twenty minutes ago?' Sherry takes the jacket, with its unfashionably large lapels and spreads it over the board.

'Actually, it's impossible to empty your mind completely. You need to have an object of focus. Something you can visualise. Something that makes you happy.'

The suit neatly pressed, Sherry puts it on a wire hanger, drapes a green plastic bag over it and takes a pink numbered ticket which she staples to a belt loop. 'And what, dare I ask, is your focus when you are meditating?'

There's a moment's silence, before Linda announces, 'a family-sized bag of cheese and onion crisps.'

The band is gathered around the kitchen table in Simon's parents' house.

'What are we going to do?' asks Adam. 'We can't carry on without Zack.'

'Can you talk to him, Clare?' asks Simon.

'I think I'm the last person he wants to see,' says Clare, solemnly.

'You're very wrong, Babe. Very wrong,' says Ziggy. Adam and Simon mouth 'Babe' to each other and shrug their shoulders.

'He's all about you, Clare. That's why he's been trying so hard. I guess it was difficult me turning up,' Ziggy continues.

'Yeah. I didn't think he'd mind. I thought we had a strong relationship.'

Ziggy reaches over and holds Clare's hand. 'You do. He's a great guy. I really like him. You're made for each other.'

'Absolutely,' chimes in Simon. 'And he's an excellent guitar player.' Adam kicks him under the table. 'As well as being a great guy and made for you and all that.'

Clare laughs. 'Who wants Zack most – me, or you lot?'

'Well, now you come to say…' says Adam.

'Trouble is,' says Simon, with a sigh, 'I've known Zack for a long time. He'll be having a major sulk. He'll take some persuading to re-join the band.'

'Well, I have an idea,' says Ziggy.

'Great, what's your…' Adam begins to speak, but is interrupted by Simon.

'Sorry, but before we hear your grand plan, Ziggy, what's with you and Clare?'

Clare and Ziggy look at each other. 'What do you mean?' asks Ziggy, looking genuinely confused by the question.

'Well, I mean, I mean, er, how can I put it…?'

'He means, do you still have feelings for each other?' says Adam, coming to Simon's aid.

Clare and Ziggy both laugh. Ziggy leans back on his chair.

'Me and Clare? We were a nightmare together, weren't we Babe?'

Clare laughs. 'A total nightmare.'

'But you both…'

'Are still good friends, Sime. We never fell out. We just decided that we weren't good together. We were only in a relationship for a month or so, but we stayed in touch. Clare said she wanted a bass player in her boyfriend's band and, well…' Ziggy spreads his arms wide.

Simon and Adam look at each other, incredulously. 'So, why do you keep calling Clare "Babe"?' asks Simon.

Ziggy laughs so hard he nearly falls off his chair. 'I call every girl I know "Babe"! Now, do you want to hear my plan?'

Back at the station, Sergeant Miller has spent the afternoon trying to piece together the movements of PC Carr and Gail Perkins. They were pretty much as Sally had described them and, despite himself, Sergeant Miller has to admire their cunning.

'You couldn't make this stuff up,' he says to Sally that evening as they are eating a plate of spaghetti bolognaise, his favourite, though he's not enjoying it as much as usual.

'It's very odd, Stephen. Was there any sign they might be attracted to each other?'

'None.' Stephen sprinkles pepper over his bolognaise. 'Though, he made her lots of cups of tea.'

'I don't think that would necessarily win a woman's heart,' says Sally.

'Perhaps not. I'm trying to think. They weren't alone together very much. I'll have to go through the interview tapes. Maybe there were some coded words between them.'

'Do you know if they had anything to do with each other before she was arrested?'

'Not that I know to. Gary always boasted about his many conquests and Gail Perkins was never mentioned. Anyway, the *whys* are not important right now. The important thing is, *where* are they?'

'He's in his bedroom – the light's on.' Simon whispers, even though he, Clare, Adam and Ziggy are standing twenty feet away from the house in the Peterson's driveway.

'Great. Let's go,' says Ziggy.

They creep up the driveway, placing each step carefully, a layer of gravel crunching under their feet. A minute later, they are standing below the window of Zack's bedroom. Zack is on his computer, idly playing a game in which he has no interest. He had refused to come downstairs when his mother called him for tea and his phone is switched off. The light outside is beginning to fade, which suits his mood perfectly. An alien appears on his computer screen and sends out a beam of red light that vaporises his adopted character. He is about to switch off the machine when he hears a guitar playing the opening chords to the song he had tried to pass off as his own, below his window. A soft and pure voice sings the first couple of verses. Just before the chorus, he gets up and goes to the window, standing slightly back, so as not to be seen. Below, in the half-darkness Clare is singing up to him, accompanied by Ziggy strumming a Spanish guitar. When they get to the chorus, they are joined by Adam and Simon, sounding like they are singing at a football match, but with every word sounding as if it comes from the heart. Zack stands and listens, a lump in his throat. When they have finished, he opens the window and leans out.

'Come back to us, Zack!' shout Adam, Simon and Ziggy, in unison.

'Come back to me, Zack!' shouts Clare.

Zack laughs loudly. 'Now I know how Juliet felt!'

'Thanks for setting this up, Nick.'

'That's alright, Frank, it is Leeford Day after all.'

'If you'll excuse me, I must have a word with the others. Cody is collecting Howard. Ethel's helping him. They should be here soon.'

Nick gazes at Frank as he moves across the hall to find out if Howard has left the nursing home. *Frank is subdued tonight,* he thinks.

'They're here!' shouts Sheri, seemingly attempting to clear excess wax from Frank's right ear.

'Do you mind, Sheri?'

'Sorry Frank, it's the excitement,' she says as she strides over to welcome the honoured guest.

'Lovely to see you again, Mr Smithson.'

Cody, in charge of the wheelchair for the day, seems desperate to ask a question.

'Door next to the kitchen. Gents first on the right.'

'Thank you, Sheri. That's not why I was trying to attract your attention.'

'What is it?'

'I think we have a problem.'

'What with?'

'Today.'

'Today?'

'Why does everyone insist on answering a question with a question?' snaps Cody.

'What... sorry Cody, but what problem?'

'I daren't tell Frank, but he'll have to know eventually. You know that Howard said today is Leeford Day, the anniversary of the creation of the village...'

'I'll have to know *what* eventually?'

'Ah, sorry Frank, didn't know you were standing behind me.'

'Well? I'm listening.'

Cody tries to stand behind Ethel for protection, but she shuffles sideways, gently nudging his arm as a signal for him to move forward and make some sort of announcement. 'Bear in mind,' continues Cody 'it's difficult to rely on everything that Howard says. To be fair to him, he's ninety-six, and his memory isn't what it was. He's been talking a lot to one of the service managers, Katy.'

156

'What Katy did next!' pronounces Sheri.

'What?'

'You know, the Susan Coolidge book.'

'I'm getting tired of this. You're as bad as Jack, quoting stuff all the time.'

'Go on, Cody, what did Katy tell you?' asks Ethel.

'Thank you for that sensible question, Ethel. She relayed some of Howard's ramblings.'

'About Leeford?' asks Frank.

'Well, yes. The first thing was the origin of the name.'

'Which is?'

'You know the brook that runs at the back of the police station? That is what remains of the River Lee, and, going back two hundred years, it crossed what is now East Banfield Road, creating a ford. It was a road of sorts, but more of a dirt track. Hence the name 'Lee-ford'.'

'So,' says Frank, 'what's the relevance of that?'

'Nothing, but it sounded interesting, and it's the second thing that got me thinking.'

'Second thing?'

'You know this date he gave us, today's date.'

'Yes,' says Ethel, very slowly and deliberately, in the style of Charles Burns from the Simpsons.

'Well, I don't think it's Leeford Day after all.'

'What makes you say that?'

'Today is the day that Howard was captured at the front by the Germans. He was in one of their camps for nearly two years. He kept a diary for ages and always marked this day as significant.'

'Good grief,' declares Frank.

'This isn't Leeford Day at all! I must talk to Nick. We've got to close the event.'

'You okay, darling?'

'Of course.'

'Coffee?' Linda slides out of bed, slipping on her short dressing gown. Allen can't take his eyes off her. 'What are you looking at?'

'What do you think?'

'Do you still want that coffee?'

'Acutally, Linda, it's you I want. Get back in.'

'Allen, we've only spent one night together, but I think I'm falling for you. Do you feel the same?'

'I want to stay here with you forever.'

'One problem, love – my kid sister.'

'Where is she?'

'Staying with one of our cousins. She's not back till tomorrow. Stay the night again and we'll have a long lie-in.'

'You don't have to ask me twice, Linda.'

As he takes her in his arms and his lips meet hers, and they shiver at the touch of each other's skin, the imperceptible sound of a key in the lock of the front door does not reach them. Their passion has no bounds, and the innocence and trust of Linda's seventeen-year-old sister is in danger of being shattered. Sherry gently closes the front door, keen to avoid disturbing her older sister. As far as she is concerned, Linda is alone, in bed, asleep. Only one of the three is true.

I'll pop my head round the door and see if she's asleep, Sherry thinks. *She's a funny old stick, but I do love her. I've missed her the last few days.* As she places her hand on the door handle, she senses that something is wrong. The shoes in the hallway, subconsciously absorbed, only just recalled. *Size ten at least,* she thinks. *Linda's got a man in there*!

'You awake, Gail?'

'Only just. You okay?'

'If I try not to think about the court case, the fact we've broken the law and that Sarge probably wants to kill me, I'm fine.'

'But are you happy?'

'Come here,' says Gary, as he pulls back the duvet and slips under. 'Do you like it here?' he asks.

'What, do you mean Sunrise Lodgings or Borth in general?'

'Both, I suppose. Funny being "Mr and Mrs Brown", isn't it? Just like the movies.'

'Bonnie and Clyde?'

'Hope not! They went down in a hail of police bullets, didn't they? Or was that Butch Cassidy?'

'I don't care, Gary. I've got you, that's all I care about. How we managed to keep it quiet for so long, I don't know. Didn't Sergeant Miller suspect?'

'Don't think so.'

'Gary, what do we do now?'

'I've got a few ideas.'

'No,' she says, slapping him playfully on his bare shoulder, 'I mean

158

about running away. Where do we go?'

'We'll work something out. For now, all I want is you.'

'You romantic police constable, you.'

'I might be romantic, my darling, but I won't be a copper much longer. Not after this.'

There was a time when Jason Owens had a lot in common with his younger brother, George. They loved to go fishing, and in conversation could drop seamlessly onto any topic, switching back and forth, instinctively knowing the point each was trying to make. It's not like that these days. Jason works in Spendfields as a till assistant but has dabbled in several businesses over the years. At fifty-nine, he is 'winding down' as he calls it. A novel is on the cards - he's threatened it for ages.

Living in the house he inherited from his parents in Green Crescent, not thirty yards from George's flat, would be enough of a red rag for any sibling. But it's not even George being left out of the will that caused a generation-length chasm between the brothers. Affairs of the heart strike deep and true. George has never recovered, and he blames Jason. However, the day of George's fifty-sixth birthday prompts Jason to attempt a fraternal reconciliation. He has an idea why George took against him, but the severity of his brother's anger and the thirty-five-year silence has always seemed an excessive punishment for something that Jason had not planned – however guilty he felt at the time.

'George.' No response. Jason waits until the lady checking out a mobility scooter for her son moves on. 'George. How are you?'

He's cornered. No customers to protect him or give him an excuse. He looks across at the other stalls. No one responds, no one gains eye contact so he can engage with someone – anyone other than the brother he claims to no longer love. On this occasion, for the first time in decades, defeat is conceded. 'What do you want?'

'At least you're speaking.'

'Get on with it.'

'George, I've never properly understood what happened. You know I'm sorry, but there must be something else. One mistake. I hurt you, yes, but how many times must I say sorry?'

'Sorry doesn't cut it, Jason. Now, I'm busy, do you mind?'

Jason pauses, and then steals away from the situation, the market, his embarrassment, and his only brother. Walking along Market Street, towards Green Crescent, he unconsciously recalls the last happy day they shared. He smiles as he remembers the joke. He links George with that play on words.

George, the younger brother at twenty years of age, and Jason, twenty-four:

'Anything?'

'Not yet, Jason. You?'

'Three tiddlers, oh, hang on. Dash it – missed the blighter.'

'I've got two.'

'That's paltry,' says Jason.

'No, it's not. It's fish!'

'I'll throw you in if you carry on like that.'

Chapter 33: The Leeford Factor

'Ahem.'

Frank Watson clears his throat and taps a gold-plated fountain pen on the table, making Ethel jump. Conversations cease immediately and all eyes focus on the chair at the head of the table, which pleases Frank.

'Firstly, we'll take a roll-call.'

'A roll-call?' laughs Cody. 'There's only seven of us. Can't we just get on with it? I've got a chip shop to open!'

Frank ignores the remark, calling the names of each councillor. In turn, each councillor responds with a 'here.' Frank puts a tick against each name on his list. 'Good,' he says, clicking the top on his pen, 'all present.' He straightens the military tie he wears for parish council meetings, which, unbeknown to those present, was bought from a second-hand shop in 1978. 'As you are aware, this is an extraordinary meeting, convened with the intention to plan the Leeford Village fête, this coming July. If anyone has any other matters, please leave them until the next scheduled meeting.'

'Which will be an un-extraordinary meeting,' chimes in Ken Taylor, a man of few words unless someone mentions EU Agricultural Policy, about which he has many strong opinions.

'Though sometimes extraordinary things can happen during un-extraordinary meetings, Ken,' says Stephen Miller. Ken nods and looks at Ethel for confirmation. In the absence of any considered response, Ethel nods back.

'Gentlemen, please!' There is a note of irritation in Frank's voice. 'Now, unless anyone has any strong objections, the date for the fête is July 10th.'

'Why that date, Frank?' asks Amanda Roberts, not a bona fide council member, but given special dispensation to deputise for her husband, Jeremy, whose on-call duties clash with the timing of the meeting, much to the annoyance of the chair and to the great amusement of Cody who loves a rule being broken, particularly if it's one of Frank's.

'I have my reasons, which will become apparent. Any objections to July 10th?' No-one objects. Frank removes the cap of his pen, writes down and circles the date. 'Firstly, we need to form a fête sub-committee, with each member having specific responsibilities.' He produces a list with a task written against each name.

'Fait accompli is it then, Frank?' says Cody, reaching over and grabbing the list. The pun is lost on the rest of the group.

'Let's see. Catering - Ethel. Makes sense. Stalls – Ken. Well, Ken does work on the market. Security – Stephen, yes, logical. Publicity – Amanda. You are mellowing, Frank! Entertainment – Reverend Peterson. You okay with that, John? Didn't have you down as a performer.' Cody winks at Reverend Peterson. Frank goes to take the list from Cody, but Cody snatches it back. 'Hold on, Frank. Cody – flowers? FLOWERS?'

'Er, yes, Cody. I'm afraid it was the only job left. By flowers, I mean all decorations: bunting, flags, that kind of thing. Making the area look aesthetically pleasing.'

Cody is speechless.

'I thought maybe your Agnes could help,' says Frank. 'And perhaps young Meredith, from the gift shop. Her place always looks lovely. I thought with her being your Adam's girlfriend...'

'No!' Cody slams his hand down on the table. Ethel jumps again. 'I'm sorry, Frank. I'm not doing it. You'll have to find someone else.'

Frank is about to fire a verbal tirade at Cody, when Ethel says quietly, 'we could do the catering together, Cody. It's too much for me and I could use your expertise.'

'Thank you, Ethel. I'd gladly work with you. That makes far more sense.' He casts a disparaging look at Frank tapping his pen on the table.

'Very well,' he writes Cody's name against catering.

'I'll ask Clara if she can do the flowers, Frank,' says Ethel.

Sherry turns and creeps quietly down the stairs. A man. Nothing wrong with that, but why the secrecy? The evening must have been planned. Linda is not the type to pick up a casual lover and bring him back home. No, this is someone who has been on the scene for a while, someone Linda has been seeing behind her back. These thoughts race through Sherry's mind as she picks up the shoes (a nice pair of brogues - this guy has some taste) and takes them into the kitchen. She switches on the kettle and takes a mug out of the overhead cupboard, dislodging the mug next to it which falls onto the tiled floor with a crash and cracks into several pieces. Almost immediately there is a bang on the floor above, followed by the sound of footsteps making their way across Linda's bedroom. Sherry looks at the broken cup on the floor, then the shoes on the kitchen table.

Apart from Cody's outburst, Frank is pleased with how the meeting has progressed so far. The other councillors accept their roles with enthusiasm, putting forward several ideas. Amanda reminds Frank that he had already asked her husband, Jeremy, to run the tombola and Ethel is certain that several of the villagers would be happy to help.

'So, just the entertainment left to think about, John. Any initial thoughts?'

'Well, I have to say Frank that my job is embarrassingly easy.'

Frank frowns. 'I think the church choir might be a bit too, how can I put this…'

'Religious?' offers Cody, now recovered from the thought of working with Meredith.

John laughs. 'That's not what I had in mind, Frank. No, the obvious choice is my Zack's band. I think they've always had it in mind to play their first gig at the fête'

'Yes,' agrees Cody. 'My Adam's in that band. He says they are brilliant, though he would say that I suppose.'

'No, he's right. I've heard them and they are very accomplished. In fact, the other day they played one of my favourites, though it did seem to cause a brief parting of the ways.'

Frank shakes his head. 'Sorry, Reverend. Cody. It's not going to happen.'

'What's not going to happen, Frank?'

'Nepotism, Reverend. Nepotism.'

Cody rolls his eyes. 'Oh, for God's sake,' he says, followed by, 'sorry Rev.'

'You might roll your eyes, Cody, but there are several entertainers that might put themselves forward. If they find they have been overlooked in favour of one, two actually, councillors' relatives then our integrity might be called into doubt.'

'Who did you have in mind, Frank?' says Stephen, looking forward to how this latest turn of events will unfold, despite still being preoccupied during most of the meeting with the whereabouts of his missing PC.

'Well, there's Ronnie Arizona, the country and western singer. He used to play all over the Midlands, though, come to think of it, I haven't seen him for a while.'

'I buried him a fortnight ago, Frank,' says John, solemnly.

'Oh dear. Poor man. Well, what about the brother and sister that play the banjos? They're still around. I heard them playing that tune from that film, you know, Deliveroo.'

Amanda laughs. 'You mean Deliverance.'

'Right. Well, that's only a couple of examples of local artistes and I'm sure there are many more. We have to give everyone the chance to participate. Do you agree? Stephen? Ethel? Ken?'

Ken jumps suddenly as if awoken from a dream.

'Never mind, Ken,' laughs Cody.

'We'll hold auditions!' suggests Stephen. 'The winner, or winners get to be star billing at the fête.'

'Like the X Factor!' says Ethel, excitedly.

The others agree with Stephen's proposal. Even Frank, to the surprise of Cody, who cannot remember the last time Frank agreed with any suggestion not put forward by Frank himself.

'We'll need judges,' says Amanda.

'Well, obviously I'll be chair of the judges,' says Frank, before anyone else has a chance to speak.

'Obviously,' says Cody under his breath.

'You'd make a good Simon Cowell, Frank,' says Amanda. 'I can see you know. Trousers pulled up to your navel, white shirt unbuttoned to show a mass of chest hair. You'll have the ladies swooning!'

Even Ken lets out a burst of laughter at this, despite having no idea who Simon Cowell is.

'Don't be ridiculous.' Frank shuffles nervously. 'I'll need a couple of assistants.'

'Don't look at me, Frank,' says Ethel, 'I'm going to be busy catering, with Cody. And, I'm no Cheryl whatshername!'

'Oh, I don't know, Ethel.' Cody winks at Ethel and she throws her pencil at him.

'We're all going to be fully occupied. And I can't be on the panel. Nepotism and all that,' says John.

'Well, who then?' asks Frank.

'Nick and Jessica. They're young, on trend, and probably available.'

Frank shakes his head. 'No, no, no. They're not on the council, though goodness knows how many times Nick Allthorpe has badgered me over the years.'

'It's not exactly a council position, being on a panel of judges, is it?' says Cody.

'I suppose not, it's just that…'

'Just nothing,' interjects Cody. 'You don't like Nick, but that shouldn't stop you working with him. And you can't think of anyone else, can you Frank?'

Frank groans.

'That's sorted them. Now, can I go and open my chip shop? This meeting's costing me money!'

Sherry sits on the floor at the end of the hallway, opposite the front door. She is correct in assuming that the man will emerge from the bedroom and quietly pad down the stairs. She is also correct that when he finds his shoes are not where he left them, he will scratch his head and turn to go back up the stairs. And, when he does turn, he will see Sherry holding up a shoe in each hand.

'Looking for these, Mr Gomez?'

Chapter 34: Fat-Pipe Parallel Thingies

'I can help you with that, Stephen.'

'What's that, Frank?'

'You mentioned it before the start of the meeting – your missing PC.'

'Oh, yes, what do you suggest?'

'I know someone who can get a top of the range model for less than £600.'

'Eh?'

'You know, six terabyte hard drive, dual disk controllers, fat-pipe parallel whatsits - all mod cons.'

'Fat pipe what?'

'Parallel thingies.'

'At times, Frank, you are too technical for me. What in Heaven's name are you talking about?'

'Your PC – you had it nicked, didn't you?'

'Well, if my computer is called Gary, and it's helped a prisoner escape, fallen in love with her – apparently – and driven off into the sunset, then, yes, it's about my computer.'

'You've lost me Stephen. Honestly, you can be obtuse sometimes.'

'Ob...'

'Obtuse, Stephen, obtuse.'

'Me? You're the one who... never mind, Frank. I'm talking about Gary and Gail.'

'Yes, you fouled up there good and proper, didn't you?'

'What?'

'Good man-managers can spot problems with staff, especially if they are up to no good.'

'Let's leave it there, Frank. I don't want to fall out with you, but you're not helping.'

'Fine, I'll leave you to it. By the way, I'd like you to chair the next council meeting. Need to get away for a few days. Business to attend to.'

'Okay Frank. Okay.'

'What are you doing here?'

George doesn't wait for an answer and tries to close the front door, but his brother blocks it with his foot. 'Those strong-arm tactics won't work with me, Jason.'

Jason was always more powerful than his younger brother, pushing his way into the house easily.

'You can't just...'

'I only want to talk.'

'Too late. You had your chance at the time, and you blew it. You'll never know how it affected me.'

'Maybe I do.'

'Get out, Jason,' says George, placing his hand on his brother's shoulder, easing him towards the door.

It happens quickly. Jason spins round, his elbow accidentally catching George on the chin. His reaction instinctive, George lunges at Jason, fists clenched, his eyes burning with rage. The left hook that connects with Jason's right cheek is enough to knock him to the floor, but he regains his senses. He grabs George's legs, rugby-style. The 1950s stereogram comes into play, the sharp corner waiting for the collision with George's forehead. Jason knows that his brother is in trouble the second he hits the twisted pile. His eyes roll, then close. Blood oozes from the wound. 'George!' No response. 'I didn't mean it. I'm so sorry.' It takes him a few seconds to gather his thoughts, but he is soon dialling the number that will bring help. 'Ambulance, please.'

'Mrs Adams for Doctor Roberts.' No acknowledgement. The receptionist repeats, 'Mrs Adams for Doctor Roberts – room nine.'

'Oh, sorry. Miles away.' All Mel needs is a repeat prescription for her anti-depressants. Jeremy Roberts has been trying to wean her off them for over a year. She taps the door twice.

'Come in.'

'Morning, Jeremy.'

'Mel – please sit down. What can I do for you?' The pause is almost imperceptible, but not to Jeremy. He knows her thoughts, her innermost thoughts.

'Er – you've been trying to stop me having my regular tablets, but they do help me.'

'Mel, dependency can be worse than the original depressive state. They are a crutch to lean on for a short while, but...'

'I need to walk on my own two feet,' she interrupts.

'Precisely.'

'I'll try, I really will.'

'What if I half the dose today, and we'll review it in a month?'

She agrees but doesn't want to leave. Not just yet. 'Jeremy, can we talk?'

'I need to get on, Mel. I have fifteen patients out there. I'm running twenty minutes late as it is.'

'No, I mean somewhere else.'

'Is there any point? It was a long time ago, Mel.'

'I think there is. I was the one who finished it, and there are things that need to be said. It's on my mind every day.'

'Did you ever tell Steve?'

'No. Does Amanda know?'

'She doesn't, and I want to keep it that way.'

'Meet me in the park – tomorrow afternoon. Our old spot, the seat by the bandstand?'

'But Gary, you said...'

'I know, love, but what choice do we have?'

'Leave the country?'

'We wouldn't last five minutes. Look, I'll phone Sarge and explain. He might listen.'

'Might?'

'Nothing to lose, is there? We need to move from Borth. Mrs Williams is starting to suspect something.'

'Has she overheard us?'

'Don't know, but at the very least she thinks that I've whisked you away from your father and we've driven off into the sunset for the rest of our lives.'

'Sun? In Wales?'

'You know what I mean.'

'Darling, I do understand, and I agree we made it worse by escaping and running away, but I could go down for five years. You know that.'

'I could do a two-year stretch for aiding and abetting.'

'Well then?'

'Look, Gail, trust me, I won't tell Sarge where we are, but I'll find out how the land lies, and we'll come to a decision. He might be angry, but he'll help us.'

'Nurse, when will the doctor let me know what's happening?'

'Are you a relative?'

'George is my brother. Is he conscious?'

'They are operating on him as we speak. Try not to worry, Mr Owens, he's in good hands. Get a coffee - the doctor will join you in the waiting room as soon as he has some news.'

After three hours in the Banfield General A&E waiting room, a receptionist calls Jason's name. 'Doctor Zofia will see you now. Come through this way.'

Jason has never stopped loving his brother, but the feeling becomes more intense as he follows the receptionist down the narrow corridor towards a small room at the rear of the main section of A&E. Used for bad news. Sometimes. *Not today, please. My baby brother - yes, he's always been that,* he thinks. He remembers the day that George was born - he was as proud as his parents. George was only six days old when he was first allowed to hold him - that warm, sweet-smelling bundle of love in his arms - and he vowed to look after him. They would fight, of course they would, but he would care for him for the rest of his life. No matter what. Jason regrets what he has done, but never meant to hurt George. It was the last thing on his mind. Not just the fight that brought his kid brother to this place. No, his feeling of regret has lasted for decades. He tries to put it out of his mind as he enters the room. This must be Doctor Zofia. 'How is he, doctor?'

'Don't alarm yourself, but your brother is in a coma. The blow to the head caused a small bleed. We've operated and managed to reduce the pressure.'

'Will he pull through?'

'It's too early to say. The next forty-eight hours are crucial. It appears he is a strong, healthy man, so he has a good chance. There is one thing, Mr Owens. The police from Banfield station want to talk to you. Just through here...'

'Oh my God, Sherry.'

'You may well say that, Allen.'

'I'm so sorry, it's just that...'

'I'm not listening to any excuses. I thought it was me that you liked, and you sleep with my sister. Can you honestly explain that?'

'Well...' As he tries to find the words he needs - what for he's not sure as he has no regrets about Linda - Sherry's anger is visibly turning to distress. Allen, fond of Sherry, places his hand on her shoulder in an effort to comfort her.

She flinches and pushes him away. 'Don't you dare touch me Gomez!' she shouts.

Linda is padding down the stairs, keen not to announce her presence, but Sherry, all too aware that her sister is approaching, calls out to her.

'Might be an idea for you to stay upstairs. Not in the mood for you just now. Okay?'

'Sherry...' Allen is attempting to calm the situation.

'You'd better sod off Allen. Stuff your job. I don't want to see you again.'

'Please don't do anything rash. We didn't mean to upset you. It just happ...'

'I know it just bloody happened, Allen. I imagine you can't keep your hands off each other. Just go.'

'Sorry.' Allen realises that any words are woefully inadequate.

As the front door closes, Linda is at the top of the stairs. Sherry is standing at the bottom, wiping away the tears. She glares at her older sister. 'Your new boyfriend hasn't taken his shoes.'

'He's got some trainers in the car.'

'Bully for him, Linda. They're going in the bin. He can whistle for 'em.'

'Sherry, I'm...'

'Sorry? Bloody sorry, are you? Leave it Lin. Not now, okay? Not now.'

Chapter 35: The Ticking of The Clock

Sherry's glare follows Linda as she brushes past her and walks into the kitchen. She flips the switch on the kettle, not sure a cup of tea will ease the situation, but she has to do something. She waits for the kettle to boil and makes two cups, one for herself and one for Sherry, whether she wants one or not. She sits at the table. Sherry hovers in the doorway. She hates falling out with her sister, but her anger has not yet abated.

'Come and sit down, Sis.' Linda motions to the chair at the opposite side of the table. Sherry is reluctant at first, but she's never been one to refuse a cup of tea and she's also curious about her sister's relationship with Allen Gomez, which has surprised as well as angered her. She puts her hands around the cup and lets the steam from the tea rise up to her face.

'Why Allen Gomez?' she asks, her voice calmer now. 'You've never liked him.'

Linda sighs. 'He's not that bad once you get to know him.'

'*You've* certainly got to know him! Very well, I would say!' Sherry's anger begins to rise again, but she manages to keep it under control.

'The thing is, Sher, I'm twenty-three years old. The clock is ticking, and I've never had a real relationship with anyone. You and I can't live like this forever, can we?'

Sherry shrugs her shoulders.

Linda continues. 'We live hand to mouth on minimum wage, with no prospect of ever making anything of ourselves.'

'I think we do fine. We have each other and living together is fun. Isn't it?' Linda detects a quiver in Sherry's voice.

'Yes, of course. And I love us living together and I'll always be there for you, you know that. It's just that at some point I need to settle down. Have a family maybe.'

Sherry bites her bottom lip, realising that things are going to change. 'And Allen, well, he's going places, Sher. He's going to make something of himself. He wants to take over the market one day and he has contacts that he says will make it happen.'

'Contacts?'

'Yes. He says there are people he knows, with money and, er, 'influence', was the word he used and that one day he's going to be rich.'

'Hang on? Are we talking about the same Allen Gomez here? Allen Gomez 'the sleazeball', 'the snake in the grass', the 'lowlife' and all the other things you have always called him, until he flashed his best grin at you. Or his money, or at least the promise of it.'

'I know,' says Linda. 'I did say all those things, but I've come to see him differently just lately. I suppose, at first, I knew you fancied him and that he was interested, so I didn't want him around. But since we've been going out together, he's told me his plans and I've got to like him more.'

'So, what you're saying is that you see him as a way out? You want to ride on the back of whatever he achieves? You want to be the lady of his manor?'

'Not exactly. I do kind of like him, so the money isn't everything. But I believe him when he says he is going to be rich one day and, yes, I do want some of that. Don't you?'

Sherry laughs. 'You're mercenary, you are, sister.'

Linda frowns. 'Is that like a nun?'

Sherry laughs again. 'Never mind. So, you see him as your sugar daddy one day, then? And you're prepared to overlook the fact that he's a sleazeball, as long as he provides you with the lifestyle to which you would like to become accustomed?'

Linda laughs now. 'Well, if you put it like that...' She reaches across the table and grabs her sister's hand. 'And you'd do exactly the same, wouldn't you?'

Allen Gomez, who had crept back into the house through the front door to retrieve his shoes and who has spent the past ten minutes listening to every word decides he has heard enough. He feels like slamming the front door shut but decides against it.

'An audition? In front of Frank Watson?' This is the third time Adam has asked the question and it's beginning to irritate Zack.

'For the last time, yes. An audition in front of Frank Watson. Nick and Jessica will be there, too.'

'Oh, yeah. Like anyone will have any say in the matter but Frank Watson.'

Clare tries to help the situation by pointing out that Jessica Townley, as well as being a hairdresser also writes songs and plays guitar. 'I've heard her. She was support for a folk group that came to Banfield a few months ago. She's fantastic.'

'Well, that's something at least,' says Adam, though he is still convinced that neither Jessica nor Nick will have any say in Frank Watson's choice of the main act at the fête.

'Do we know who we're up against, Zack?' asks Simon. 'I can't think of any other bands around here that would want to do the gig.'

'Well, my dad says there's a band from Northeast Banfield called The Kingsnakes. I've never heard of them.'

Simon and Adam shake their heads. 'Me neither,' says Clare. 'What about you, Zig?'

Ziggy is busy tuning his bass. 'Sorry, what?'

'The Kingsnakes. From Northeast Banfield. Do you know them?'

Ziggy shrugs his shoulders and continues his bass tuning.

'We'll take that as a 'no' then, shall we?' laughs Simon.

'Let's get started then, guys. We've got a lot of work to do if we're going to impress Frank Watson.'

Zack and Adam pick up their guitars and Simon sits behind his keyboard. Clare adjusts her seat and, after a count of four, they launch into a ballad that Zack has written, one which he thinks might impress even Frank Watson, even though the others in the band are not keen on playing so slowly. Playing this slowly and with such a straight beat gives Clare time to look around at the others: Zack, singing his heart out, totally dedicated to the band and his music; Adam, contorting his face with every last squeeze of emotion from his guitar solo; Simon, trying not to play like his piano teacher keeps telling him he should and Ziggy, mean and moody, a man of few words, head down, red in the face.

Red in the face! The same colour of red that used to spread up from his neck whenever he lied to her about where he had been, or who he had seen when they were going out with each other. *What are you not telling us, Ziggy*? she thinks.

PC Carr looks out to sea. There is a line of small black rectangular shapes on the far horizon, on their way to somewhere distant and, right now, he wishes he could be on one of them. The idea of running away to sea always appealed to him when he was a boy. He once considered joining the navy after he finished school, but his father persuaded him to join the police force, as he had done. How his father must be ashamed of him now that his career is in ruins, with a prison sentence looming and goodness knows the national press are going to have a field day. He can imagine the headlines now and shivers at the thought. Still, despite Gail's protestations, he is convinced that giving

173

themselves up is the right thing to do. He reaches in his jacket pocket for his phone, but it is not there. After a brief moment of panic, he remembers that he had put it on charge when he woke and heads back across the beach to the guest house.

'A fête! What a glorious idea!' George Dennis clasps his hands together.

'Yes, love. I can't ever remember Leeford having a fête. Can you?' Clara is preparing dinner, slicing carrots and dropping them into a pan of potatoes boiling on the stove.

'Let me see…' George disappears for a while into the past. After a couple of minutes, he concludes there has not been a fête in Leeford, as far as he is aware.

'I'm going to make lots of things for the craft stall,' announces Clara.

'You're going to be very busy, indeed.' George is genuinely excited about the prospect and Clara is pleased to see him happier than he has been for a few days, during which he had sunk into melancholy, hardly moving from his study and falling asleep for most of the evening.

'Well, I already have a lot made. I might try some new designs, stretch myself a little.'

'You do that, my pumpkin. You do that.'

This is the type of conversation they used to have, George encouraging Clara in everything she did. Somehow, having this conversation makes their present situation seem even sadder than usual.

'You know what, Clara. Maybe the sixth formers could put on a bit o a review. I'll ask them tomorrow.'

Clara sighs. 'You do that, George, my dear. You do that.'

PC Gary Carr runs down the stairs into the kitchen where Mrs Williams is clearing up after breakfast.

'Have you seen Gail, Mrs Williams?' There is desperation in his voice.

'Gail?'

'Er, Joanne,' says Gary, remembering they had given false names.

'She paid up and left twenty minutes ago. She said she was taking her stuff and you'd be back to take yours.'

'Did you say where she was going?' Gary can hardly speak the words

Mrs Whitehouse shakes her head. 'No, Tony, she didn't.'

Chapter 36: Let's Be Frank

'Which one are you joining then, Cody?' asks Jack, as he pushes back his chair to join the queue at the bar.

'Don't know yet.'

Aware that Meredith had joined the Leeford Writers' Group, and taking into account his distinct lack of interest and talent in any area of literacy – many years have passed since he last read a Colin Dexter novel - Cody is leaning towards the Readers' Group. He hasn't read a book in ten years, only dipping into Top Gear magazine when Agnes isn't around to nag him into yet another chore. There is another reason for his indecision. Recent events have not dulled his yearning for the owner of Park Cards and Gifts (renamed from the original Meredith's Cards). However, realisation has not only dawned but has smacked him squarely on the nose; Meredith doesn't fancy him, simple as that. He knows it, but the conscience sitting on his left shoulder is still dragging the pieces across the board in the chess game it is having with his right-shoulder conscience. Cody not only 'does' conscience, he is paranoid, jealous (at one point, of his son, Adam), unsettled in his daily life and typically middle-aged. This, in the sense that the co-owner of 'Leeford Plaice' no longer has the desire or the energy – Cody would say the 'oomph' – to continue running a fish and chip shop.

As Jack saunters off for liquid supplies, Cody thinks back to the weekend – when he had browsed his Oxford English for just the right word to complete the Sun crossword. Brushing past the letter 'O', having already decided he had no 'oomph' left, he reached for the drinks cabinet after discovering the true meaning of 'oomph': 'the quality of being exciting, energetic (*okay so far*, he mused) and sexually attractive'. *That's it,* he thought, *the dictionary is right. No wonder I'm getting nowhere with Mere...*'

'What planet were you on?' Agnes had said.

'Eh?'

'Customers in the shop, Cody. You said you'd be five minutes.'

He wants more. He still loves Agnes, the mother of his child, his life partner, business partner, possibly his best friend, but he wants more.

He wants what he can't have. Meredith.

'Ground control to Major Tom, commencing countdown.'

'Eh?'

'Where did you go just then, Cody?' enquires Jack.

'Just daydreaming.'

'Well daydream your gob round this pint then.'

'Thanks, Jack.'

'Well?' says Jack.

'Well, what?'

'Readers or writers? Jessica's running both clubs at the Community Centre. Tuesday evening for writers, Wednesday for readers.'

'Think I'll join the writers.'

'I'm sure we could sort something out, Sherry. I'll have a word with the lads. Would you be prepared to work on any stall at short notice?'

'I'm very grateful, Jason – thought you'd have enough on your plate. How is George?'

'No change. They say he's stable and breathing on his own now. There are tubes everywhere.'

'He needs fluids as he can't take food himself, apart from antibiotics and other drugs.'

'You sound like you've been through this, Sherry.'

'An aunt of mine. In a coma for two months.'

'Did she...'

'Oh, she's fine now. Nearly eighty. When she recovered, she went to live in Jamaica with her two cousins. Anyway, Jason, must dash. Send my love to George, you know, when he wakes up.'

'I'll speak to the lads this afternoon - see which stalls need some help.' As Sherry walks away, waving to Jason, he calls out, 'I'll see Allen in the cafe at lunchtime. His stall is always busy.'

The double-take took less than two seconds to register in Sherry's brain. *No, I don't want to help Allen with his stall, thank you very much*, she thinks. *I've just quit my job because of him. Come to think of it, have I? Must write my notice letter. Linda wants me to give it another go. I don't know.*

'No, Jason, leave it for now, but thank you so much. Please don't mention it to Allen or the others just yet. Give me a couple of days. I'll get back to you.'

'What's with the old briefcase, Frank?' enquires Nick.

'What? Oh that, it was my grandfather's. Found it in the loft yesterday. Nothing special.'

'You seem preoccupied.'

'No. Just busy, you know,' replies Frank.

'What can I do for you?' asks Nick.

'Could you let Jessica know that I'm interested in her new groups?'

'Oh, she will be pleased.'

Frank does not pick up on the sarcasm. 'Thanks, Nick. Tell her I'll join both groups.'

'With pleasure, Frank,' knowing that Jessica would not be that pleased.

As Frank opens the main door and makes his way down the slope towards his car, Nick feels that he has encountered a different Frank Watson; a man not presenting his usual bluster, pomposity, and sarcasm, though Nick is convinced that Frank doesn't mean to be sarcastic. It's just the way he is. Now, Jessica on the other hand...

He watches him through the main window of the Community Centre, noticing how carefully he opens the side door opposite the driver's seat and places the briefcase on the passenger seat. *Carried out with a good deal of deference,* thinks Nick.

'Penny for them,' says Suptra, passing Nick's mid-morning mocha to him, as Frank drives away, heading towards East Banfield and the local archives office.

'Black coffee please, Ethel.'

'Black? Not your usual, then?'

'I need the caffeine kick and I want it as hot as possible,' replies Jason.

'How is he?'

'I've just been explaining to young Sherry – George is still in a coma. I feel so guilty.'

'What did the police say to you at the hospital?'

'Well, they're not pressing charges. At least not yet. They want to talk to George when he wakes up.'

'What difference will that make, Jason? They believed you, didn't they? It was an accident, and we all know that you love your brother. You'd never hurt him.'

'That's the thing, Ethel, I have hurt him. I nearly killed him.'

Simon Brown doesn't venture into Birmingham very often, but the Facebook posting he'd read on the Yamaha page entices him into the city. He used to play acoustic guitar, but always struggled with the more difficult chords. His parents suggested piano lessons, and, after initial doubts, he soon took to the new instrument in his life. He plays piano at home, but the portable Yamaha keyboard is his favourite. However, he dreams of owning a Roland RD-2000 stage piano, in parallel with Simon's literary hero, Harry Potter, who craved for a Nimbus-2000 broomstick. As these thoughts flow, he arrives at the shop. A poster in the window grabs his attention:

Keyboard players and guitarists wanted for auditions.
Apply in person.
The Dive, Digbeth

He notes the number but decides to have a walk down to the club. He's heard of 'The Dive'. *It's been going for years*, he thinks. *Didn't UB40 once play there?* Turning the corner at the end of Digbeth High Street, not fifty yards from the club, he stops and instinctively steps into a shop doorway. He can see Ziggy standing outside the entrance of the club. He is shaking hands with a man whose suit suggests a certain level of authority. Dark glasses and a cigar add to the image. 'He's shaking hands with the manager,' he says to himself, receiving odd looks from the lady inside the wool shop whose doorway Simon has occupied. 'What's he up to?' As Ziggy walks down the hill, away from the club, presumably to the bus station, Simon approaches the entrance. As he did at the Yamaha shop, he spots a poster attached to the main door.

Bass guitarist required for The Kingsnakes – apply to The Manager, The Dive, Digbeth

'What the?' Simon exclaims out loud, as the man he assumes to be the manager approaches.

'We've been watching you on our CCTV for a few minutes. Can we help you?'

'No, er, sorry, bit of a mix up. Someone told me you needed a keyboard player. Sorry.'

Wait till Zack hears about this, thinks Simon.

Greg Withall is trouble. Ten years in Wandsworth for grievous bodily harm, assault, and drug trafficking, and he's back. Impeccable behaviour has given him the maximum discount, and he's out on licence for the next eighteen months. People in Leeford Village know Greg. He used to drink in The Cross. Heavily. And, he's Mandy Cleeve's first husband. She is fully aware that he is due out, but no one in the Cleeve family knows he has arrived in the village. When Vera had a close call over her gnome trading, she begged Sergeant Miller to leave Mandy out of it, and told him 'she's got enough problems'. Vera knows how worried Mandy is about what Greg might do, and also how her husband, Nigel, might react.

Chapter 37: Liar! Liar!

It's difficult for Dr Jeremy Roberts to leave the surgery for an hour, partly because he has to lie, which is not in his DNA, but mostly because the thought of meeting Mel Adams, other than in his consulting room, fills him with dread. He's never been sure who instigated the relationship they had a couple of years ago, but he suspects it might have been a 'grass is greener' situation for both of them. Mel and Jeremy's wife are good friends, as are he and Steve, Mel's husband, and they very often attend concerts or go for a night out in Birmingham, as a foursome. If pushed, Jeremy would say that he flirted with Mel first, in all innocence (if flirting can ever be totally innocent) and that Mel picked up on it and reciprocated. The point at which it turned into something more serious, something he bitterly regrets, is more debatable, though he can remember the first night they spent together when he was supposedly at a conference in Wales. The affair had been brief yet intense, and it was Mel who had called it off, unexpectedly and without any explanation. Would he have continued had she not? He's not sure, but what he is sure of is that it must never happen again. As he sees her walking across the park towards the bandstand, he feels a sickness in his stomach.

'He was shaking hands with the manager of The Dive?'

Simon sighs. 'Yes. Who, I've since found out, is also manager of The Kingsnakes.'

Zack feels a mixture of anger and confusion. 'And they were advertising for a bass player?'

'Yes. It said to apply to the manager of The Dive.'

Adam shakes his head. 'I always thought he was a bit suspect.'

'Really?' says Clare. 'Is this the same Ziggy you said was the greatest thing that ever happened to this band?'

Adam blushes. 'Well, I'm not saying he's not a good bass player, but that doesn't make him a good person. Does it?'

Clare rolls her eyes.

'What do you think, Clare? You've known Ziggy longer than we have,' asks Simon, casting a glance at Adam.

'Well, he was always a decent sort of guy. I'm surprised he would do something like this. Though, when we mentioned The Kingsnakes at the last band practice, he did go very quiet.'

180

'Well, there we are then. A guilty conscience,' says Zack, pleased to find a flaw in Ziggy's decency.

'Do you think he'll tell us? Or just not come again?' asks Simon.

'Here's your answer,' says Zack as Ziggy pushes open the basement door with his bass case and shouts, 'hi guys!'

Sergeant Miller leans back in his chair, his fingers threaded together in front of him. A quiet outpost they had told him when they offered him the position. A sleepy suburb. A backwater. The land that time forgot. If only, he thinks, if only! He considers his current case load: a PC who has absconded with a felon, a case of arson, the return to the village of a dangerous criminal and Vera Cleeve's gnome stealing habit. Then there is the fête to police as well as trying to control Frank Watson on the parish council. His train of thought is interrupted by a phone call.

'Hello. Sergeant Miller.' Silence on the other end of the line. 'Hello. Sergeant Miller. Who's calling?'

More silence. Then a muffled male voice. 'Sergeant Miller. I have some information for you.'

The accent is strange, thinks Sergeant Miller, though there are definite Welsh inflections. 'Go on,' he says, pressing the record button on his phone.

'I might know something about your missing PC. PC Carr, I think his name is.'

Sergeant Miller sits up straight and picks up a pen. 'Who's this calling?' he asks.

There is a short silence before the voice says, 'Anomy…anonym… anonymous.'

'Okay. What do you know?'

'First of all, I want to know something.'

'Go on.'

'I want to know what'll happen to your PC if I told you where I am.'

'Where *you* are?'

'Yes. No. I mean where *he* is. Yes, where *he* is.'

'Well, you can tell him that he'll have the book thrown at him and, depending on what the courts decide, he might even be put away.' There is a sound on the other end of the phone that Sergeant Miller suspects is what panic sounds like. 'You can also tell him that if he was to return in the next twenty-four hours, with Gail Perkins, then I will do all I can to plead mitigating circumstances.' Sergeant Miller has noticed that the voice on the other end of the phone has grown weaker as the conversation has progressed.

'Thank you,' says the voice, less Welsh now.

'And, Gary…'

'Yes? Argh! Damn!'

'Come straight to the station.'

'Yes, Sarge. Thank you,Sarge.'

Sergeant Miller puts down his pen and sits back in his chair. *Only in Leeford,* he thinks. *Only in Leeford.*

Ziggy makes a few minor tuning adjustments to his bass and plays a sequence of fast arpeggios that impresses Adam, though he makes sure no one knows.

'I'm ready,' says Ziggy smiling.

There is an uncomfortable silence while the others look at the floor, their equipment, then each other. Eventually, it's Zack who nervously takes control. 'Are you sure you're ready, Ziggy?'

'Yeah. What are we playing?'

'Maybe we should play a Kingsnakes' song?' says Adam, surprised by his own sarcasm.

'What? Why would we do that?' Ziggy is no longer smiling but looking very confused. Clare is watching him intently.

'Maybe their songs are better,' offers Zack, more confident now.

Ziggy shrugs. 'Dunno. Never heard them.'

Zack looks at Adam, who looks at Simon, who looks at Clare who is still looking at Ziggy.

'What a liar!' exclaims Zack.

Ziggy unstraps his bass and rests it against his amplifier.

'Liar? What? What are you on about?'

'The Kingsnakes. Snake being the operative word, eh?'

'What? Man, this is weird' says Ziggy, throwing up his arms.

'How did you think you were going to play with us and The Kingsnakes. Didn't you think we'd notice?'

'What the hell are you talking about, Zack!' Clare has not seen Ziggy this animated before, but she is beginning to find it attractive.

'I saw you,' says Simon, 'shaking hands with the manager of The Dive. The same guy that's manager of the Kingsnakes. Who happens to be looking for a bass player!'

At this, Ziggy explodes into fits of laughter. When he recovers, his voice has resumed its calm, authoritative tone.

'Yes. I did shake hands with the manager of The Dive. And, yes, he is also the manager of The Kingsnakes.'

'Told you!' says Simon, gleefully.

'I shook hands with him because he had agreed to give us our first paid gig at The Dive.'

'Us?' says Clare.

'Yes, our band. I know him from a few years ago and he trusts me. I asked him for a gig. He said we could take the up-and-coming bands spot on a Sunday night.'

Simon coughs. 'Oh, really?'

'Yes, Simon. Really.'

Clare notices that Simon's face is as red as Adam's Stratocaster.

'You idiot, Simon,' says Zack, echoed by Adam.

'I'm sorry, Zig. I thought…'

'Yeah,' says Ziggy picking up his bass and putting it in the case. 'I know what you thought. And The Kingsnakes did ask me to be their bass player, a couple of weeks ago. I turned them down.''

'What are you doing, Zig?' asks Adam.

'I'm off. If you can't trust me, there's no point is there?'

He pushes past Adam towards the door. Before he opens the door, he turns and points at Simon.

'And, talking of trust, did you pass the keyboard audition at The Dive?'

Vera Cleeve checks the date on her calendar. Five years to the day, half his sentence served. *It should have been longer,* she thinks, and Sergeant Miller had agreed with her. 'But the law is the law', he had said, and Greg Withall had shown remorse and behaved perfectly while in prison, meaning the parole board had no option but to release him. Maybe he has changed. *Maybe he is no longer a danger and should be given a second chance. Maybe.* She doubts it. She doubts it very much.

Sherry stands outside the launderette, a sad-looking building, neglected for many years. The topcoat of paint is peeling off and the sign has been missing a 'd' for as long as she can remember. There is a crack in the corner of the large front window, where someone had once tried to break in, unsuccessfully. It's four o'clock and the place should be open until six. Linda must have closed early. To spend time with Allen Gomez? At first, Sherry had bought Linda's story about using Gomez for his money, or at least his potential money, but now she was no longer sure. She has always believed that you can only be with someone you love. She had loved Allen once; from afar, but it was love. She now regrets it. She regrets everything. She regrets most of all the nerves that made her freeze when she auditioned for the TV talent show last year. How things could have been so different. She pulls a flake of paint from the windowsill. This is all I have now, she thinks, and feels a tear run down her cheek.

As she starts to walk towards home a car pulls up alongside her. She carries on walking, not looking at the car until she hears a woman's voice, friendly and clear.

'Sherry? Sherry Cross? I've been looking for you, everywhere!'

'Sorry, do I know you?'

Sherry quickly works out that the woman is alone. She is ready to run or reach into her bag for the pepper spray she has carried since being attacked crossing a dark North Banfield car park when she was barely fifteen. Sherry admits that she does tend to put herself in vulnerable positions, and that she is too trusting. Allen and Linda, a case in point.

'Don't you remember me? Julie. Julie Gregson, Beladon Productions. The audition?'

'That was ages ago. Anyway, you turned me down.'

'I didn't, Sherry. I liked you but found myself in a minority of one.'

'Out-voted then.'

'You could put it that way, but here is your chance to put it right. Can I buy you dinner? There's a lovely new restaurant in the centre of Banfield. I'll drop you home afterwards.'

'Well... I'll have to call my sister. Tell her where I'll be.'

'No, I can't stay for the meeting, Nick. Just popped in to drop off paperwork for Stephen Miller.'

'Are you following set procedures from fêtes organised in the past?'

'Nick, you really don't listen, do you?'

'What do you mean by that?'

'Don't you remember when I booked the room for the fête sub-committee, I told you it would be the first one ever held in Leeford?'

Jessica, taking an hour's break from the salon, hears the last part of the conversation. Frank's part. She has never liked the man and is constantly irritated by Nick's acceptance of insults, sarcasm, back-biting and generally being walked over.

'Who the hell do you think you are, Frank?'

'Sorry?'

'I doubt it very much if you are.'

'Leave it, Jessica,' intervenes Nick.

'No, I won't leave it. He's an arrogant bully and he needs telling.'

Jessica turns back to face Frank, but all she sees is his back as he exits the Community Centre.

'Well. How rude!'

'You were a bit, er, straightforward, Jess.'

'Straightforward? You mean I was rude.'

'Look love, there's things you don't know about Frank. And he seems to have a lot on his mind....'

'Never mind what's on his mind,' Jessica interrupts. Then, bursting into tears, she blurts out, 'I wanted to see you!'

'Jess, what is it?'

'Oh Nick, I've just had confirmation from the doctor. I'm pregnant.'

'We don't see you in here very often.'

'How long have you been running *Billy's* on your own?' replies Agnes.

'Fourteen years. Since my darling Bill passed away.'

'What happened, Ethel? I've often wondered but not wanted to ask.'

'His heart. He'd had problems for years. More and more tablets, but he was getting weaker.'

'Was it sudden in the end?'

'No. He went into hospital after an attack. He was in Banfield General for three weeks. Bill even organised his own funeral and had time to tell me what to do with the business.' Ethel lowers her head, tears filling her eyes. Agnes leans forward and takes Ethel's right hand in hers.

'There, love, it comes and goes, doesn't it?'

'Yes, after all this time and I still think of him every day.'

'Of course.'

'Never mind me, Agnes. How are things with you?'

'Shall I just say "Cody", and leave it at that?'

'He's a good man, your husband. You know that don't you?'

'Well, I do, but things have changed lately.'

'In what way?'

'I think he might be having an affair.'

'Who with?'

'Meredith Park.'

'He can't be. He wouldn't – would he?'

'Oh, Ethel, he's lost interest in me, and he is over the road at the card shop with all sorts of lame excuses. You know he bought me fifteen birthday cards?'

'Never! Why?'

'Not sure, Ethel, but I have my suspicions.'

'Anything else?'

'He's joined that new writers' group that Jessica's running.'

'What's wrong with that?'

'He thinks I'm stupid, but he switched from the readers' group when he heard that Meredith was joining the writers.'

'What are you going to do, Agnes?'

'Well, for a start, I'm joining the writers' group as well.'

If you were to walk through Leeford Village on any given day, wait for the traffic noise to die down, and, if necessary, unplug your Walkman (if you're old enough and if it still works), you might hear the hum and chatter of voices. Village voices. What are they chatting about? The upcoming fête. Cody and Agnes, with all their problems, are no exception. One thing they both agree on – they like to do their 'bit' for the community. Cody has already taken both Frank and Stephen to one side at a meeting and lobbied them for a stall. The Thorntons want a book stall. They've done it before at car boots (at Taylor's Farm) in the summer and fund-raisers throughout the year held in the Community Centre.

Cody is never sure with Frank. He nods his head or sighs and coughs, and Cody is not the best at reading body language. Stephen is much more straightforward. 'I think we should allocate the book stall to Cody and Agnes, eh Frank?' Even the local police sergeant / parish council deputy chair can only elicit a 'huh' from his superior. At least Frank thinks he is superior. Here's where the problem starts. Mel and Steve Adams also want a book stall, and Frank likes Mel and Steve. 'Good, solid business types, the Adams family,' he says. He has repeated this a number of times and it invariably brings a smile to his deputy's face. Herein lies the difference. The owners of 'Leeford Plaice' don't want a penny from the proceeds. It would all go into the village charity fund. Mel and Steve, on the other hand, have 'generously' offered 50% of any profit for the fund. They want to use the stall as an extension of their book selling business. The official list of stalls (and their respective allocations) is due to be announced at the next parish council meeting. Stephen Miller is to chair that meeting. Whether or not Frank Watson esq will allow such a momentous decision to be taken in his absence remains to be seen.

Greg walks into The Cross as if he's never been away. Ted, Jack Simmons, Cody, and Ken Taylor, deep in conversation, all pause as one.

'Greg Withall, if I'm not mistaken,' whispers Ken.

'I heard you, Ken. No, you're not mistaken. It's me. I'm back.'

'We don't want any trouble, Greg,' says Ted.

'Trouble? Why should I be trouble?'

Greg Withall is a man whose appearance defies his reputation. The girl he married, Mandy Smith, is now Mandy Cleeve. She considered him to be quite a catch back then. Relatively clean cut (except for a jagged scar to the left of his lower lip), a firm jaw, deep, dark blue eyes than can latch onto a person's glance, if someone dares glance. Short, dark brown, wavy hair that Mandy used to love. Not anymore. He's aged but hasn't changed that much. A facial expression more accountant than hired thug turns in a second if someone riles him.

'I'm just saying, Greg. Do you want a drink?'

'That's kind of you, Ted. Giving out freebies now?'

'I didn't mean...' splutters Ted.

'Don't get your knickers in a twist, Edward. I can pay. I could afford to buy your pub, let alone a drink.'

'You're not welcome here, Withall.'

Greg spins round, to see Jack rising from his chair.

'Sit down, Jack. He's not worth it,' says Ken.

'I could take you both on, but I'm just here for a quiet pint. Okay?'

'Leave it, lads,' says Ted. 'Here's your pint, Greg.'

'You remembered – my favourite brew.'

'Hello Jeremy, or should I say "doctor"?'

'Mel, I don't have much time. What is it?'

'Please sit down. I need to explain.' Mel had been the one who brought the relationship to a dead stop, with no explanation. She has wanted for so long to talk to him properly and provide him with that explanation. He now understands that she doesn't want to revive the passion they felt for each other, but she does want to end any awkwardness. 'So, you see, we were going through a bad patch. I had suspected that Steve was seeing someone else. He wasn't – I'm sure of it – but he had lost interest in, well, bed.'

'I see.'

They sit quietly for a few minutes and don't see the man in the blue anorak leaning against an old oak, not thirty yards away.

'Jeremy, I'm so glad we have come to an understanding. Steve never knew about us. He would have gone crazy.' She reaches over, places her hand on his left shoulder and gently plants a soft kiss on his cheek. 'Goodbye, Jeremy.'

'I'm so glad you're okay,' he replies.

Steve Adams moves behind the oak tree, waits for the couple by the bandstand to part then makes his way back home.

'Glad he's gone,' says Cody. 'Now, where were we? Jack, I think you had the chair.'

'Thank you, Chairman Cody. All you need is a little red book.'

'Eh?'

'Never mind,' Jack continues, grasping his pint glass, ready for another. 'I'm going to ask for a stall at the fête.'

'You as well?' says Ken. 'Doing what?'

'The Pound Challenge.'

Chapter 39: I'm going to make you a star!

'What would you suggest? The Merlot, or the Cabernet Sauvignon?'
Julie Gregson runs her finger down the wine list.

'I've never eaten either. You choose.'

Julie looks over the top of her glasses. 'They're wines, Sherry.'

'I know. I was joking.' Sherry folds and unfolds her napkin, as she
has been doing ever since she sat at the table.

'Oh, I see. Well, which one?'

'Neither.'

'Something else, then. How about a nice Rocha? Maybe a pinot...'

'I'm seventeen.'

Julie's finger pauses at a bottle of Châteauneuf-du-Pape. 'Of course.'
Julie folds the wine list and picks up the menu.

'The nearest I've been to anything alcoholic is a packet of wine
gums.'

'I'm sorry, I'm just used to, well, you know, in my job...'

Sherry is beginning to wish she hadn't said 'yes' to Julie's meal
invitation.

'I'll tell you what. I'll order for us, shall I? Is there anything you
don't eat?'

'I'm vegan.' This announcement is as much a surprise to Sherry as it
is to Julie.

'Oh, well, I'm sure they'll be able...'

'Why have you brought me here?'

Julie puts the menu down and leans back in her chair. 'I detect a bit
of an attitude. That's good in the right circumstances and it's certainly
a selling point, but not when you're talking to someone who could
change your life forever.'

'Change my life? How?'

'How? I'll tell you how, if you'll stop being so rude.'

Sherry looks down at her hands. She needs her nails manicuring and
will make an appointment with Jessica's beautician in the morning.
'I'm sorry. It's just that whenever I think something good is going to
happen to me, I always get let down.'

Julie leans forward. 'I won't let you down, Sherry. I promise. When
I saw you at the audition, I knew we could work together. I've been
trying to find you ever since and I'm glad I have. Your voice is on
trend, your sense of style is what kids relate to and, as I have witnessed
today, you have attitude. It's the perfect combination.'

Sherry feels a rush of adrenalin.

'So, Sherry Cross, what would you like to eat?'

'A steak,' says Sherry, smiling.

Sergeant Miller is parked in a lay-by on the outskirts of Banfield. A familiar blue Clio pulls in front of him. A couple of minutes later, PC Carr is sitting in Sergeant Miller's car, explaining why he helped Gail Perkins escape from custody. The more he explains, the more ridiculous it sounds. Sergeant Miller waits until PC Carr has finished.

'I don't know what to say, Gary. You know I can't let you get away with this, don't you?'

'No, Sarge.'

'We're going to have to go to the station, where I will charge you. I'm not sure what with yet, but it could be assisting an offender. Or it could be harbouring an offender. Or even perverting the course of justice. Or with being an absolute and complete idiot!'

PC Carr lowers his head.

'We'll sort it out when we get to the station. There's one more thing you have to tell me, Gary. Where's Gail?'

PC Carr bites his bottom lip. 'Sorry sarge. I've no idea.'

There are six people in the room when Cody arrives and none of them is Meredith. He sits at a table in front of Jessica Townley who is flicking through a pile of papers ready to hand out during the evening. He pulls a pen and notepad out of his bag and begins to doodle.

'Hi Cody,' says Jessica, looking up briefly. This is the first time she has run a writing group and she wishes she wasn't feeling so sick. 'I thought morning sickness only happened in the morning,' she had said to Nick when she emerged from the bathroom for the third time, earlier. She looks up again. 'Hi Meredith. Take a seat, we'll be starting in a minute.' Cody hears the scrape of a chair behind him but resists the temptation to turn around. He feels a knot in his stomach, a feeling he has not had since Emily Curtis planted a kiss on his cheek at the youth club when he was twelve.

Jessica coughs, which makes her feel worse. 'Thank you, everyone, for coming. I'm sure you're going to enjoy it and I'm looking forward to sharing our work. We'll introduce ourselves to each other shortly then I'll explain what we are going to do this evening. But first, I'd like us to just spend five minutes writing whatever comes into our minds. It doesn't have to be Dostoevsky and it's not something anyone else will see, but it'll get the creative juices flowing.'

Cody picks up his pen. What to write about? "Whatever comes into our minds" Jessica said. There's only one thing in Cody's mind and he certainly couldn't write about that! He sucks on the end of his pen, trying to erase the image of him and Meredith, at least temporarily. Just as he is about to write his first sentence, he hears the door close at the back of the room followed by the voice of the last person he thought would be there tonight.

'Sorry I'm late.'

'Agnes! Welcome. Please take a seat. I'll come over and tell you what we're doing.'

'What are we going to do without a bass player?' asks Simon. It's been three days since Ziggy walked out on the band and not even a call from Clare could persuade him to return.

'We'll advertise for someone,' says Zack.

'Right,' says Adam, 'and we're going to get someone to audition and learn all the songs before the fête?'

Zack sits disconsolate on the floor in front of his amp. 'I don't know. Maybe we should forget the whole thing. Anyway, Simon. It's your fault. You were the one who told us Ziggy was playing with The Kingsnakes.'

Simon's face reddens.

'And you never answered Ziggy's question. What were you doing at The Dive keyboard auditions?'

'Don't have a go at me!' Simon puffs out his chest, but he is so skinny it makes him look like he is leaning backwards. 'You're the one who called him a liar!'

'Yeah, because you had got it all wrong!'

'We could have just asked him why he was there before we accused him.'

'Actually, it was you that accused him first, Adam!' says Zack.

Adam throws up his hands. 'Only because Simon got it totally wrong, just like his keyboard parts!'

Simon points at Adam, 'Oh, that's great, coming from the guitarist who can only play three-string chords!'

Adam lunges at Simon and the two of them grapple, knocking over amplifiers and guitar stands before crashing into Clare's drum kit.

'Enough!' shouts Zack. 'Out! You're both fired!'

Adam picks up his guitar case and storms out of the room. Simon goes to pick up his keyboard, then realises he needs his mom to come and collect it. 'I was leaving, anyway,' he says, brushing past Zack on the way out of the room. The room is suddenly quiet. Clare straightens up her kit.

'That's it, then. We're finished,' says Zack slumping to the floor. Clare puts her drumsticks into the bag her mother had made for her when she first started having drum lessons.

'You haven't said anything,' says Zack.

She comes from behind her kit and sits behind Simon's keyboard. 'Play that new song. The one you wrote at the weekend,' she says.

'Eh, why?'

'I like it.'

He reaches forward and grabs his acoustic guitar which has been knocked off its stand in the melee. He tunes it roughly then strums the introductory chords. He sings the first verse. When he gets to the chorus, Clare joins in, in perfect harmony. It's a beautiful sound that sends shivers up his spine. They finish the song together, with a chorus.

'Wow, Clare, that was amazing. I didn't know you could sing like that.'

'I used to have singing lessons before I switched to drums,' she says.

'Let's do another,' says Zack jumping to his feet and strapping on the guitar. They work their way through two more of Zack's songs and a couple of covers, in one of which Clare sings the verses.

'This is it, then,' says Zack as they finish the final song.

'This is what?'

'This is the new band. Me and you. Zack and Clare. We don't need the others!'

The front door closes. Allen Gomez jumps up from the settee. He is tucking in his shirt when Sherry steps into the room.

'Don't panic, Allen. I'm not bothered,' she says, sitting down heavily in the armchair.

Allen looks at Linda, who shrugs her shoulders. 'What's up with you? Was the meal no good?'

'Yeah. It was very good, actually.' Sherry sighs and slowly unbuttons her coat.

'So, why the glum face?' Linda pats the settee and Allen tentatively sits down beside her, his eyes on Sherry.

'Julie Gregson wants me to make a demo in her recording studio.'

'Oh, wow, Sher! Fantastic! When?'

'Next week.'

'So why are you looking so miserable?' asks Allen, feeling a little more confident though still suspicious of Sherry's sudden acquiescence.

'She wants me to go and live with her for a year.'

'And what's the problem with that?'

A single tear runs down Sherry's cheek.

'She lives in Las Vegas.'

Chapter 40: Schrödinger's Cucumber

'I am so sorry, George. Can you forgive me?'

George sighs and takes a deep breath. Jason waits.

'Just tell me you're okay.'

There will be no reply today. Doctor Sahid moves to Jason's right side and gently touches his shoulder. 'He's stable, but this could take some time. His vital signs are good, and, if he can come out of this in the next few weeks, there's no reason why he can't make a full recovery.'

'I feel so helpless. Is there nothing I can do?'

'Talk to him. Just talk to him.'

'Nice walk in the park, love?'

Mel flinches as Steve's eyes seem fixed in a gaze, tracking her line of sight so he misses nothing.

'How did you know I'd been in the park?'

'You said you might this morning. Y'know, just after breakfast.'

'Oh. Yes.'

'See anyone?'

'No, just clearing my head. Heh, any news about the book stall? You've got Frank on board, haven't you?'

'Everyone else is rooting for Cody and Agnes.'

'Popularity contest?'

'No, not so much that. Word is, they think we are the selfish business tycoons. Mr and Mrs Cod are doing it all for charity.'

'We're offering 50% of our profits, Steve!'

'You don't have to tell me that.'

Mel takes refuge in the kitchen, making their evening cocoa. 'Does he suspect?' she mutters under her breath.

'It's like Schrödinger's cat,' says Jack.

'He's off again.'

'I might be off, Ken, but I know a thing or two about marrows.'

'Excuse me for breathing, but have you noticed what I do for a living?'

'You might be a farmer - doesn't make you a specialist.'

Roy Cohen collects the used glasses, taking a keen interest in the proceedings. 'What's Schrödinger's...'

'Cat, Roy. Schrödinger's cat,' snaps Jack.

'Come on then, Jack, never mind Dad's lack of marrow expertise...' says Doug.

'Do you mind, Doug!'

'You know what I mean. Anyway, please explain about this flippin' cat.'

'It was a thought experiment. In the 1930s, he developed a theory, following on from an idea by Albert...'

'Tatlock!' shouts out Roy, laughing at his own joke.

'Einstein, thank you very much,' sneers Jack.

Roy hovers by the table a little too long and is ordered back to work by Ted, who can't help but get involved himself. Sally tilts her chin slightly and tuts. 'So, what does this cat do?'

'Schrödinger puts him in a box, seals it, and does something, say, blasts it with radiation. Something that may or may not kill whatever's inside the box. You've got no way of knowing whether or not the cat will survive. You won't know till you open the box, so at that point the cat could be dead or alive - it could be thought to be dead and alive.'

'Bloody rubbish,' shouts Ken.

'What's this got to do with marrows anyway?' asks Doug.

'My point is...'

'You're nuts, that's what your point is,' interrupts Ken.

'My point is last year's marrow growing competition was a farce. No one had any idea what they were doing. Did you see the state of some of the exhibits?'

'Mine wasn't too bad,' shouts Roy from a table at the far end of the lounge.

'Too bad? You've proved my point, Roy. It could have been dead or alive. Probably dead *and* alive. It was pathetic.'

'It came second.'

Frank Watson has been standing by the bar catching the back end of the lads' intellectual debate. 'Cucumbers!'

They all spin round as one. Doug is the first to respond. 'Cucumbers, Frank?'

'That's what we're doing at the fête. This year, we want you to grow prize cucumbers. Easier than marrows.'

'You'll be sorted, Dad,' says Doug. 'You've already got loads growing. They look smashing - it'll be a shoe-in.'

'Commercial entries not allowed. Sorry, Ken.'

'Good grief, Frank, why do you have to spoil everything?' replies

Ken.

'I'm in,' states Ted.

'And me,' jumps in Roy.

The others all stake their claims - Ken allowed a private entry on condition that the cucumber is grown in his garden and not on the farm.

'Well,' says Jack, 'let's hope some of your cucumbers survive the treatment you lot give out.'

Frank steps forward again. 'That's settled then. I'll let the committee know that another stall is organised. I'll judge it.'

Ted mutters, 'democracy in action then,' a comment heard, but ignored by Frank.

A groan finds its way from the lounge towards the bar as Frank slams his glass down for Ted to refill. 'Watson in charge yet again.'

'Another pint of your best, young Ted.'

'He sounds cheerful enough, doesn't he,' whispers Jack.

'Never mind him,' says Roy. 'I'm off to the allotment when I've finished my shift.'

'Are you ready to chair the meeting, Stephen?'

'I've done one before, Frank.'

'Yes, but not one at this level. The first fête - remember that.'

'I'm quite aware of the historic significance.'

Frank, ready to bite at the barely disguised sarcasm emanating from the lips of the local police sergeant / deputy chair of Leeford Parish Council, is distracted by the dulcet tones of Pink Floyd - his new ringtone. 'Yes?' There is a pause as he takes in information that, to Stephen, appears to animate Frank to a level higher than his usual demeanour. 'Thank you, I'm so grateful. 1734 you say?'

Trust Frank to have found a friend who gives such precise times, Stephen thinks. Why can't they say, 'twenty-five to six' or 'just turned half-past five'?

He enters the shop as the solitary customer collecting their Sunday joint is preparing to leave. Doug Taylor and Percy Lloyd spot him simultaneously, catching each other's knowing look. The door closes, swinging towards the frame powered by the hydraulic door closer that Nigel Cleeve had fitted two weeks before. No longer the almost permanently open door, the winter draught, and the characteristic bang as it is periodically slammed shut by a diligent customer.

'Is he in?' enquires Greg Withall.

Doug's left eye twitches. It does that at short notice if its owner finds himself in a stressful situation.

'Cat got your tongue, Doug?'

'In the back. Wait here. I'll fetch him.'

'Take your little pal with you and send Mr Cleeve out to me. If you don't mind.' Having witnessed the exchange between his dad and Greg in The Cross, Doug has no appetite for further antagonism between himself and the new arrival.

'Ah, Nigel Cleeve, as I live and breathe. No, before you say it, I didn't do poetry in the Nick, although I did make one or two inmates sing if you get my drift.'

'What do you want, Greg?'

'Not much. Just half of the investment my dear wife sank into your business. I would say my share is now worth forty grand. I'll settle for the original thirty, if it's alright with you.'

'That was always Mandy's money. You know that.'

As Greg moves closer to the counter, close enough that he could reach Nigel, if necessary, he snaps back. 'No Nigel, you're not listening. She took my share when we divorced - without my permission. Have I made myself clear? You've got two weeks.'

'Two?'

'You heard. If you value your business, and the state of your face, you'll be a sensible boy.'

'Are you threatening me?'

'You might call it that. I would say we've had a frank and fair exchange of views, and I've put you right on a few matters. Two weeks. Got it?'

As Doug and Percy peer round the curtain at the rear of the shop, Greg opens the door, giving Ethel, who is keen to collect her weekly treat of a lamb chop and a couple of Nigel's delicious pork pies, a polite smile as she enters with her Spendfields bag-for-life. He waves a hand in a sarcastic, majestic fashion to usher her towards the counter.

'See you in two weeks, Nigel. Nice talking to you.'

'Where the hell are you, Gary? You said you'd come into the station.'

'Sorry, Sarge, I hope you'll understand. I've spoken to Gail overnight. I know I've done wrong, and I want to fix it.'

'How, for God's sake?'

'You might say I've had a tip-off.'

'From Gail?'

'Yes, and she doesn't realise.'

'Where are you?'

'London.'

'What?'

'She's meeting Martin Frobisher, and thinks I'll help him as well.'

'The Swede.'

'Half-Swede.'

'Leave it, Gary. I'll call the local station.'

'No Sarge, please. Let me do this. I'll bring them both in. You'll see.'

'I don't like this, Gary.'

'One chance, Sarge. Just give me this one chance. Twenty-four hours.'

'You'd better not foul up. My head's on the block as well.'

Chapter 41: Well, it ain't Shakespeare…!

Cody bites the end of his biro, a habit formed in his schooldays and one he has never been able to break. Cody's biros are chewed to destruction long before they run out of ink. 'So, fourteen lines, written in iambic pentameter. Shouldn't be too difficult,' he mumbles to himself. He can't remember what Jessica Townley, the writing tutor had said about iambic pentameter, so he decides to ignore it and just stick with the fourteen lines. 'Have a look at Shakespeare's sonnets, for inspiration,' she had said, but he hasn't time to do that now. Anyway, he wants it to be an original piece of work and does not want to be influenced by anyone else. In any case, what does Shakespeare know about writing a love poem? Didn't he write plays about kings and fairies? Cody sets to work on his poem:

It is you I love, in so many ways.
It is you I love, for always.

Rhyming 'always' with 'ways' is probably not a good thing, he thinks. *Days? Would that be better?*

It is you I love, for all my days.

Perfect! He takes a bite out of his biro in celebration. He remembers Jessica saying something about describing the person you love, pointing out the things you love about them. He sucks the end of his biro. *Here's the problem,* he thinks. *How to describe Meredith, whom the poem is about, while letting Agnes think the poem is about her?* Then, as he spits out another piece of plastic, inspiration hits. 'The eyes,' he whispers, 'they both have the same colour eyes!'

From the early morning when I rise
I think of you and your clear blue eyes.

Beautiful! Another ten lines like this and I'll be the star of the next writing class, he thinks, as the ink chamber drops out of the bottom of the biro.

They are sitting in a cafe in Euston Road. Martin Frobisher is talking animatedly to Gail Perkins, who is in two minds whether or not to order a second piece of cake, seeing as Martin is paying and he owes her, big time. PC Carr positions himself behind a lamp post on the opposite side of the road. He peers round it and takes a quick photograph with his phone to use as evidence later. He checks the picture - an old man and a dog walking in front of the cafe. He takes another. This time he captures the two of them perfectly. Gail looks out of the window. *Where is he?* she thinks, expecting Gary to have turned up at the cafe fifteen minutes ago. She has not told Martin Frobisher about Gary because she is not sure what Gary's plan is for the three of them. All Gary had said was to meet Frobisher in the cafe and wait for him there. Gail looks out of the window again. Gary jumps quickly to his left, so that the lamp post obscures his thin frame completely. As he is about to make his move, a young man wearing a grey hoodie approaches him.

'Got a light, mate?' His voice is gruff and there is an urgency to his request.

PC Carr is flustered. Gail is bound to see him now. He instinctively fumbles in his pocket, then remembers he gave up smoking two years ago. 'Er, no. Sorry. Don't smoke.'

The young man pulls his hood further over his head, covering most of his face. 'Give us a twenty quid then.'

'What?'

'Twenty quid. Give us twenty quid and I'll leave you alone.'

PC Carr looks over to the window. Gail and Frobisher are still talking. The waitress is bringing Gail another piece of cake. He looks at the young man and then at the outline of a knife in the pocket of his hoodie. Under normal circumstances, the man would by now be handcuffed and pinned against the lamp post. But, today, PC Carr pulls out his wallet, takes out a ten-pound note and two fives and gives them to the man. 'On, your way then. And be quick about it.' The man looks incredulously at the money he has been handed without even having to produce the knife, shrugs his shoulders and walks away. PC Carr turns to look at the window. Time for action. Or at least it would be if he could escape the grip of the two police officers that have appeared from nowhere and are now pinning him against the lamp post.

'What the …'

'You are under arrest on suspicion of dealing in illegal substances. Anything you say…'

PC Carr does not wait for the rest of the warning, a warning he has handed out hundreds of times. 'But I'm a police officer!'

'Yeah, and I'm the prime minister,' says one of the officers.

'We've been watching you, sir, and you've been behaving suspiciously for the last fifteen minutes,' says the other.

'Honestly, I am a police officer. I'm about to arrest those two in the cafe over the road!' pleads PC Carr.

'Which two?'

'Those two at that…oh, no, please, no! They've gone!'

'Well, sir. Maybe you'd like to come and play at being a police officer down at the station. It'll be right up your street.'

'You have to go, Sher! This is your big chance, Sis!'

Sherry sits down on the sofa and holds her head in her hands. Linda puts her arm around her. 'I know, Lin. But Las Vegas? That's a whole life away from Leeford!'

'Well, yes. I grant you there are not many similarities, but this is your opportunity to make the big time. It's a no-brainer, surely. Tell her, Allen!'

Allen Gomez clears his throat. 'If this lady is asking you to stay there for a year, she's pretty serious about it.'

'Yeah,' agrees Linda. 'You can't say "no", Sis. You'd be mad if you did.'

'I know.' Sherry wipes her eyes. 'It's all I ever wanted to do for so long. Then after the audition went wrong, I thought that was it and I gave up on my dream. I'm happy here, with you, my job, my friends.'

'Yes, but you'll have new friends. And money. And fame. Think of the clothes, Sher!'

Sherry laughs.

'What have you told this, this…'

'Julie. Julie Gregson.'

'…Julie Gregson?'

'I told her I'd talk to you about it. I'm under eighteen, so I have to have your written permission.'

'Well, you've talked to me, girl and you have my permission a thousand per cent!'

Sherry blows her nose, very loudly. *Not very superstar-like*, thinks Allen.

'What say you, Allen?' says Linda. He is looking pensive. He coughs again. Then he grins at Sherry. 'You'll be needing an agent!'

*

Though you may never love me as I love you,
all my life, to you I will be true.

Cody puts down his second biro of the day and sits back in his chair. 'Beautiful', he says to himself. At least it would have been to himself if Agnes had not walked into the room at that moment.

'What's beautiful?' she says, wiping the coffee table with a duster.

At the sound of his wife's voice, the blood drains from Cody's head. 'You are, my love' he says, weakly.

'I'm what?' Agnes lifts each ornament off the mantelpiece and dusts underneath.

'Beautiful. You're beautiful.'

'Thank you, dear. Just don't start singing it, will you?'

Cody turns the sheet of paper over.

'What's that?' asks Agnes, squirting polish on the desk. Cody is about to say 'nothing' when Agnes snatches it out of his hand. She reads the first line:

From the early morning when I rise.

'Oh, it's your homework. Aren't you a girly swat? I haven't even thought about mine yet.' Cody wants to leave the room but knows that if he stands up now, the room will spin around him. Agnes reads the rest of the poem, mouthing each word silently. 'Well, it ain't Shakespeare,' she says, handing him back the piece of paper. She picks up her polish and duster. Cody feels relieved. *Got away with it*, he thinks.

'Who's it about, Cody?'

Cody frowns. 'You, of course.'

'I see.'

'Yes, I thought this was a perfect opportunity to express my, er, love for you. I'm going to read it out aloud...in the class...next week... to show people how much I...Agnes, why are you staring at me like that?'

Agnes' face is six inches away from Cody's and her eyes are wide open.

'This is very strange behaviour, Agnes...I don't know why...oh... oh...oh, my God...your eyes are brown...aren't they? Very brown.'

*

'Was that...?'

'Yes, Ethel. Greg Withall. As large as life.'

'Well, I never. I thought he'd a few years to do, yet.'

'They must have let him out early on good behaviour,' says Nigel, still looking towards the door through which Greg had left.

'Good behaviour? Greg Withall? I'd not associate him with that phrase.'

Doug and Percy appear from behind the curtain. 'He can be a charmer when he wants to be,' says Doug.

'I bet he did everything the screws wanted him to, pretended he was a reformed character,' says Percy.

'What did he want, Nigel?' asks Ethel.

'Oh, nothing. Just came to let us know he was back.'

'Does Mandy know?'

'No, Ethel. And she mustn't know.'

Chapter 42: Awaiting Their Fête

Six weeks to go. Six weeks after Leeford Parish Council finally revealed the identities of the allocated stallholders to the world, the festivities of the first ever Leeford Village fête will begin. Celebrations for some, devastation for others. They do tend to take it rather seriously in the village. Months of planning, arguing, lobbying, cajoling, lunching and bribing have now come to an end. Frank Watson, in particular, has sampled the best that Banfield's restaurants can supply, tasted Italy's finest offerings from Marchesi di Barolo to Azienda Agricola Valentini. Not for Sergeant Miller. No, he is impervious to the attempts by stallholder applicants to sway him in their direction. No Charbroiled Kobe Fillet for Stephen, nor a Macaroon Haute Couture. Indeed, he plays a straight bat, and Frank's absence from the current parish council committee meeting not only fills him with a new sense of importance and responsibility, it also furnishes the local police sergeant with a spring in his step.

Also, there are six weeks in which successful applicants - having received the wonderful news of their acceptance to Frank's inner circle of stallholders - have to work with him to organise and prepare their respective stalls.

'Are you sure you're ready for this, Stephen?'

'Of course, I am.'

'You have my proxy vote?'

'Yes, Frank. All in the file.'

'You'll not let the Thorntons get the book stall?'

'Frank, we've talked about this. There are seven committee members at the meeting. It will be decided by a simple majority. Whatever they vote for, it stands. You know that. Integrity, Frank. Integrity.'

'Are you saying I don't have any?'

'Won't you be late for your appointment, Frank? Where did you say you were going?'

'Never mind that, but don't let me down, Stephen.'

'Okay, so you've proved you're a copper, but a suspended copper. What's going on?'

PC Carr pauses, lifts the hot cup of coffee to his lips and sips gently, his gaze lowered to avoid eye contact until he's ready.

'Officer...'

'Smithson. *Sergeant* Smithson,' interrupts his interrogator.

'Sergeant Smithson. You must understand. I got myself in a tangle. A complete mess.'

'A woman?'

'Yes.'

'Figures. Been there. Was she the one in the cafe?'

'Yes, but you've blown my chance of sorting this by arresting me.'

'Not so fast, PC Carr. We called in to the station earlier and checked you out. My guv'nor has spoken to Sergeant Miller in Lee...'

'Leeford Village.'

'Yes, well, we've spoken to him. Seems your story checks out.'

'I can go then?'

'No. We're holding you on suspicion of assisting a felon. Anything you say may be...'

'All right, Sergeant. I know the drill,' jumps in PC Carr. 'I've just had about enough. I don't care about myself anymore, but Gail Perkins and Martin Frobisher?'

'Don't worry about them. They were tracked on CCTV from the cafe to a flat in Ossulston Street, near the Shaw Theatre, off the Euston Road. We've got 'em, Gary, we've got 'em.'

'Have they said anything?'

'Full confession. Frobisher resisted at first, but Ms Perkins told us everything. Put a good word in for you as well.'

'What happens now, Sergeant?'

'Your gaffer is coming down to pick you up. You've been bailed. Could be career over, but your actions prove your intentions were honourable. You might avoid jail.' For a few moments, words escape PC Carr. He doesn't care anymore what happens to him. He has done the right thing.

'There's a call for you, PC Carr.'

The telephone is passed to him across the interview desk. 'Gary, it's me,' says Sergeant Miller. 'You've been a right berk, haven't you?'

'Sorry, Sarge.'

'I'll look after you, mate, whatever happens.'

'Thanks, Sarge.'

'You're lucky you were allowed in, Ken.'

Leaning over the wall at Taylor's Farm, only half a mile from the turning to Leeford Village on the Kidderminster Road, Frank takes time to admire the view in both directions as he sees Ken approaching. To the east, behind the farm boundary, he takes in the imposing array of English oaks, beech, and sweet chestnut trees, reminding him of his childhood fascination with flora and fauna: ribbonwood, seringa, cypress, jarrah, whitebeam - he would study and memorise them all, much to the disdain of his industrious father but eliciting an equal measure of veneration from his doting mother. To the west is the land that sweeps away across the country villages of Quatt, Neenton, Munslow into the Welsh border towns, past Kerry and Staylittle to the coastline and the Irish Sea.

'Everyone keeps telling me how busy you are,' barks Ken.

'Eh?'

'You and your mystery appointments.'

'Excuse me? What's that to do with you?'

'Pardon me, Councillor Watson, but you seemed preoccupied. No offence intended.'

'None taken.'

'That's alright then. Anyway, what can I do for you?'

'Just taking in the air and the view. I must say, Ken, you live in a beautiful spot.'

'When I've got time to appreciate it. Too flaming busy to think about the view.'

'How are your cucumbers doing?'

'You trying to be funny, Frank?'

'Look, I've accepted your application. Can you let it go? You're in the competition - your cucumbers will be on the stall. Okay?'

'Sorry, Frank. Let's call a truce.'

Keen to do well in the 'Leeford Best Cucumber' competition, Ken quickly realises that antagonising the chief judge would not thrust him into the fast lane of success. 'Do you want to have a look?'

'Oh no, that would be unethical. I can't look at them till judging day.'

'Don't you mean Judgement Day, Frank?'

'Thought I'd catch you in here.'

'Greg. What do you want now?'

'If you weren't being so friendly, Nigel, I'd think you didn't like me.'

'My friends are in the bar. They'll be expecting me any minute.'

'Perhaps you could tell them you've had a little too much to drink.'

'Please, Greg - if you've got something to say...'

'Not so fast, butcher man. Oh, and by the way, I know all about your dodgy dealings with that meat wholesaler in Coventry. Naughty. If the Food Standards Agency got to know...'

'Okay, okay. What do you want?'

'I like to be fair. I gave you two weeks. Let's make it six. I've got to go away for a while, but I'll be back on the day of your silly little village fête. Bring the money then. Cash. In a briefcase. I'll settle for thirty grand.'

'But...'

'No 'buts' Nigel. The day of the fête. Okay?'

'Good start, Roy.'

'I know it doesn't look much. On the packet it says four to six weeks to grow them from seed.'

'Where did you get them from?' enquires Percy.

'Amazon.'

'Actually Amazon, or one of those companies that just use Amazon? Not official, you know.'

'Not official?'

'Well, you don't always know what you're getting, do you? Do you have the packet?'

'In the bin at the back of the shed.'

Intrigued, Percy whistles as he shuffles round the small, slabbed path that Roy has made. Tripping twice on the uneven surface, he curses Roy under his breath as he finds the bin. 'What have we here?' he says to himself. *He hasn't read that properly,* he muses. The leaflet included with the seeds proclaims:

LAST YEAR YOU GREW MARROWS. THANK YOU FOR YOUR BUSINESS.
WE ALSO SELL CUCUMBER SEEDS, BUT WHY NOT TRY COURGETTES?
ONLY TAKES 4 - 6 WEEKS. YOU'LL LOVE 'EM.
CUCUMBERS_TO_DIE_FOR.COM

'Courgettes. Blimey,' mutters Percy, sniggering, as he makes his way back to the red and green-striped deck chair and a heavily-sugared hot brew that Roy has prepared.

'Did you find it?'

'Yes. Lovely. You should have a good crop.'

'Hello there, young William! Don't see you in here very often.'

'Morning, Ted. I knew you were the man to see. Tell me about the cucumber competition.'

'Well, I'm in it myself. What do you want to know?'

'How do I join, and who else is entering?'

'Frank's in charge. He's left some forms on the bar with all the information you need. Is your dad entering?'

'Too busy with his sermons.'

'What about that brother of yours?'

'I give up on him sometimes. Makes a dreadful racket, quits the band, re-joins, sacks everyone and now the audition is due.'

'What's he going to do?'

'Who knows, Ted, who knows. Anyway, thanks for the info. Who else did you say was in the cucumber competition?'

'So far, there's me, Ken, Roy, Percy, George, with Clara, Edward, Suptra and Vera.'

'Bit of competition for you this year then, Ted, eh?'

'No problem. Last year's marrow was a disaster, but I know my cucumbers. Talking of cucumbers - Percy, pint is it?'

'Thanks Ted. Hey, you'll never believe what I've just seen.'

The committee, led by Stephen Miller, is more relaxed than usual. No one mentions Frank. Conclusions are reached after minimal discussion - just left for Stephen to read out the results of the votes to decide who will run each stall.

'In no particular order:

Pound Challenge - Jack Simmons

Book stall - Cody and Agnes

Cake stall - Ethel and Clara

Leeford's Best Cucumber - Frank Watson

Tombola – Dr Jeremy

Soft drinks and nibbles - Ted and Sally

Chuck the sponge - Nick and Jessica

Home-made cards - Meredith and Adam

Pies and pasties - Nigel and Mandy

Coconut shy - Jason

Any questions?'

'Stephen, you said there were fifteen stalls. You've listed ten.'

'Still space for five more if anyone expresses an interest in something different.'

Chapter 43: You Have Four Yesses!

'That was lovely. Absolutely lovely. Moved me to tears.' Jessica flaps her hands in front of her face.

'Moved me to tears, too', says Nick, adding, 'but probably not for the same reason.'

'Nick!' Jessica thumps him on the arm.

'Just kidding. I thought you were both great. And you go so well together. You'll be the next, er, er…well, I'm sure you'll do very well.'

Zack and Clare high-five each other. 'Does that mean we've passed the audition?' asks Clare.

'What do you think, Jessica?' asks Nick.

'It's a "yes" from me!' she shouts, raising a hand.

'And it's a "yes" from me. You've got four "yesses"!' Nick sits back in his chair.

'Four? There's only two of you,' frowns Zack.

'Sorry, having a Simon Cowell moment. Always wanted to say that,' laughs Nick.

'I thought Frank Watson was going to be on the panel,' says Clare, relieved at his unexplained absence but curious, nonetheless.

'He was supposed to be, Clare,' says Jessica, also relieved, 'but he left a message to say that he wouldn't be able to make it.'

'Oh, good,' says Zack. 'I mean, oh, dear, what a shame.' When their laughter has subsided, Zack asks, 'who else are you auditioning?'

Nick and Jessica look at each other, then at the sheets of paper in front of them. Nick appears to run his finger down a list. 'Let's see. There's…hmm…and…hmm…and, of course, hmm…they were excellent…'

Jessica interrupts. 'What he's trying to say, Zack, is there were no others. You were the only ones that auditioned.'

'But you are the best we've had!' says Nick, prompting another thump from Jessica.

'Don't look like that, Zack,' says Jessica. 'You and Clare were great. Are great. And you'll make brilliant headliners.'

Zack shakes Nick's and Jessica's hands. 'Thank you both for your support. Come on Clare. We've got a show to put together!' He picks up his guitar, grabs Clare by the hand and they run out of the Community Centre.

*

Five minutes to go. Five minutes before she embarks on her new life, a leap into the unknown, a leap that is frightening and exhilarating, not necessarily in equal measure. She has said her goodbyes to her sister at the house, saying she couldn't bear the idea of watching her out of the window of the bus as it takes her to Birmingham Airport. Linda will be fine, she thinks. She has her man, even though Sherry would prefer Linda's man to be anyone other than Allen Gomez. She checks her handbag for the tenth time that day: ticket, passport (hurriedly applied for), money (pounds and enough US dollars to buy some food and drink when she arrives at Las Vegas Airport), work visa. She sees the bus arriving and her heart skips a beat. A couple of minutes later, she finds an empty seat at the back.

'This is it, girl. No turning back now,' she says to herself, feeling a lump rise up in her throat. 'Don't cry!'

The bus leaves Banfield. Sherry looks out of the back window as the place she has known all her life falls away into the distance behind her. In her suitcase she has all the cards sent to her from well-wishers, some of whom she doesn't even know that well. She has never thought she was particularly popular, but the number of cards she has received proves otherwise. As the bus travels through Leeford Village, it passes Jessica's hairdressers, now fully restored after the fire, Meredith's card shop (where she knows many of the wellwishers'cards have come from), the library, Dr Roberts' surgery and George and Clara Dennis's house. Sights so familiar, she has taken them for granted. How I'll miss all this, she thinks. Finally, she passes the church, where she first sang in public. 'What a voice!' Reverend Peterson had exclaimed. 'You'll be on the stage one day. Mark my words.' She marks his words, with tears streaming down her cheeks as the bus gathers speed towards Birmingham.

Zack and Clare sit at the Peterson's kitchen table, drinking a celebratory shandy.

'Did you notice that Jessica's a little, you know, around the…' Zack points to his stomach.

'Do you mean, did I notice that Jessica's pregnant?'

'Well, yes. I think that's what I mean.'

'You've gone red. You're blushing!'

Zack takes a swig of shandy. 'It's not a word I've ever said before!'

'When we walked into the audition, I noticed, and she noticed me noticing. She mouthed "yes, I am", but then she put her finger to her

211

lips, like she was telling me to keep it a secret.'

'Won't be a secret for very long, Clare. It's pretty obvious.'

'Well, I'm not going to tell anyone. Are you?'

'Definitely not,' says Zack, emphatically.

'Why do you say it like that?'

'Like what?' Zack walks over to the sink and drops his empty can in the recycling bin.

'Like you don't agree with it, or something.'

'Let's talk about the fête,' he says, returning to the table with a couple of packets of crisps.

'Don't change the subject. You don't agree with it, do you.'

Zack opens a packet and takes a large crisp from the top. 'No, if you must know. I don't agree with it!'

Clare leans back in her chair. 'Why?'

'Because they're not married.'

Clare sits with her mouth wide open, a look of incredulity on her face. It's a while before she speaks, during which time Zack noisily eats half the packet of crisps. 'Well, aren't you the vicar's son?'

'Yes. I am actually. And I think it's wrong to have children before marriage.'

Clare goes to take a crisp from Zack's packet, but he pushes her hand away. 'I don't think stealing's right, either. Eat your own!' He pushes the second packet across the table. They burst out laughing.

'You're so last century, but I love you, Mr Morality.'

'So you should, you wicked woman. So you should.'

Cody is preparing the batter, stirring it around a large white plastic bucket. Agnes is filling the chip fryers with fresh oil. They have not spoken for two days. Cody knows it is down to him to breach the impasse. He puts a lid on the bucket and carries it to the back room. 'I made a mistake, Agnes. Of course, I was thinking of you when I wrote the sonnet.' Agnes switches on the burners. After a few minutes, bubbles rise up through the oil and she closes the covers. 'And I wrote "blue eyes" because I had been listening to Elton John earlier. His song was stuck in my head. An "earworm" they call it. I think.'

Agnes stands with her arms folded. 'You must think I'm stupid. Next, you'll be telling me you'd just heard Crystal Gayle singing "Don't it make my brown eyes blue?" on the radio.'

'No, it was definitely…oh, I see what you did there. Very funny. That's what I love so much about you. Your humour. Among other things of course. Many…other…things…where are you going?'

'Out. You can do the shift on your own tonight. Or maybe you can do it with Frank.'

'Frank? Frank Watson, do you mean? Or Frank Reed?'

'Frank Sinatra, Cody. Ol' blue eyes!'

Zack and Clare are sitting in the basement, working through the songs they intend to play at the fête.

'Do you think we'll carry it off?' asks Clare, as Zack is retuning his guitar.

'Carry it off?'

'Without a band. There'll be lots of people there and we're very quiet.'

'We're only quiet in here. They'll be loads of amplification. And lights. And pyrotechnics. And a laser of course, spelling our names out in the sky. I think we'll be noticed.' Zack strums an E-chord. Clare shakes her head.

'It's a real shame there was no one else to audition,' says Nick, stacking the table they have been using at the back of the room. 'I mean, Zack and Clare are great, but I'm not sure an acoustic duo will be able to entertain everyone for an hour.'

'Simon and Garfunkel did. The Everly Brothers. The Proclaimers,' says Jessica.

'Yes, but they were already well-known by the time they were filling concert venues.'

'Well, Zack and Clare are all we have. I think they're great. They go so well together.'

Nick carefully wraps his arms around Jessica's waist. 'Like us, you mean?' he kisses her on the back of the neck.

'Yes, like us.' She squeezes Nick's hand.

'Let's go. I'm starving. Fancy some chips?'

'Absolutely. It's what Simon always has after the X-Factor.'

'Of course, it is. And I bet Nicole has been known to have a chip, or two.'

As Nick is switching off the lights, Jessica hears someone moving about in the entrance. 'Hello?' calls Jessica. She walks towards the door. No-one there. 'Strange. I'm sure I heard someone,' she says. Nick joins her. They hear the toilet flush. Then a door opens.

'Sorry, I'm a bit nervous. That's the fifth time this afternoon. Is this where the auditions are?'

Nick and Jessica look at each other.

'Well, they were. But we're just on our way out,' says Nick. 'I'm afraid you're too late. Next year, maybe?'

'Yes, this is where they are,' says Jessica, 'in the hall.'

'Jessica!' whispers Nick. 'Surely you're not going to…'

Jessica ignores him and switches on the hall lights. 'So, what would you like to start with?' she says. Nick puts his head in his hands and groans.

Chapter 44: The Big Day Arrives

Frank Watson has been conspicuous by his absence. His appearance at the 'Cucumber Prize' stall is not exactly a surprise to the residents of the village, but a few of his closer associates have started to wonder if the metaphorical flag of residence would ever be hoisted up Frank's flagpole again. But he's here now, proudly displaying what he considers to be the best banner at the fête. 'Leeford Village Prize Cucumber Competition' it boasts. Rumour has it the owner of a small printing company in East Banfield had made a spelling mistake in his first effort. Predictive text gets everywhere these days, but Megan, Frank's daughter, had her work cut out to pacify her father after he was presented with 'Leeford Village Privy Cucumber Competition'. Frank imagined the comments by the regulars of The Cross – the men he considers to be 'friends' (unfortunately not reciprocated) – and cringed at the very thought of facing Cody, Jack, Roy, Ted, Percy, and particularly Ken. 'We have to keep 'em in the loo then, Frank?' he would say. 'Alright if we get caught short while we're tending to our cucumbers,' Cody would chime in. Frank, however, did spot the error, so all is well.

'He's here, Jason,' whispers Cody.

'Who?'

'Your brother. He's coming over. I'll make myself scarce.'

George, looking much slimmer than when Jason last saw him, stands beside him. 'Jason.'

'George. Oh, hang on, the vicar's about to open the fête, alongside Frank.'

Reverend Peterson clears his throat and blows into the microphone to make sure it is switched on. 'When I first came to Leeford, someone told me there had never been a village fête. Hilda and I have had great pleasure in helping to set up the stalls in our garden, and I've enjoyed being part of the parish council.' A barely audible noise emanates from the area occupied by Nick and Jessica. A few heads turn, wondering if there would be a repeat of the 'harrumph' once made famous by Anthony Buckeridge's Mr Wilkins, that almost, but not quite, throws Reverend Peterson off his stride.

'I promised Frank that I wouldn't preach, but I would like to read the lines of a text I discovered some forty years ago in something called

"600 Magazine", about the six most important words in our language. They are: "I admit that I made a mistake".'

'That's seven,' mutters Nick, attracting a frown from Jessica.

'When we are dealing with people, we must also remember the five most important words: "You did a good job".'

Frank's expression, as he shuffles from one foot to the other, is not exactly a glare – more of a scowl – and a mind-reader would hear him say 'is this about me, John? How dare you!' The vicar continues:

'The four most important words are: "what is your opinion?" The three most important are: "if you please". The two most important: "thank you".

Finally, the least important word is "I". Something to think about?'

A pause from Rev Peterson, then an intake of breath from the audience as he concludes:

'Food for thought, but, moving on, it gives me great pleasure to open the very first Leeford Village Annual Fête. I will now hand you over to Frank who will tell you all about the stalls and various events, including music!'

Meanwhile, the entries for the Leeford Village Prize Cucumber Competition have been placed on Frank's stall. He returns from announcing the running order for the day to find an array of what can only be described as pathetic specimens. As with all statements in the English language, it has to be said there is invariably an exception. In this case, Vera Cleeve provides the exception with a cucumber that could not possibly have been grown in the six weeks since the competition was announced in The Cross. Frank knows only too well that one needs a minimum of fifty days with plenty of water and tender loving care to achieve a specimen the length of a standard school ruler. Vera's is twice that length.

'But I knew that marrows wouldn't be on the agenda after last year's debacle. I used my brain and anticipated what you would do, Frank.'

'Sorry, Vera, I'm afraid I must disqualify you. Twenty-four inches is not possible in six weeks. It's anatomic... er, horticulturally, well you know, darned impossible.'

'I'm lodging a protest!' she shouts.

'Who to?' replies Frank.

'The head judge, arbiter, whoever!'

'Well, you've come to the right place. That's me!'

'Frank Watson, you are the one who's impossible, not my cucumber.

You won't find me entering your competition next year.'

As Vera flounces away from the stall, Ken Taylor steps forward, smiling. 'Ten inches, Frank. There's nothing here to beat it, is there? The trophy's mine!'

'I need evidence that your entry is home-grown. Anyway, what's this next to yours?'

Roy has placed his effort next to Ken's potential champion. Everyone takes a step forward - Cody, Percy, George, Clara, Edward and Suptra. Frank's eyes appear to glaze over.

'What the...'

'It's my cucumber, Frank,' says Roy.

Ted and Percy look at each other.

'Sorry, Roy,' says Percy, 'that ain't no cucumber, old pal.'

'What is it, then?'

'Courgette.'

Frank, with more important matters to deal with, does what he's good at. He makes a decision. Dispensing with the formalities of documentary evidence to prove Ken's worthiness as Prize Cucumber Champion, he announces that Ken Taylor, farmer of this parish, is indeed the new King of the Cucumbers.

'To the victor the spoils!' Ken declares.'Drinks on me at Ted's Soft Drinks and Nibbles stall.'

Trophy awarded, handshake speedily given, Frank shuts the stall and makes a beeline for the main stage. He's got something to say, and he needs a microphone.

'Nigel. Have you got it?'

'No idea what you're talking about, Greg.'

'Thirty grand. We had a deal.'

'I didn't agree to anything. I heard what you said, but as far as I'm concerned, you can get stuffed. That's Mandy's money. We're partners in the business. Do what you have to do, Withall.'

Greg takes a step forward, pushing Nigel into the tent that has been constructed to protect their supply of pies and pasties. As Nigel falls to the ground, Greg kicks out, catching his victim behind the left knee. The music blaring out across the vicar's garden masks the cry of pain emanating from Nigel's lips. He feels that a knife has seared through the tendons and instinctively rolls into the foetal position while Withall aims a second slug to his lower back. As Withall attempts to grab Nigel by the arms to haul him to his feet, Jason Owens appears to his left.

'Leave him, Withall.'

George, his brother, is standing by his side. 'I can take you both on. You look like you couldn't go three rounds with a ten-year-old and you're only just out of hospital. Anyway, I thought you were sworn enemies!'

'Never mind that, Withall,' spits George.

'I will stand by my brother whatever the circumstances. Take him on and you'll have me to deal with.'

A shrug of the shoulders from Greg and, as he moves towards George, a voice calls out,

'And me!'

Cody enters the tent, followed by Ted, Jack, Adam and Nick. 'Want to take us all on, you slimy toad?' roars Ted. 'Tell you what's going to happen. You're going to forget your thirty grand, get out of Leeford and never come back.' Everyone knows that when Ted says something, he means it.

'You can't speak to me like that. I'm breaking no laws. It's my money.'

'Couldn't give a monkey's,' says Sergeant Miller as he joins his friends in what is now a very cramped space. 'You can do what you like, Withall, and you can report me to my superiors if you want, but if you so much as breathe on any Leeford resident, I'll break your legs. Don't worry, we all know what you're trying to do. Nigel and Mandy are our friends. Threaten all you like. You're finished here. Now, get out!'

As Greg brushes past Sergeant Miller, Nigel lunges at him, swings his right fist and connects with the back of his shaven head. 'Leave my family alone!' Withall thinks better of retaliating, and slinks away to leave the fête, battered and defeated.

'If I could have your attention. You will be aware that, based on false information from, er, a certain party, the first Leeford Day celebrations were curtailed.' A few sniggers and coughs cause Frank to pause. I have carried out extensive research into this matter and was inspired to take this further after finding an old briefcase in my loft. The case belonged to Benjamin Watson, my grandfather. He held documents in the case that bear out some of the things that Howard Smithson told the care home manager.'

'What's that then, Frank?' enquires Cody.

'Exactly two hundred years ago today, the River Lee ran behind the

'Crux Inn', crossing what is now East Banfield Road. People called it the 'Lee Ford'. I delved into the archives and found something truly amazing. In a letter from the Earl of Banfield, he invited King George IV to visit the town.'

'Did he come here?' asks Nick.

'Actually, no. Instead, he decreed that the parks of Banfield were to be used by the King's swans, making particular reference to the park near the Lee Ford, declaring the area as a village in its own right. The village of Leeford. I am proud to announce that today, the day of the first Leeford Village fête, is officially Leeford Day!'

The garden is filled with applause and the cheers of an appreciative audience. Frank Watson, for once, has got it right.

It seems that the whole of Leeford Village has turned out for the fête. If it wasn't for the fact that Leeford nestles between several large conurbations, the scene would be quite pastoral. Frank Watson, flushed by his achievement in determining the true date for Leeford Day, is circulating among the stalls, shaking hands with all and sundry and basking in the compliments being paid to him for a successful fête, as though he has been solely responsible for the whole thing.

A small stage, adorned with bunting of all colours has been erected on the large patio in front of the vicarage. Large speakers capable of projecting sound across a ten-thousand-seater stadium produce ear-splitting feedback that whistles across the whole of Leeford as each microphone is tested, repositioned then tested again. Zack is sitting at the edge of the stage, tuning and retuning his guitar. He has not spoken to the rest of the band since it folded, though he has heard rumours they have found a new singer and are rehearsing for their first show at North Banfield Social Club. At first, he regretted leaving the band, but as he and Clare sang and played together in preparation for today's performance, he realised that this is what he wants more than anything: Clare.

How lucky he is to have her, he thinks, as he sees her walking towards him, looking like Sir John Everett Millais' painting of Ophelia, though not submerged in water. *Beautiful, intelligent and musically talented.* Yet, in the back of his mind there is always the nagging possibility that she could find someone better than him.

'You've been tuning that all day.' Clare sits down next to him.

'I know. The heat affects the neck and puts it out of tune.'

She rests her head on his shoulder.

'It'll be fine,' she says.

Yes, it will, he thinks.

Allen Gomez and Linda Cross are walking hand in hand around the Peterson's well-manicured garden, away from the crowds.

'I miss her, Al. I can't believe she's gone,' says Linda, her voice wavering slightly.

'I know you do. But she'll be back.'

Allen tries to reassure her, though having to reassure a woman on the verge of tears is not something with which he is familiar - he wishes Linda would get over Sherry's move to America as soon as possible. This moping Linda is not the Linda he committed to, largely against his better judgement at first, though he would now admit that there is a connection between them that he never thought would be possible, given his previous track record with women.

'And just think. She'll be rich. She'll be able to look after you in your old age. Look after us.'

Linda halts in front of a patch of purple salvias. 'Us? Do you think they'll be an 'us' when we're old, Allen?'

Allen feels his face burning and not just from the sun. 'Of course,' he says, with a conviction with which he surprises himself.

Linda kisses him. 'I don't believe you. But it's lovely of you to say it.'

Frank Watson is receiving congratulations on the success of the fête from Ethel and Clara on the cake stall when the sound of tapping on a microphone causes him to turn towards the stage.

'Now what's he doing? Not another sermon!'

Reverend Peterson is standing at the front of the stage.

'One-two-one-two. Can you…? Ladies and gentlemen. If I could have your attention.' All eyes turn towards the stage. 'I wish I could get the same amount of attention on a Sunday morning!' he says, laughing. 'Right, well. We are nearly coming to the end of the day and the main entertainment, Zack and Clare.' Ripples of applause break out at various points across the lawn. 'But first, a late addition to the programme. Singing that timeless Dolly Parton classic, 'Jolene', we have the wonderful Agnes Thornton!'

Cody Thornton, alone on the bookstall since Agnes slipped off to 'buy an ice cream' ten minutes earlier, drops the book he is passing to

Nita Sangra.

'I never knew Agnes was a singer, Cody,' says Nita, picking the book up from the grass.

'Neither did I, Nita. Neither did I,' says Cody, a look of bewilderment on his face.

At the handmade cards stall, Adam Thornton is deep in conversation with Sergeant Miller. Meredith taps him on the shoulder. 'Adam. Your mom's on the stage.'

Adam pauses mid-sentence. 'Oh my God. What's she doing?' He looks across to his father. His father shrugs.

Agnes walks up to the microphone to enthusiastic applause from the audience that has gathered around the front of the stage. 'Thank you. This has always been a favourite song of mine and I'd like to sing it for you today. As those of you who have heard the song know, the lyrics are an appeal by a woman to another woman for her not to take her man. I've always found them to be a bit demeaning to women to be honest, but in recent days they have come to mean something to me. So, I'd like to dedicate this song to the lovely, very blue-eyed Meredith Park over there.' Agnes points over to Meredith's stall. The whole fête turns to look at Meredith.

'What's she on about, Meredith?' asks Adam.

'I've no idea. Honestly,' she says. She looks over to the bookstall. Heads turn to look at Cody, standing with his head in his hands.

'Meredith?'

'Honestly, I have no idea, Adam.' Adam storms away from the stall. Cody marches after Adam. Meredith calls him as he passes her stall, but he just shakes his head. The backing track starts up and the audience turn back to the stage. Agnes belts out a fine version of 'Jolene', her eyes fixed on Meredith throughout. When she finishes, the audience is not sure whether to applaud.

'I knew we should not have let the Thornton's have the bookstall,' says Frank Watson to anyone within earshot.

'Well, well,' says Nick Allthorpe, squeezing out a wet sponge one of the primary school children has just thrown at him. 'Who'd have thought? Meredith and Cody. And Adam!'

'Shut up, Nick,' says Jessica, 'we don't know anything.'

'I'm glad you didn't fail her at the audition, Jess! This is priceless!'

Jessica picks up a soaking wet sponge and squeezes it down the back of Nick's shirt.

Agnes bows and leaves the stage. She walks back to the chip shop, ready for opening time.

The shock of Agnes's accusation dampens the spirit of the crowd for a while, while at the same time setting tongues wagging. 'Quick, Zack. Get on there!' says Reverend Peterson to his son, still trying to tune his guitar.

'But we've got another ten minutes, Dad. Anyway, Clare's not here yet.'

Reverend Peterson sighs. 'Well, as soon as you can. Let's try to avert a disaster.'

It's twenty minutes before Clare arrives. 'Sorry, Zack. I saw Meredith's stall was unattended, so I took over. Amanda's doing it now.'

Zack and Clare take the stage, much to the relief of Zack's father, who approaches the microphone. 'And now ladies and gentlemen. From the sounds I've been hearing from my basement over the past few weeks, you're in for a real treat. Will you please welcome...' he turns to Zack and whispers, 'what are you called?'

'Er, Zack and Clare?'

'Oh, of course. Will you please welcome Zack and Clare!'

Before the audience has chance to welcome Zack and Clare, they launch into their first song, a stripped-down band number. This is immediately followed by a couple of covers and then one of Zack's own songs. They are going down well with the crowd, who are dancing along, waving their hands in the air. Even Frank Watson can be seen tapping his brogue and slightly bending a knee. After an up-tempo number enhanced by a virtuosic performance by Clare on the tambourine, Zack announces that the next song is an addition to the original set they had planned that he is going to sing solo. Clare, looking confused and a little miffed, moves to the side of the stage.

'This song is dedicated to the girl I love and is called, "Clare"'.

Clare feels her face redden. There are whistles from the audience, which Zack ignores.

The song is a lilting love ballad that has the crowd swaying in unison in front of the stage. Zack sings it perfectly, looking all the time at an increasingly embarrassed Clare. Halfway through the final verse, Zack stops. He puts his guitar down and walks to the back of the stage, where he opens his guitar case and takes out a small box.

'Get on with it!' shouts someone from the hushed audience.

Zack goes to the side of the stage and drops down on one knee in front of Clare. There's a collective gasp from the audience. He takes a ring out of the box and holds it up in the air.

'Clare Adams, will you marry me?'

Clare puts her hand to her mouth.

'Oh, my God. Oh, Zack, I...I... don't know what...'

'How lovely,' says Ethel to Clara.

'She's only seventeen!' says Steve, Clare's father.

'She's still at school!' says Ted Coleman. 'I can't even serve her alcohol, yet!'

'They'll make a lovely couple,' says Linda, pulling Allen worryingly close to her.

'He's done what?' says Hilda Peterson as she is led out of the kitchen by her flustered husband.

'Wow, Jess. A marriage break-up and an engagement, all in one hour. Only in Leeford, eh?' says Nick Allthorpe.

'Harrumph!' exclaims Frank Watson.

~ ~ ~ FIN ~~~

Acknowledgements

Michael would like to thank Lesley and Philip for putting up with him; Jon for his support and friendship – the writing partnership giving Michael a new focus and purpose at a very difficult time. Also, the local libraries at Kingswinford and Wordsley for their support in helping to promote the Leeford Village serial, and The Express and Star for publishing the episodes.

Jon would like to thank: Nicky and Annie, for everything; Pen to Paper writing goup in York for their support; Michael, for his friendship and coming up with the idea in the first place.

Michael and **Jon** would like to thank Lesley Clayton for the cover artwork.

Author Biographies

Michael Braccia is a writer and musician living on the Staffordshire / West Midlands border. After working in I.T. for twenty-two years, part-time lecturing at the local college and running three small businesses, Michael retired early to look after his wife and son. He self-published two books in 2015 and went on to create the concept of a village in which the local residents argue, live, love and generally behave badly, but not too badly. Based on a small town near the Staffordshire border, Leeford Village was born.

After being widowed in January 2019, the writing partnership with his friend and ex-colleague, Jon Markes, was formed, and from September that year to the time of writing, the serial 'Leeford Village' has been published fortnightly by the regional newspaper, the Express and Star, on their website.

Jon Markes is a writer and shopkeeper, living in York but originally from the Black Country. Jon has written prize winning short stories and two illustrated children's books.

michaelbraccia.co.uk

jonmarkes.com

Printed in Great Britain
by Amazon

19154848R00129